KU-331-485

VIVIENNE COULDREY

The Swans of Bryder

Collins

FONTANA BOOKS

First published in Great Britain by Fontana Books 1980

© 1980 Vivienne Couldrey

Made and printed in Great Britain by
William Collins Sons & Co Ltd, Glasgow

The Swans of Bryder

VIVIENNE COULDREY, a successful journalist, lives in Tunbridge Wells in Kent.

Describing herself as an 'incurable romantic' she has long been an admirer of the great Victorian writers and is currently at work on a new novel.

Now sleeps the crimson petal, now the white;
Nor waves the cypress in the palace walk;
Nor winks the gold fin in the porphyry font.
The fire-fly wakens; waken thou with me.

Now droops the milk-white peacock like a ghost,
And like a ghost she glimmers on to me.

Now lies the Earth all Danae to the stars,
And all thy heart lies open unto me.

Now slides the silent meteor on, and leaves
A shining furrow, as thy thoughts in me.

Now folds the lily all her sweetness up,
And slips into the bosom of the lake.
So fold thyself, my dearest, thou, and slip
Into my bosom and be lost in me.

from THE PRINCESS
Alfred, Lord Tennyson

CHAPTER ONE

He had danced with her five times at the ball. Under the chandeliers of the Assembly Rooms, glittering in a score of mirrors, the same two figures had come together in quadrille, cotillion, galop and two waltzes, and with each successive dance shock waves of disapproval spread round them, outraged ripples on the quiet waters of Bishop's Linden society.

All along the gilded chairs, the chaperoning ladies kept watch and kept count. Heads turned and lips tightened and breath was drawn in sharply. Keen eyes followed their every movement.

They were not unaware of the effect they had: Arabella Curtis, the local girl, proud and beautiful daughter of a man of modest means, and Neville Rossiter, the stranger to the town, heir to an earldom, with a fortune to match. He had a lean and tawny look, dangerous, disdainful. She had a way of tilting her head back proudly on her long neck. With her high forehead and finely arched eyebrows, she always looked assured and supremely self-confident. But there was a tell-tale brightness in her eyes.

The agitation was at its greatest in Hester Curtis's corner of the ballroom. Arabella's mother, who could have the vapours over burnt toast, clutched her hands to her heart as she watched a man who filled her with tremulous alarm, play flagrant havoc with her daughter's reputation.

She was already shaking like a jelly when the Dowager Lady Darnley advanced upon her, impressive and formidable as a ship of the line, prodding the air with a closed fan as she announced very loudly, her opinion on the subject.

'To dance three times with the same man is extremely forward, four times is outrageously rash, five times may well prove to be fatal. The only hope for her now is for her engagement to be announced forthwith.'

Lady Darnley had never in her life waited to hear anyone else's opinion. She made an even more impressive departure; the elaborate magnificence of her bustle swaying after her through the double doors.

Mrs Curtis's clutching hands moved from her bosom to her throat, and someone found her a chair to collapse on to.

'That was the first time Lady Darnley has condescended to speak to me in years,' she said, moaning quietly to herself. 'I don't understand Arabella,' she kept repeating. 'I don't understand her.'

Bishop's Linden society declared it didn't understand either. Hadn't Neville Rossiter come to stay there with the clear intention of courting Elizabeth Mansard? She was the local heiress and was also acceptably pretty in a modest and demure way that did her credit, and her mother was a close friend and confidante of Lady Darnley. Hadn't Rossiter also been heard to declare that balls were elaborately boring and he didn't care for dancing?

So what did he mean by it, dancing again and again with Arabella as if there was no one else there? And what did she mean by it, shamelessly accepting? Society called to mind one or two other items that it had chalked up against her. Several proposals of marriage she had been known to turn down, from young men of Bishop's Linden perfectly good enough for her. How on one occasion she had ridden to hounds, flouting polite standards, riding much too fast and too daringly for a woman.

And the white dress she wore at the ball, made of white figured silk with a lace overskirt fashionably drawn back, left the underskirt decidedly too tightly form-fitting for respectable approval. There seemed to be more of her pale skin visible above the corsage too, than there should have been. That might have been caused quite simply by the fact that she had an unusually long and graceful neck, but Society in Bishop's Linden had been affronted and wasn't prepared to give her the benefit of that doubt.

Worst of all she seemed not to care, dancing exultantly, not smiling, yet radiant as she held out her hand to her partner, tilting her head back, walking proud.

Hester Curtis had shuddered as she watched.

'I shall faint,' she said, pressing a lace handkerchief to her lips and preparing to do so. But they had persuaded her not to, just in time.

6

Neville Rossiter with a stiff bow had announced to her curtly that he would call on her tomorrow at twelve.

So at eleven, Arabella Curtis sat before her mirror, preparing for his coming, her mother fussed around her and from time to time they both looked at Arabella's reflection in the mirror with unspoken satisfaction.

For Hester Curtis it was a recurrence of a familiar feeling of amazed wonder, that this radiant creature was her daughter. She herself, faded, portly and timorous, came barely to Arabella's shoulder and her daughter seemed equally above and beyond her in beauty, confidence and intelligence. Often it seemed to her Arabella was like a goddess in temporary mortal form; that she could only serve her, and only the very best was good enough for her. Other times when Arabella was being particularly contrary and difficult and demanding, she was well aware that her daughter was human.

'The white dress?' she asked. 'You want to wear white again? Why not the ruched green silk?'

'No,' Arabella said; her decision of will showed itself in everything she did. 'The white dress is the right one. And I shall not wear all my hair up. A few curls would be suitable this morning.'

From the rich luxuriance of her hair a cascade of curls came down on to one shoulder. The white dress this morning had a pleated bodice and twenty tiny buttons to the neck.

Arabella had slept very little, kept wide awake by excitement, still up on a high plane, joyously flattered and full of anticipation. She had re-lived the hours of the ball, every exchange of words and quizzical glances with Neville Rossiter, savouring the triumph of it in unspoilt secrecy. She knew she had shocked them all, last night, dancing with him so many times, but she also knew that it was envy that really made them so cross with her; it followed her wherever she went. There was a very thin line between personal success and social downfall; to walk that line was to live dangerously, but she loved the danger. It added extra quality to the excitement and she exulted in life's excitements.

So far in her sheltered world, these had been few. The

social life of Bishop's Linden was staid and limited, balls at the Assembly Rooms were infrequent and her father's modest means restricted her scope. But she had made some powerful friends; Sir Hugo and Lady Faversham had taken her under their wing and invited her to join them on a forthcoming visit to Reisbaden; and she had ridden to hounds, despite everyone's protests. That had been the high spot of her enjoyment of life so far – the glorious feeling of a spirited horse under her, the rush of cold bright air dashed with sunlight, the thrill of the chase.

Such a marvellous feeling – an effervescence in the blood, a tightening of excitement round the heart, a shiver of rapturous delight up and down her spine. She had not experienced such feelings before, but similar feelings had returned to her last night when Neville Rossiter advanced towards her again and again at the ball, when she had looked up and found his strange amber-flecked eyes intent upon her, when he had taken her hand, when he had held her arm. A soft warm glow of vitality had spread through her. The same feelings of excitement, and new more disturbing ones.

How dared she accept his invitations, all of five times, the chaperoning ladies had said each to each last night. How would I have dared refuse? Arabella asked herself. There had been challenge in Neville Rossiter's every look; he had dared her to accept and she had dared and danced, conscious of all the watching eyes and the gathering frowns about her, danced with assured grace even though she knew the polished floor was thin ice under her.

The elation had lasted through the night hours and this morning there was the triumphant knowledge that he was coming to her. That was how it should be, she thought with a superb kind of satisfaction. She didn't formulate any very coherent thoughts beyond that. She knew and her mother knew what Rossiter's call meant. But neither of them spoke out about it.

'To think, all these weeks we've been talking of nothing but your visit to Reisbaden and preparing for that,' Hester Curtis said, trying to find something helpful to do as Arabella dressed. Her nervous excitement and apprehension were so great by now that she couldn't sit still for a minute. 'To think my dearest wish was for you to agree to marry George Hetherington – and now, *this* –'

'You see, Mama, how careful you must be about what you wish? Your dearest wish come true might be a disaster for us all.'

'Oh now, you mustn't say things like that. You set such high standards for people, you are so very hard to please. Poor George isn't a disaster – just a bit slow perhaps –'

'Very slow,' Arabella said. 'Exceedingly slow.'

'But gentle,' Hester said. 'And kind.' Neville Rossiter didn't strike her as kind. She tried to think of how to describe him, but all she could think was he was heir to an earldom, almost a lord, with great wealth beyond the bounds of her imagination, and large estates in Sussex and Wales and a house in London – and he alarmed her. Alarming, she thought, that's the word to describe him.

Her thoughts ran erratically from that point, thinking how modest this house must seem to such a man. 'Perhaps we should receive him in the drawing room, Bella, and then you could walk with him in the garden, take a turn in the shrubbery.'

The same thought had occurred to Arabella. The drawing room of the family villa in Lansdowne Road, Bishop's Linden, was cramped, over-full of heavy plush and padded furniture, crowded with bric-à-brac. He would seem caged there. The garden wasn't much improvement; it would be a very short turn in the shrubbery, altogether too confined for him. Yet he was not such a big man, physically. His strange eyes had only been a couple of inches above hers as they danced, his lean face with the strongly marked lines had been very close to hers in the waltz –

She shivered suddenly, disturbed at the recollection. His physical presence had changed the familiar and humdrum Assembly Rooms, transformed it into a dramatic place, tense with challenge and excitement. What would his coming here do?

It also occurred to her that for the first time, she wasn't in complete control of events. Up to now her life had been ruled by her own decisions; since she was three years old her mother and father had given in to her wishes and her demands, and been dominated by the need for her to have the best. She had implicit confidence that all would be well and that her own destiny was assured and splendid. Her assurance was boundless and had always been so, she had no fears of the future, no doubts in the present. She was spoilt and indulged by her parents, all her sisters were younger and completely overshadowed by her; the young men she knew in Bishop's Linden flattered her and wanted to marry her; her young woman friends envied and admired her and copied her dresses and if the older women disapproved of her, she could shrug her shoulders and disregard them.

Only last night, only with Neville Rossiter's demanding attentions, she had the feeling that she had encountered someone she could not predict or direct to her whim or satisfaction. She thought, no one must know that.

Arabella stepped into her petticoats, fewer petticoats than her mother thought proper, and fastened the buttons of her white dress from her small waist to her long neck. She took a last look in the mirror, checking the smooth coils of her hair and re-arranging the vagrant curls straying over one shoulder. Yes, in the garden where the sunlight was mild and the elation of spring was in the air – she would walk there with Neville Rossiter and listen to what he had to say to her.

All Arabella's sisters had been banished away out of sight, with instructions to remain out of sight until Rossiter had come and gone. They stood together in bunches at the upstairs windows, waiting for a sight of him, whispering and giggling together.

Downstairs in the privacy of his study William Curtis, Arabella's father, waited, sombre and selfcontained, but gnawed by the terrible anxiety that hung over him day and night. A gentleman of independent means, he was respected in Bishop's Linden, though he took little part in the life of the town beyond attending Holy Trinity Church where Canon Gore-Stanley preached fire and brimstone sermons every Sunday. He was considered to be of a studious turn of mind, from the amount of time he spent in his book-lined study, but he never turned the pages of any of the books. He had no friends, no associates, no one to whom he talked with frankness and sincerity. He lived a wholly domestic life, surrounded by women and yet he was constantly irritated by the domestic scene, escaping from it to his study, there to calculate endless figures on endless sheets of embossed and watermarked paper, trying, desperately, to discover whether he had a chance of financial survival.

No one in Bishop's Linden guessed that William Curtis was hanging on to his modest means by his finger nails, hanging perilously over a pit of poverty. No one had any idea of the nightmare of destitution that haunted him, all the more real because he had never personally experienced it. He was not a man of imagination, and yet his fear was terrible because he could picture so vividly the mire into which at any moment he and his entire family might be plunged. He saw them reduced to joining the pallid ranks of the destitute that filled the squalid streets of London, gin-sodden and ragged. He himself flinched from the beseeching faces and the out-stretched hands of the destitute as he knew others would flinch from him if he were one of them, if he once lost his source of income. He knew so well the trap of hideous desti-tution, the crime and punishment that poverty created – he lived with the fear of it all the time.

Sometimes when he made his calculations, entering the figures in the columns of a ledger with a precise and pains-taking hand, he was cheered; it seemed he had exaggerated his alarm, that he was holding out, that he had nothing to fear. Then for a while he could feel easy in his mind, caress his daughters and spare a kind word for Hester no matter how silly she was being. Other times, when the figures were so much worse than he had thought they could be, he felt the pain physically in the pit of his stomach. He was bent double with it, and then he took it out on his family, on Hester most of all, crushing her mildest observation with a mortal blow of cruel sarcasm, hurting his daughters with sadistic verbal scorn.

'Your father is suffering with his stomach,' Hester said over and over. The girls grew up in the shadow of their father's indigestion. The cook was blamed, the maid who waited at table, even the slavey who washed the dishes. The new butcher was blamed, the baker who had supplied them for twenty years was blamed, the weather was frequently held entirely responsible. Never once did he tell anyone the real reason for his anguish. Whom could he tell? Certainly not Hester, he knew her poor silly mind would break apart under the strain of it. Certainly not Arabella because the one thing that really mattered to him was that Arabella must have the best in life. Arabella must have the newest Paris bonnet to reach the milliners of Bishop's Linden, Arabella must have a new French-made dress for the Assembly Rooms ball, and an amethyst necklace of special design, Arabella must have a bigger and better horse, not a mere pony. There was no question in his mind about it, he just went on swallowing his bismuth and wincing at his pain and his face turned grey and became tense and drawn, tightly drawn, like parchment.

Sometimes as he calculated his figures, he calculated the future too, trying to think what would become of them, all the girls growing up, a whole house full of them. Arabella – well, of course, it was only a matter of time before Arabella married well; one of the procession of George Hetheringtons would be the lucky one. But the other girls – he ran down the list in his mind, hesitating over the names because their faces merged into one face in his mind and they all looked like Hester, pale and indistinguishable – what would become of them all?

As William Curtis waited, like the rest of the household for Neville Rossiter's arrival, his tension was the greatest. He knew Rossiter was a wealthy man beyond the understanding of Bishop's Linden society. William Curtis had an odd way of knowing things, despite his isolation from the world. He knew the extent of the Helvyn family estates to which Rossiter was heir. He knew that Copper Down Manor was a Jacobean mansion of impressive size and grandeur and that the present Lord Helvyn, Rossiter's uncle, owned extensive mining rights and market rights. He also knew a little about Rossiter.

He paced his study thinking about what he knew and trying to reassure himself. Young men with money to burn, as Rossiter had, were entitled to sow wild oats. From what he'd heard, Rossiter had passed his time at Oxford in profligate spending, his time in London in brilliant seduction and his time in the country with gambling and racing fast horses; he had sown a bumper harvest of wild oats. So perhaps he would settle for a winter of matrimony without discontent and straying to other pastures. The time came for all young bloods to cool. It might well be this was the time for Rossiter to quieten his pace.

When Arabella came to his study to speak with him as she awaited Neville Rossiter's arrival, he looked at her with an anguish of contradictory emotions, seeing her as Rossiter himself would see her – a fair flower of girlhood, untouched by life, intrepid, unaware. The words burst from him: 'There is no one in the whole world good enough for you.'

Arabella agreed with that, smiling, familiar with her perfection in his eyes. 'But that does make it difficult for me to choose a husband, father.'

'I fear so, very difficult,' he said. That Arabella knew anything of Rossiter's taste for fast living or his reputation as a seducer, William Curtis thought extremely unlikely. But should he warn her? Arabella was high spirited and headstrong, to tell her, even to hint or warn her, was to risk a rash refusal and marriage to Rossiter represented wealth, success, position and security beyond anything that her father could ever provide for her. That was worth so much, he thought, taut and tense, wincing as a new wave of nausea built up in him, so much –

'Difficult, but not completely impossible, father,' Arabella said lightly. 'I shall not insist upon perfection on all counts. There must be some who approach perfection and I shall select the least disagreeable.'

'And do you imagine that Mr Rossiter might be among the less disagreeable?' asked William Curtis. 'You danced with him, apparently without distaste. I imagine you must look on him with some favour.'

'And if I look on him with favour, father,' Arabella said, airily still but taking note. 'It would find favour in your eyes?'

The contradicting anxieties raced through his mind then – the alarming figures in the ledger, his doubts about Rossiter, all his hopes and fears for his dearest daughter. If Arabella were to marry Rossiter she would be safe from any financial danger, and so he must overlook the man's colourful reputation and be thankful.

'Young lady, you know very well that you have always found favour in my eyes and always will.'

She knew it to be true and the knowledge moved her, almost bringing tears to her eyes. Quickly, lightly, she kissed his deeply furrowed brow.

At Westwood, four miles outside Bishop's Linden, where his friend and host Charles Sankey was taking his time over his breakfast, Neville Rossiter wasn't giving anything of his feelings away. He sat by while Sankey ate prodiguously and at the same time gave him the benefit of his advice and opinion, as a friend. Rossiter was abstemious in the matter of breakfast. Only in the matter of breakfast, as Sankey pointed out.

'Tell you what m'dear fellow,' Sankey said. 'I'll ride over to Bishop's Linden this morning. Pay your respects to Ma and Pa Curtis, saw how sorry you are not to be able to call on them as arranged, but you've been called away to London. Urgent matter of business, and it couldn't wait. What do you say to that?'

'No.'

'It would be much the best way to do it. The girl's reputation will survive, she'll marry old George Hetherington and the tabbies of Bishop's Linden will forget the five dances when she's a respectable wife. You've no need to concern yourself over it. Leave it to me, I'll smooth the ruffled feathers for you.'

'No.'

'I wish you wouldn't keep saying that.' Sankey mopped up the last of the devilled kidneys and ordered more toast. 'Anyone would think you were hellbent on marrying the girl –'

'You could say that –'

'What? Say what?' Sankey wiped the crumbs from his trailing Dundreary whiskers, flapped with a napkin at the maid, and lost the thread of what he was saying.

'That I'm hellbent on marrying the girl.'

'For God's sake man. What has happened to you? Matrimony is a disastrous decision in any case – and that girl! I know she's a beauty, but she's as mettlesome as they come. A

14

spirited horse is one thing, but a spirited wife – God help you! It's not just grievous folly, it's madness. Think – give it time. Look at me, look at my ruined life. Consider this remorse-ridden life I lead because I was fool enough to marry. Let me prevent you making the same mistake, my old friend, or what kind of a friend am I?'

Sankey had married a girl with winsome charm and an enthusiasm for playing practical jokes that had amused him vastly on first acquaintance. But very quickly her charm had turned to whining and fretting when he wasn't home to dine and her jokes lacked any originality whatever. The tenth time a bottle balanced on top of a door spilled milk all over him, he found he had come to the end of his amusement and the only thing he had ever had in common with her. Marriage was now something to be endured. He stayed in London, left her in the country and only returned home to Westwood with friends to keep him company, constantly lamenting his own foolishness and offering half his worldly goods to any-one who would get him out of the prison of matrimony.

'Consider again – think what you are doing,' Sankey con-tinued, warming to his theme. 'You are throwing yourself from a rock into a turbulent sea from which none of us can rescue you. What is the reason for marrying? Even more, what is the reason for marrying this girl? She has no fortune at all. Why don't you wait till you inherit – then, if you must, turn respectable. You are not old and played out and ready to settle. You! No! Never! And she's going to be hard to handle, that much I can tell you. If you must marry, choose some docile little maiden, one you can put back on the shelf and just take down and dust when you've a mind to, like the little heiress. How well do you know Miss Arabella Curtis – ask yourself that?'

Rossiter did ask himself that, as he rode the four miles down the hills to Bishop's Linden, although he had turned a deaf ear to the flood tide of Charles Sankey's grandiloquence. His strong face had set into a kind of impassive taciturnity, that was his way of masking his feelings and blocking any inter-ference in his affairs. He left Sankey muttering lugubriously that he'd be sorry, he'd regret it, when he found himself roasting on the spikes of matrimony.

Rossiter thought about Arabella all the time. She occupied every corner and crevice of his mind in a way that astonished him. How well did he know her? He had only seen her on two occasions before the Ball last night.

First he had noted her riding with the hunt. He could scarcely fail to notice her in her black riding habit that fitted her like a glove, her hat rakishly set, a bunch of violets in her lapel. He had admired her graceful courage as she rode and asked Charles Sankey who she was.

Then he had been introduced to her at a grand dinner party given by the Dowager Lady Darnley, the party at which he was supposed to focus all his attention on the heiress, Elizabeth Mansard, but he couldn't take his eyes off Arabella. At dinner she had been some distance from him, but he had been able to observe her and had watched the way she turned the flattery of the young men aside with a light touch and a quick wit.

Lady Darnley had considered that Rossiter's mode of looking at Arabella was more conspicuously admiring than was consistent with good taste and for that she blamed Arabella entirely. It was a girl's duty to repress excesses of ardour in any form, didn't she know that?

Lady Darnley had decided to have a word with Arabella. In the drawing room, while the men remained at the dinner table passing the port, they had sat together on a chaise longue, Arabella in unadorned white voile, Lady Darnley in spotted tulle with bows and streamers, pearl trimming and three humming birds strategically placed.

Rossiter, observing them when he joined the ladies, had been in time to hear the Dowager Lady say: 'Your approach to society is altogether too bold, in my opinion. You should address yourself with more diffidence on occasions such as this. A quietness of manner, a polite detachment, a certain indifference would be in order and would deter the attentions paid to you when they become too marked.'

'I am surprised that is your ladyship's opinion,' Arabella had said speaking with a demure air. 'I have found that a polite detachment and a certain indifference has the reverse effect.'

'You must not forget,' Lady Darnley had reminded her in ringing tones, 'that you are a young woman without fortune or background. And also I note without useful accomplishments. I would advise you to take up needlework, domestic accomplishments could prove invaluable to a girl in your position. Tapestry work, I have always found is extremely good for those of a mettlesome nature.'

'How interesting – that is something I have never tried. There are so many pursuits to follow, are there not? – music, dancing, riding, archery, croquet, acting, reading – all these things I appreciate, but in an abundance of variety, otherwise they reduce one to such dullness.'

'Too much variety suggests a fickleness of mind. In my opinion you should apply yourself to your accomplishments more earnestly and with single-mindedness. I am sure you would find it agreeable –'

'Ah well if it is agreeable, then I should pursue the matter most happily,' Arabella had said.

Rossiter had listened to the exchanges with a pleasant feeling of satisfaction spreading through him, for the girl, firmly refusing to be patronized, had quite the best of the encounter. Rossiter was convinced by now that she was a girl of rare quality with a radiant vitality, a lovely face and a lively mind. He pictured her in scenes and situations in his own life and found she fitted there remarkably well.

At the ball he had been drawn to her side five times by a powerful stimulus that over-ruled all objections – and there were many – that could be produced against her. They were over-ruled again now as he rode down into the sedate town of Bishop's Linden to the square and solid grey stone villa with a semi-circular drive designed for the carriage they did not own, where Arabella Curtis and her family were awaiting him.

'What an honour, what a pleasure, how very kind,' Hester Curtis said, advancing and retreating between the ranks of furniture, until she reached the farthest corner and could retreat no further. She bobbed forward again and nearly bumped into the still figure of Rossiter, as he stood firm in the biggest space of carpeting. Sudden close confrontation with his waistcoat and cravat unnerved her completely and she

17

subsided into silence leaving Arabella's father to do the sycophantic honours. He proceeded to overdo them at tedious length until Hester gathered her scattered wits and joined in again.

'What a nice day it is, don't you agree, Mr Rossiter? Not too warm, not too chill. Just the day for a ride from Westwood – such an agreeable distance – not too near, not too far –'

'Mr Rossiter knows how far it is, Hester.'

Rossiter waited with impatience for his chance to talk to Arabella. She impressed him more each time he saw her, and her appearance in a white dress startled him. It seemed to him not so much the white of innocence and demure naïvety, as a statement of availability. White, to begin with, he thought, and found it excited him almost unbearably, he who had seen successions of dresses, white and all other colours, on and off and disarrayed.

Arabella was quiet, only because she found herself seized with anger directed towards all the people in the room. With her parents for being so humble, for fawning and flattering, with Rossiter for his contempt for them and the way he didn't trouble to hide it. She was also annoyed with herself. She had found her heart beating fast at the first sound of his horse in the drive. It had needed all her self control to walk into the room to meet him with an air of calmness and poise. She felt impatient with her own embarrassment, and also with him because no one else had ever made her feel so uncertain of what she was going to do. She had an awareness as she looked at him of power held in check. She knew instinctively that this cold and courteous manner of the man was no indication of his true self.

The polite exchanges had already gone on too long. With an effort she was able to suggest that Rossiter might care to walk in the garden, but her voice despite her efforts sounded too bright and too hard in her own ears.

There was so much tension in the air; it was not lessened by walking out of doors. They stepped out stiffly along the gravel walks, Rossiter with his hat in his hand, Arabella with gravely downcast eyelids and an air of waiting. She felt herself strongly opposed to the idea of asking him conversational questions, a contrary urge to make no small talk. He had made it clear he wanted to talk to her, let him talk then. She walked in silence and waited for him to begin.

He seemed to be in no hurry to do so now. They walked to the boundary of the shrubbery and the path came to an end at a small lily pond, circling it. They turned back towards the house and watching figures there moved hastily away from the windows. They circled the pond in formal fashion, then Rossiter stood still contemplating the aspect of the house.

'A pleasant enough house,' he said. 'A comfortable home. And Bishop's Linden is a most pleasant place to live, don't you find?'

'Yes, most agreeable,' Arabella said, smiling a little that he had produced small talk as banal as any of her mother's. 'Though I should not like to think I was always to live my life in this house and in Bishop's Linden.'

'That is unlikely, surely.'

'Unlikely? My parents have no thought of moving.'

'Your parents, perhaps not. But you – you will marry. There must be many who make you offers.'

'I have no plans to marry,' Arabella said, fairly and squarely. She looked up, conscious of the fact that his eyes had been on her throughout this preliminary. As before, his eyes startled her. Now in daylight, she could see how strangely coloured they were, with amber light in them and flecks of brown. Watchful eyes, very quick, very intent, missing nothing. His expression was formidable and it disconcerted her, she said quickly: 'I think the advantages of marriage are much exaggerated.'

He smiled at her then, suddenly and Arabella could see how very sure of himself he was. It was a lordly, superior, arrogant smile. 'Sadly – there is little chance for a woman to extend the boundaries of her life without marriage, either socially or geographically. For a woman, a single life must essentially be lacking in status and satisfaction, wouldn't you say?'

'Life is poorly managed that it is so.'

'I agree – but it is not of my managing. What I can manage

is to make my own life full of variety and interest – and to let it be so for my wife.'

He spoke graciously, turned towards Arabella and seemed about to say more, but she had half turned away, taking a few steps from him. She had never felt such constraint as he imposed on her, never felt her spirit so subdued by anyone, and she resented it. When he stood near her there was a sophisticated scent of masculinity and tobacco that was strange to her. It must be that, she decided, that produced this uneasiness in her.

Scarcely aware of what she was doing, Arabella reached out and picked a few spring leaves at random. She stood shredding them with tense, distracted fingers.

'I know that most women consider marriage their main purpose in life – it is not necessarily mine.'

'What is your main ambition then?' Rossiter might almost have been teasing her, indulging her, and she felt a moment's helplessness because she didn't in fact know exactly what her ambition was in life. To lead, yes, to shine, to succeed, certainly, to live life vividly and in rich degree. But such ambitions, though clear enough to her were only outlines and generalities. Exactly what form her leading and shining and succeeding was to take she couldn't say. To some extent she was already achieving her ambition. To be much sought after as a bride, to be hopelessly signed for by a succession of George Hetheringtons, that in itself was a proof of womanly power. Was this present moment then the height of feminine success, the achievement of her girlhood's aim and ambition? Neville Rossiter walking with her here, an offer poised on his lips? To be Mrs Neville Rossiter would certainly arouse the admiration and envy of the whole county.

And wasn't this living life vividly? She had never before been so intensely aware of the quality of the moment – the spring sunlight glossy on the rhododendron leaves, the wisps of clouds swept across the placid blue of the sky, a flight of small birds about the grey corners of the house roof, a goldfish suddenly brilliant in the dark water of the lily pond. She had never before been so aware of every distinct detail, or felt anything so keenly as the nervous anticipation and the excitement he inspired. Her lips felt numb, her breathing seemed unnaturally fast and her fingers pulled at the leaves, crushing and shredding them in her white hands.

'What are you doing to those poor leaves?' Rossiter's voice changed suddenly. He spoke quite differently, naturally, quickly, impulsively, but as if he was humouring her. He put his hand over hers, keeping it there, and the watchers in the windows back at the house, seeing the gesture, felt the finishing post was in sight. She opened her fingers, at his touch, and the torn leaves fell to the ground, scattered and bruised, ignored. Firmly, as if he would put her out of her misery of not knowing his intentions, he said with kindness:

'You must know why I've come today. I want to ask you to be my wife.'

All Arabella's doubts and uncertainties crystallized at the touch of his hand and the lordly condescension in his tone. She felt possessed by a powerful fury – that he should be so sure of her, that he should be so contemptuous of her parents. Does he think he has but to beckon and I shall come? All thoughts of luxury and dignity he was able to offer her went out of her mind, and all thought of how impressed her circle of family and friends would be at such a marriage. If she recalled them, at that moment of decision, it was to reckon up the advantages of the marriage and make her rejection of it even more splendid. Condescendingly, he had made his offer, seeing her anxieties and fears. He should realize that she was the one with the power, she had hold of the leading rein. Maybe a single life didn't hold much hope of promotion for a woman; maybe she was so placed that she depended on making a good match in order to achieve brilliance of any kind. But the choice was hers. He at this juncture could but make her an offer, and beg her to accept it. She at this moment was the one in control of their destinies. He should have more awareness of her power.

She drew her hands back, her eyelids lifted and the demure and downcast eyes were suddenly brilliant with her anger. Her head tilted back on her long neck. She turned so suddenly that her white skirts swung out round her and Rossiter, his expression of patronizing complaisance startled on his

21

face, took am amazed step backwards.

'You mistake the cause of my anxiety of mind, Mr Rossiter. I was endeavouring to turn the conversation aside. It was my aim to avoid for you the embarrassment of making me an offer that I cannot possibly accept.'

She could hear the crisp decision in her tones and could see his incredulous disbelief. He said in a low voice:

'Would you refuse me then?'

'As I said, I have no wish to marry –'

'I imagined you were speaking in general terms, a matter of theory. I imagined that an offer such as I am able to make you –'

'Your imagination was incorrect. My generalized feelings against marriage are in no way altered by your particular circumstances. I beg you to excuse me from further discussion –'

'My presence is abhorrent to you then?'

'I did not say that,' Arabella's anger as she looked at him then, became mixed with real alarm. The feeling of power held in check that she had acknowledged in him each time they met, was now confirmed. There was savagery in every line of his face, and his face was white with anger, his eyes shining with tigerish ferocity.

'I don't think you know what you are saying.' She thought for a moment he was going to take hold of her – grab her arm, her hand, her shoulder; her limbs seemed to shrink at the thought of his touch in anger. But instead he held his hat in both his hands and looked as if he would pull it apart.

'I believe I know very well what I am saying –' As her alarm increased and his anger became more evident, Arabella's own self control increased. In the serene brow and the proud tilt of the head and the composure of her clasped hands there was no hint of her feelings; only the brightness of her eyes and the momentary trembling of her lips betrayed her emotional state.

'You are sending me away? You want me to leave and never return to you?' Rossiter was determined to make certain once and for all whether it was just coquetry. 'If I leave you now – I will never return.'

'If the only way to persuade you to stay, is to consent to become your wife, then, I regret, Mr Rossiter, that you must leave.'

He stared finally, furiously amazed into her face, then he left, by-passing the house and she heard the sound of his horse ridden quickly away down the gravel of the drive.

She ran into the house and as her parents came towards her their faces remarkably alike in their distress at this outcome of events, her control broke, and she cried: 'Leave me alone. There is nothing to say.' She rushed up to her room and her mother followed her there.

'I don't understand,' Hester Curtis said piteously. 'I thought you – liked him, Bella. Can't you tell me what happened?'

'No. I can't tell you anything at all.'

'Will Mr Rossiter call again?'

'No. And if he does I will not be here to receive him. I shall go to Reisbaden as planned.'

'But, my dearest –'

'There is nothing more to say, Mama. I do not want to talk about Mr Rossiter or hear his name ever again.'

'I don't know what to do,' Hester said hopelessly.

'You could begin to pack my clothes for me, Mama,' Arabella said. Her voice was very hard with decision; she was quickly in control again. Her mother left her alone at last and as she went out of the room even her bustle was drooping with disappointment.

Downstairs in his study, William Curtis had his head bowed between his hands in utter desperation. 'That she could be such a fool,' he groaned. 'How could she be such a fool?'

Neville Rossiter rode his big black horse a great deal too fast up the hills from Bishop's Linden, unable to give word to coherent thought. His vision was full of Arabella in the garden with the light of the morning on her, tall and proud and lovely in her white dress, like a lily just coming into flower.

'Damn her,' he said aloud, again and again and again. 'Damn her. Damn her.'

CHAPTER TWO

The magnolias were blossoming in splendour at the rotunda of the spring colonnade, and Reisbaden, with its arcades and steep flights of steps, Gothic churches and gabled houses had altogether a most satisfactorily foreign look about it. Arabella was wholly delighted to be there.

The invitation from Sir Hugo and Lady Faversham to accompany them that spring to the German watering place had been made many months before and Arabella had been able to savour the prospect of it all winter. She would have been happy to accompany them anywhere. She had responded immediately to the Favershams and the world they represented and she took great pleasure in their urbane company.

Sir Hugo was a tall impressive figure with a fine head, white hair, white beard and a patrician look about him. He took an extraordinary amount of care of his own health and well-being, but he was a kindly man and he took very nearly as much care of the health and well-being of a chosen circle of friends, relatives and employees. Recently retired from a busy political life to the peace and tranquility of Bishop's Linden, he had found more time to contemplate his own state of health and to discover his greatest need was something to relieve the boredom and monotony of retirement.

Lady Faversham, his sweet Emily, dignified and fastidious, also devoted herself to the cossetting of his health and she spared no efforts to relieve him of the burden of boredom. She collected about them in the quiet comfort of their home, people who could talk, amuse, and please him with their company and among these people was Arabella Curtis. Just the sight of Arabella made Sir Hugo feel better on even the most rheumatic morning. He liked the way she always had something to say for herself, told him things, responded when he talked to her with lively animation and – most of all – didn't upset him with talk of sad, disquieting things he could do nothing about. He insisted upon remaining ignorant of anything upsetting. 'Don't tell me. I don't want to hear,' he would say, deliberately turning his deaf ear towards the speaker.

With no children of their own clamouring for attention or vying for favours, Sir Hugo Faversham and sweet Emily found an honorary daughter in Arabella, one they felt they couldn't have improved upon if she had been their own.

Sir Hugo might fuss tediously over draughts and chills, but he talked of politics and power and people who were famous and his talk fascinated her. Lady Faversham had moved in Society, in a world beyond Arabella's experience that she was eager to know. She drank in their discourse thirstily.

A visit to a German watering place, not dissimilar in size and style to Bishop's Linden, in their elderly over-protective company, might not be a whirlwind of excitement, but to Arabella it was a first glimpse of life beyond familiar streets and well-known circles. She had scarcely been more than a day's drive distant from home in her twenty years and was acutely conscious of the fact that there was a whole world out there to see.

For her even the initial train journey to Dover was vivid with novelty. The Faversham's party was well equipped for the greatest possible comfort in travelling, with footwarmers and rugs and luncheon baskets and Sir Hugo took an inventory at each stage of the journey of dressing cases, flasks, opera glasses, telescope, umbrellas and canes, waterproof and wrappers, overcoat and comforter, books and newspapers. He was Sir Hugo, a man stationmasters and staff hastened to see accommodated, to give his ladies and his luggage precedence at all times.

He checked departure and arrival times with his gold hunter watch, pointing out to the stationmaster at Ashford the discrepancy between the timetable and the appearance of the connection they were awaiting, and complaining when the train was ten minutes late at Dover that South-East Company trains moved at the speed of a glacier. But Arabella had never travelled so far or so fast before and had no complaints to make.

The Channel crossing was her first sea voyage and it was

a calm initiation, the sea an untroubled grey without a hint of a white wave top, and it passed in a hazy dream for Sir Hugo insisted that all the ladies took a dose of chloral for seasickness. Every mile of foreign soil as they travelled across Europe had so much to interest her that it helped her to push the whole episode of Rossiter and the rejected proposal into the background of her mind.

But there were times when, unable to sleep for some unknown reason, the vivid recollection of their encounter took over her thoughts and she remembered the white fury of Rossiter's face as he had left her in the garden, the strong lines of his face so deeply marked. She seemed to hear his voice and how it had changed from formally polite to condescending and then suddenly to amusement at her nervousness: 'What are you doing to those poor leaves?'

She could remember every word he had said – every single word. He had been so sure of her. She smiled into the darkness, thinking of his incredulous amazement at her rejection of him, his anger, his disbelief. There had been enormous satisfaction in rejecting him; she could savour the triumph of it over and over again. '... You are sending me away? You want me to leave?' ... 'If the only way to persuade you to stay is to consent to become your wife, then, I regret, Mr Rossiter, that you must leave ...'

How very satisfying, Arabella thought with a kind of triumphant retrospective relish. How I enjoyed that.

She had certainly not been slow in proving to herself, if proof was needed, that she had no need of him. Here she was speeding across the Continent in superior company, appreciated for her own sake by her dear friends Sir Hugo and Lady Faversham. She didn't need to become the wife of Neville Rossiter in order to move into a wider world and find appreciation.

And had she really meant what she said to Neville Rossiter 'I have no wish to marry'? Arabella asked herself, going over the scene again in the sleepless night. The words she had spoken seemed to spring from a long held conviction, something thought over and carefully decided upon. But that wasn't in fact the case. She hadn't known what she was going to say to him. She had found herself saying those words; they seemed to be the right ones. It had been instinctive, a feeling that now she had emerged from sheltered girlhood, life should open out and expand into a vivid kalaiedoscope of interest, variety, and sensation. Observation of marriage in her experience had led her to the conclusion that for a wife, life closed in; the married woman's world was closely confined to the home; her dominion extended only over the servants; her knowledge of the outside world was only through the medium of her husband. Her days were made up of household decisions, supervision of the pantry and the linen cupboard; the climax of her week maybe a morning call from a neighbour. Children inevitably followed upon marriage and children meant claims on her health and strength and tedious occupation with their well-being. What pleasure would there be attending balls at the Assembly Rooms or dinner parties, meeting new and interesting people and attracting the flattery of the young men? Once married, one could have no stake in that, no part, no action.

Arabella thought of her mother's marriage, constantly overshadowed by her father's indigestion, producing nothing but daughters and a state of timorous anxiety about everything. She thought of other marriages she knew, even of Sir Hugo's and sweet Emily's. Emily was a perfect wife, devoted, and completely docile to her husband's needs and whims. Could she ever have made herself docile to Neville Rossiter?

A shiver ran through her at the very thought. And what about love then? She asked herself, twisting and turning in the darkness. If it was impossible to believe from real-life observation that Mr A had ever loved Mrs A and burned with passion at the thought of her, Arabella had read novels – she knew that where meetings of men and women were concerned, love was the ingredient that couldn't be accounted for, love was the match to the gunpowder, love let the heart rule the head of the coolest heroine. She had read Tennyson, had felt herself melting with longing at the lyric loveliness of lines that haunted her with a kind of rarefied promise of inspired feelings yet unknown to her. The half-remembered words went round and round her brain – 'Now sleeps the crimson petal,

now the white ... The firefly wakens; waken thou with me ...
Now lies the Earth all Danae to the stars, And all thy heart
lies open unto me ... Now folds the lily all her sweetness up,
And slips into the bosom of the lake, So fold thyself, my
dearest, thou, and slip Into my bosom and be lost in me.'

Perhaps that was what Neville Rossiter was really saying to
her: become my wife – be lost in me.

Arabella found herself grasping at something that eluded
her the more she tried to pin it down. Was it possible that
love was the strange constraint she had felt when Rossiter
stood close to her, the prickling uneasiness that even the light
smell of tobacco he used provoked in her, the nervousness, the
uncertainty of what she was going to say or do, the beating
heart? No, surely that wasn't the same thing at all. Not at all.
That was weakness, not love. She had risen above her weakness. She had taken the brave, bold course. She had chosen
the romance of life instead of the security of marriage.

But it was three o'clock in the morning, a time when doubts
and uncertainties take on a fatal hopelessness. Something far
back in her mind came to the surface inexorably at such an
hour; a vague uneasy feeling that she had had her chance and
she had missed it, that a time would come for regrets. Arabella
pushed the long falling hair out of her eyes, and sat up to
address the darkness with more forcefulness. 'I don't regret
what I said,' she declared valiantly. 'I don't regret one word.'
The darkness remained unimpressed.

'Or if I do feel any regret at all,' she finally conceded, 'it is
not that I refused to marry him.' The feeling she was forced
to admit to, was a feeling of disappointment that her impulse
to refuse him had at the same time ended the possibility of
future meetings. He was, by far, the most exciting, disturbing, challenging person she had ever met. She had felt the full
force of his demanding presence and matched herself against
it; she had enjoyed the battle. If she must acknowledge regret
it was that in indulging her one moment of glorious power,
she had to pay the price of seeing him ride out of her life with
such complete finality.

The first days of Arabella's visit to Reisbaden were days of
discovery. At a fashionable spa – one of Europe's most

gracious – life was quietly ordered and pleasingly entertaining. The climate was mild and the city was set among orchards and vineyards with forested hills about it and the mighty Rhine to the north of it. Fine prospects and beautiful views of the city could be enjoyed from surrounding vantage points.

The warm springs at Reisbaden were beneficial for rheumatism, gout, intestinal complaints and excessive obesity, but there was an outstanding difference, Sir Hugo explained to Arabella, between taking the waters and taking a cure. Sufferers who were determined upon taking a cure had a whole range of vapours, warm dips and hot mud baths, stinging douches, hosings and ice cold plunges, therapeutic sulphur and brimstone and salt to experience. Taking the waters was a social affair, a matter of imbibing the waters at the pavilion over a matter of several leisured weeks, and this was performed with grace, elegance and precise etiquette. Apart from the morning ritual at the pavilion springs, the days were dedicated to a pleasant and cultured indolence, concerts and card parties and generally mingling with one's social equals and superiors – preferably superiors.

Arabella's first reaction to the spa water was one of surprised distaste, for in Reisbaden the waters boiled and hissed from the earth at such high temperatures that very often the beakers cracked when they were lowered into it by the attendant dippers. Confronted with a beaker almost too hot to hold, Arabella then found that the water tasted unnaturally and disagreeably like chicken soup. She determined that one beaker of spa water each day would be quite adequate for her needs during her stay.

Lady Faversham admitted that she had a preference for the pure waters of Malvern, but. 'It is so unpleasant it is most certainly doing us good,' she insisted.

Sir Hugo visited the thermal baths in the hotel and drank the spa waters in moderation, but he preferred the champagne for which Reisbaden was also world renowned. He maintained that champagne was an excellent tonic for the blood and his partaking of the local vintage had a medicinal solemnity.

Reisbaden's fame had been founded upon its baths but the

city fathers had built so lavishly upon it that the baths in a cavernous underworld below the city were now the least part of its attractions. Classical halls, formal gardens, fine churches, lavish shops, exquisite colonnades and promenades were the glory of Reisbaden and attracted visitors from all over Europe. Under the chestnut trees the fashionable visitors to Reisbaden would promenade and take note of who else was there. The social etiquette of the watering place was as strictly defined as that of Bishop's Linden, but more complex and of a higher order.

Visitors on the promenades would walk and talk, meet and greet each other and part with a fine formal courtesy like a scene from a French opera. Invitations and acceptances were made with the strictest precision. It was possible for the experienced to convey the exact level of rank by the angle of a nod, for the practised to impart a snub by the mere movement of the eyelids. And most of the visitors to Reisbaden had had a lifetime of practise.

The Favershams occupied a comfortable suite of rooms at the Schwarzer Bock Hotel in the Kranz Platz. Massive meals were served there and throughout the hotel there was an army of servants, and at every door a flunkey, deferential and eager to serve. Arabella accepted that utterly as her due.

Lady Faversham, impeccable and fastidious, never nodded when she should have remained aloof, never introduced Arabella to anyone who was not certainly well connected, and never bestowed an invitation on anyone who might prove tedious to Sir Hugo's finely balanced peace of mind. The people Arabella met in Reisbaden were therefore elderly and aristocratic without exception, almost all were interested predominantly in their own state of health, but refrained from discussing it quite continuously.

One or two diversions were planned: expeditions to the romantic castles in the area, a drive through the great forests to the gold-domed Greek chapel, and to the Platte – a conspicuous hill to the north of Reisbaden where there was a shooting lodge and a fine collection of antlers. Sir Hugo was convinced Arabella would be interested in the antlers. Arrangements were also to be made for her to ride in the palace park, the residence of the Dukes of Nassau, and Lady Faversham was doing her best to persuade Sir Hugo that attending a performance at the splendid Hessian State Theatre would not be injurious to anyone's health.

Arabella would understand, they said, that the balls held during the season were not to be considered. 'Everyone gets so hot, d'you see, they are tempted to open the windows and that's when the trouble starts.' Evening parties under lanterns in the spa park came under the same ban. 'There's always some dampness around, it comes up from the river and the grass is always damp of an evening and very unhealthy, d'you see?'

Arabella swallowed her disappointment and smiled sweetly. What came as a complete surprise to her was the discovery that after the taking of the waters and the constitutional walks, the party regularly attended the casino and played roulette. Sir Hugo found roulette was the best cure yet discovered for his boredom, so Arabella was duly conducted through the grand pillared portico of the spa casino to find a crowded and colourful scene within.

In the stifling heat and brilliance of gas light, a couple of hundred people were gathered, concentrated around the gaming tables where the lights were brightest. The atmosphere was unlike any other, hushed with nervous expectancy, tense with drama, excitement, despair and wild exhilaration uneasily suppressed. The rows of spectators and players several deep around the tables had all their attention riveted upon the play, utterly engrossed.

In the centre of the crowded circles she could see the dark croupiers presiding, hear the rattle as the wheel turned, the exciting clinking of coins and the expressionless voices repeating and repeating: 'Faites vos jeux, mesdames and messieurs, faites vos jeux ...'

Arabella watched keenly, immediately fascinated by the entirely strange new world revealed to her. This, she thought with pleasure, was indeed a far cry from sedate Bishop's Linden.

She had never encountered such a cosmopolitan crowd, olive complexions from the far south mixed with fair-skinned

northerners and visitors from England; old and faded mingled
with youth and beauty; the dresses with sweeping trains that
some of the women wore were the finest she had ever seen.
In this place the aristocrats and the fashionable mingled with
a rabble of gamblers and hangers-on of no rank or pretension
whatever.

There was a blankness in the faces of the players, in their
uniform absorption, but their hands were eloquent. One hand
that reached out across the table was plump and white and
encrusted with rings, another clawed like a vulture, another
scuttled sideways across the baize like a frantic insect. Often
impatient hands from the back rows would push through
between the rows in front to place a stake. While one hand
hung hesitant over a few francs, another heavy hand remained
impassive and unmoving while a pile of gold and banknotes
was raked away from it.

Sir Hugo took pleasure in explaining the rules of the game
to Arabella, the various combinations of rouge et noir, pair et
impair, manque et passe, and how some of the numbers were
a greater risk but a richer reward.

'You can place your stake on odds or evens, on black or
red. You can take a chance on zero and if you win the amount
is thirty five times as much – but zero only rarely comes up.'

Sir Hugo himself played a sober game, essentially a gentleman's game, played strictly in order to experience the process
of winning and losing, never out of a vulgar desire for gain.
He played out of academic curiosity to discover how great a
win or loss would upset his equilibrium.

Lady Faversham, looking all the time very dignified and
English, inclined her silver head as she risked a ten franc
piece and her hand as she reached out to place her stake was
delicately gloved in dove-grey.

Arabella stood watching, instantly fascinated by the brilliant, vital scene and the human dramas being enacted there.
Her attention was held first by a rouged and raddled old
dowager mumbling to herself, piling her stake money on to
zero again and again and again and watching it swept away,
then by a fat German shopkeeper who was winning showily,
greedily, his avaricious eyes blinking all the time with nervous

excitement, then by a pale and priest-like figure playing with despair as if he had no hope in life but roulette. All the time, jostling for position, the riff-raff of hangers-on tried to be in the right place when the winner who was beside himself with triumph threw his money in the air.

But it was not in Arabella's nature to remain a spectator, and in her purse she had all the money her father had given her. She stood behind Lady Faversham's chair for just so long, and then she leant forward and tentatively put down her stake on red. The numbers confused and mystified her, but the colours she could respond to. As the wheel turned she could feel her heart beating faster, and when red came up she was so pleased she confidently staked all her winnings on red – to win again.

The heart beats became louder in her ears, there was a trembling in her arms and legs, a throbbing in her head. She thought: here it is again, this amazing feeling, this surge of excitement, this catch in the breath, this exaltation. Her eyes were brilliant as she watched the spin of the wheel, utterly absorbed in the little white ball bouncing there, but her hand was steady as she leaned forward again and then again to put down her stake on red with an air of calm decision. Already she had a superstitious faith in red.

Lady Faversham beside her, breathed words of quiet caution.

'But I am winning,' Arabella said. 'And I am not risking more than my original stake of ten francs, I am only risking my winnings.'

She went on winning, a chair was found for her beside Lady Faversham, a number of lorgnettes were focused on her, for the combination of her youth and beauty and her immediate good fortune made an impression on this sophisticated gathering, even though her stakes were modest. The very brilliance of the lights seemed to spotlight her as she sat serene in her place, queenly in her success.

For this occasion she was wearing a new and flattering gown of deep crimson velvet, the skirt elegantly draped to the back, the neckline wide and low. The colour glowed richly in the gaslight and it enhanced the warm pallor of her skin. Her hair was piled proudly up and away from her face without any vagrant ringlets tonight, and the coils of hair were burnished with a rich gleam. The fine, full length of her graceful neck was accentuated by a necklace of the newest and most fashionable design. It was a simple ribbon of crimson velvet and in the centre of it a brooch like a star of amethyst and gold and pearls, richly ornate. It had been her father's gift to her on her twentieth birthday and it was worth ten times more than he could afford.

All Arabella's concentration was on the play. She was rapidly losing herself in the game she played, seeing only the little ball running on the roulette wheel, bouncing over the partitions, hearing only the clink of coins, the sweeping sound and the monotone voice repeating the same words over and over: 'Faites vos jeux, mesdames et messieurs, rien ne va plus.' As she continued to win, the excitement grew inside her, lifting her out of herself till she felt a fever of jubilant triumph. Now she could do no wrong, now everything was on her side. How absurd to calculate the chances with pencil and paper and careful sums, as some were doing! How tedious to be careful when it was so glorious to take risks! She staked her francs on red at random. Expectation of winning and confidence of success shone in her face.

'Beginner's luck,' Lady Faversham said, putting a hand of caution and discretion on her arm. 'Don't go on until it runs out.'

But she went on with a triumphant eagerness to win again, and then again, conscious of all eyes on her, radiant in her success, and the croupier called out: 'Rouge!' and again 'Rouge' as if he was arranging it all for her. Money was thrust towards her, piling up in front of her on the table, a roll of bank notes in a sealed blue paper wrapping and a pile of gold coins all for her.

Then suddenly she saw a hand – one of so many hands stretching forth on to the baize – this one a thieving hand closing swiftly over her gold coins. She gasped and made a helpless gesture of protest. Tried to identify the thief among the close-packed throng. Appealed to the croupier: 'Monsieur, je pense –', but she couldn't make him hear. She looked to right and left, startled, angry, confused.

'Permit me, mademoiselle.' The man standing at her side leaned over the table and seized the plundering hand forcefully, pulling the thief forth into full view, displaying the crime and calling on the croupier to take action. His voice was authoritative, English, and immediately effective.

Shouts broke forth all around. Arabella looked up at her champion and found herself looking into a young face of handsome and ardent seriousness, with eyes that were dramatically dark.

Officials of the casino seized the thief, he was made to turn out his pockets and all the time the illicit coins were pouring forth from the folds of his cape, he protested his innocence. He declared that he was insulted by wrongful accusation, he was a Polish count of noble lineage.

'If you are a Polish count, I am the King of England.' The voice at Arabella's side was as rich and dark as the dramatic eyes and it stirred her senses even in the bewilderment of the moment – one could take fire from such a voice. There was confusion and unintelligible gabble on all sides. The trance-like absorption of the roulette players had in a moment erupted into a thousand voices shouting and disagreeing.

'We should withdraw, my dear,' Lady Faversham said, recoiling at such brawling vulgarity.

The thief was sent packing from the casino with his pockets empty and Lady Faversham and Arabella rose to their feet. Sir Hugo hastened over to them and Arabella's defender brought to her all the money he had rescued for her.

'We are much indebted to you, sir,' Sir Hugo began, and then broke off. 'God bless my soul – Conroy. What are you doing here? Damned good job you were here – isn't that so, Emily? Arabella?'

He was introduced to her then. James Conroy. He was a man she found she very much wanted to know. And in his grave regard of her she could read his profound interest, such an intense gaze deep into her eyes as if he would read her very thoughts. She had to make a conscious effort to hide her own interest under a semblance of polite decorum.

'I am most grateful to you, Mr Conroy.'

'Indeed, it was my pleasure, Miss Curtis.'

When the party withdrew from the gaming room to an

adjoining salon where the ladies could rest on the ottomans and recover from the unpleasant occurrence, Mr Conroy accompanied them.

'This is a strange place to find one of your persuasion,' Sir Hugo observed to Conroy, and his voice, partly from deafness and partly from the habit of making himself heard in the Chamber of the House of Lords, had a carrying quality like a clarion. Arabella didn't miss a word. 'Have you come here to convert us to yet another new cause?'

'I've come to Reisbaden to meet a colleague. Looked in on the casino purely from curiosity. We're on our way to an important meeting at Berlin University –'

'That's where the young revolutionaries meet these days, is it? All the disciples of that dreadful fellow John Stuart Mill?'

'The disciples of Engels rather.'

'Engels is it? And what is his theory?'

'That capitalism is inefficient, unfair, cruel and immoral. He and Marx –'

'Bah!' Sir Hugo snorted with lordly disgust. 'Don't talk to me of Marx –'

Arabella had not the least idea what they were talking about, the names meant nothing to her. But there was a stirring quality in Conroy's voice that appealed to her strongly, an ardent assurance that she responded to. On the ottoman beside her, Lady Faversham with a lace handkerchief pressed to her lips, whispered: 'Mr Conroy is a writer with some very odd and advanced ideas. But he is quite well connected. I'm sure I'm right in saying he's distantly related to the Duke of Monford.'

Mr Conroy, it appeared, did not approve of gambling. He expressed his scorn for people who needed the application of the most gross and violent stimulants such as the fear of losing their ill-gotten gains, before they could feel any sensation.

'You would condemn us all then?' Sir Hugo enquired, bantering, relishing a debate. 'You would even begrudge Arabella the winnings you rescued for her, you stern socialist moralist?'

'By no means. It is possible for gambling to be a most interesting test of character.' Conroy bowed and his dark eyes smiled at Arabella. 'How could anyone begrudge her pleasure? And I am certain the money is in good hands, that Miss Curtis intends it for a worthy purpose.'

Arabella had been entertaining the thought of spending her winnings on one of the new sealskin jackets that she had been coveting ever since they became the fashion. She re-arranged her ideas and said: 'I haven't had time yet to consider how I shall use it, Mr Conroy. How would you have me put it to good effect?'

'I could tell you a thousand ways. If you could have seen, as I have seen, the poverty and the distress of the industrial towns of northern England –'

For a moment Arabella had a vision of herself as Lady Bountiful gracefully distributing largess in the slums, but Sir Hugo interrupted again.

'Enough. Enough. Arabella doesn't want to hear. You and I and Arabella can no more stem the tide of poverty than King Canute could stop the sea coming in.'

'We can try,' James Conroy said. 'We live in changing times,' and he looked at Arabella as if all things were possible.

Sir Hugo decided that he too would rest awhile after the excitement of gambling and the drama of the captured thief. The salon was very warm and to partake of a little refreshment in their quiet corner would be best for him and for Lady Faversham.

'But Arabella would perhaps prefer to take a little exercise, a stroll through the salons if you would escort her, Conroy,' Sir Hugo said. 'A little fresh air would be beneficial, in moderation.'

The salons of the casino outside the gaming rooms were a constantly changing pattern as the players came and went and the onlookers sat at their ease or strolled about.

Conroy led Arabella to a window leading on to the terrace. Beyond the balustrade, the outline of spires and gables against the starry sky was a dramatic backcloth and the lights of Reisbaden gleamed.

'How fine the city looks from here,' Arabella exclaimed.

'A romantic viewpoint. I thought it would appeal to you,' Conroy observed her rather than the view. 'You are enjoying your visit to Reisbaden?'

'Indeed yes. It is full of interest. It is in fact my first visit to a foreign city, so it is all new to me.'

'You see it with a responsive and unprejudiced mind and that is so refreshing to encounter. So many compare the boredom of Baden Baden with the monotony of Marienbad, the tedium of Carlsbad with the ennui of Aix-la-Chapelle –'

'Though I should like to visit all these places –' Arabella cried with immediate enthusiasm. 'You yourself are widely travelled, Mr Conroy?'

Mr Conroy described for her his early education in Switzerland, his years of study at Berlin University, his meeting with the great philosopher Karl Marx and how it had changed his life completely. He had heard Karl Marx address a mass rally of workers and felt himself stirred, inspired and deeply impressed.

Arabella only partly understood him, but he spoke with such eloquence and fervour his voice thrilled her, his eyes burned with zeal and his idealism uplifted her.

'I think you too can inspire, Mr Conroy,' Arabella said. He seemed to her a man of great depth and intelligence and wide understanding. When he gazed into her face as he was doing now, it was not with the vacant adoration that she had seen on the faces of the young men of Bishop's Linden, it was as if he would know everything about her.

'If you really think that, Miss Curtis, nothing could please me more. But if it is so, then it must be because I recognize in you a responsive spirit, a mind capable of new horizons. I wonder if you will allow me a great privilege in honour of this meeting? I would like very much to make a presentation to you of a volume of my own work on the subject that is so important to me.' Conroy produced a slim volume and handed it to her.

'The Decline of Capitalism and the Development of the Communist Answer'. Arabella pronounced the title with some difficulty. 'How fine and splendid your name looks upon the spine, Mr Conroy.'

With her permission, James Conroy inscribed the copy of his book for her – dating it 'On the occasion of our meeting at Reisbaden' and signing it 'With the compliments and admiration of the author.'

'I shall study it with great interest,' Arabella said, and as she took the book from him he leant forward to see that the ink was dry on the page. His face for a moment was so close to her's that the book outstretched between them seemed to tremble and as if in response to that uncontrollable tremor their eyes met above the opened page in a moment of surprised recognition. Only once before had she felt that strange spontaneous uncontrollable rise of emotion, only once before dancing five times, but she could not think of that now –

'And while you are staying in Reisbaden, Miss Curtis,' Conroy was saying, 'There are many places of outstanding interest that you should visit.'

'Sir Hugo has made plans, I believe, for us to visit the Platte. There is a fine view of the city from there, he tells me, and in the shooting lodge a quite exceptional collection of antlers.'

'The antlers are quite exceptional, as you say,' James Conroy said seriously, but then they smiled at the same moment with friendly conspiratorial understanding. 'I was thinking of somewhere more romantic,' Conroy continued. 'I feel you should experience the great beauty of the Greek Chapel in the heart of the forests. It was erected as a mausoleum for the first wife of Duke Adolph of Nassau and there are five gilded domes surmounted by Russian double crosses.'

'I have heard this spoken of,' Arabella said, 'But I think Sir Hugo considered it in some way hazardous to the health –'

'I should be the one to introduce you to the beauty of the place,' Conroy said. 'It is my misfortune that I have so little time in Reisbaden, but there is tomorrow –' Suddenly to her astonishment he seized her hand, clasped it to his heart and spoke with urgency. 'Will you – dare you – meet me tomorrow, at the Greek Chapel in the forests?'

It would be indiscreet, it would be most unseemly, indeed quite shocking for her to go alone, to meet this man, unchaperoned. It would be very exciting. All the reticences and taboos of her upbringing flashed warningly before her eyes. But she had not been subdued or repressed by the restrictions of the society in which she lived. She was eager for excitement, extending a universal welcome to life in all its fullness and variety.

'I am not certain that would be possible,' Arabella said, but the light in her eyes belied the doubt in her words and she realized that he knew that.

'I shall wait for you, at noon tomorrow. You will find me there.'

She stood facing him, the book he had given her clasped close to her, breathing quickly and aware of the quickening of her heart.

When Arabella left the casino with the Favershams she said with warm appreciation: 'Oh how I admire a man with intellect and aspirations.'

'Indeed?' Lady Faversham said, smiling. 'I hadn't noticed that you had any marked preference for intellectual company.'

Arabella spoke with the fervour of someone who had only just discovered the fact herself. 'Oh I realize now that is what I most admire – intellect and lofty ideals.'

'I feel sure,' Lady Faversham said still smiling, 'that as James Conroy is staying in Reisbaden for a day or so, we shall see him again.'

And shall I see him again, alone, in the forests, a secret assignation? Arabella asked herself and that night she couldn't sleep for wondering. Of course, it was impossible for her to go, impossible for her to mention the suggestion to the Favershams, impossible for her to find her way quite alone from Reisbaden to the Greek chapel It was shocking that he should make such an invitation and she would not consider it for a moment...

It might be possible to hire a carriage, she thought suddenly, they were waiting for hire at the railway station and it would not attract attention.

But it was unthinkable that she should deceive her hosts, her kind friends and escape their protective care ...

Yet their morning routine was unalterable, the ritual of

thermal baths occupied Sir Hugo; Lady Faversham never varied her taking of the waters and her constitutional promenade. It would be so easily accepted if Arabella were to say she preferred to remain at the hotel, and she could return in time for luncheon...

But what manner of a man was he, James Conroy, that he extended such an outrageous invitation to her? Sir Hugo had acknowledged his advanced political ideals yet the Favershams accepted him and his background must be socially impeccable for them to do that. She could recognize in him a daring free spirit – and how she could admire that.

Arabella stared bright eyed into the darkness, with an elation of heart and mind that made sleep impossible. She was up on the high plane again that she ascended to after her five dances with Neville Rossiter. This passionate excitement she could recognize now, delighting in it. It was a surge of exultation through her veins.

And yet – and yet – Arabella had to rise from her bed and pace about the room to keep up with her changing thoughts. She felt anger suddenly: he had insulted her by his unseemly invitation.

But even as she thought of him with anger, she saw again, clearly and vividly, the ardent admiration in his dark eyes that was almost like tenderness, heard the fervour of his compelling voice. She must match his daring and accept the challenge – just as she had accepted the challenge of the five dances – she must be his equal in response and be above the confines of discretion.

Then doubts assailed her once again. For to go at his invitation, heedless of convention and the damage to her reputation, was that not a complete sacrifice of her power? She would not be in control of the encounter, to come running at his invitation was to surrender, to acknowledge her own eagerness and desire, just as if she had meekly accepted Neville Rossiter's offer of marriage...

Again and once again, Arabella paced the room. The ruched green silk dress would look well for the occasion she thought. She could see herself descending from the carriage at the Greek Chapel, seeing him waiting for her, a dark and intense figure below the splendour of the golden domes, walking to meet him, head held high, walking as she always walked as if a carpet of honour was spread before her feet.

When it was light, Arabella sat by the window and turned the pages of the treatise James Conroy had presented to her. The paragraphs were exceedingly long. She struggled for a time but though it inspired her admiration for James Conroy's intellectual powers, her real enthusiasm for the book was for the fly-leaf and the words scrawled there with such a bold flourish – 'On the occasion of our meeting in Reisbaden'. Who could tell what would happen at their next meeting?

But it was not to be. When Arabella woke from a brief snatch of sleep, she gave instructions to the maid that she would take breakfast in her room. But scarcely had the maid departed when a telegraph was brought to her with news from England.

She stared at it with horror and alarm. A telegraph had never entered her life before and her first reaction was of astonishment that her mother had managed to send one, then the words chilled her. 'Father gravely ill – not expected to live – asking for you – return home if at all possible – haste essential.'

Arabella thought of her father as she had so often known him, grey-faced and taut, a muscle twitching in his cheek, gripped by the nervous tension of his complaint, refusing all food and speaking only in irritable monosyllables. He often seemed a bleak and solitary man but she knew all about his kindness – she better than anyone. Though stern in manner, he had never refused her anything. Dismay and affection overwhelmed her.

In her distress she turned naturally to her dear friends the Favershams, showing them the telegraph. 'I think my father must have some kind of stroke. I must go home at once.'

A pained look came over Sir Hugo's fine patrician face. 'Why must you? What is the use? However quickly you hasten your journey you are unlikely to be in time. Quite likely he won't know you and there will be precious little you can do.'

And Lady Faversham said: 'How very unfortunate that it should have happened now.'

When Arabella insisted that she must go immediately, the look on Sir Hugo's face told her that she was being tiresome. More than anything else, he looked peeved. To interrupt their pleasant sojourn in Reisbaden with her domestic problems was irritating of her and moreover deprived him of her company. He was put out by it; he felt disappointed in Arabella.

Lady Faversham was preoccupied with the fact that Arabella hadn't travelled with her own maid. 'You cannot possibly travel home to England alone. And I don't see how I can spare my Molly to travel with you.'

'No, of course you can't,' Sir Hugo said, very brusque. 'That is out of the question. It's very difficult d'you see? Now we will have to find someone suitable, travelling to England . . .'

Arabella withdrew feeling hurt and disconcerted in addition to her anxiety for her father. All too well she could imagine the scenes now in Bishop's Linden – her mother tearful and distraught, her sisters fearful and ineffectual. Of course she must go at once. She was the one who could help her father, if only by her presence. She knew so well the light that came into his face at the sight of her, she could restore his spirits, and sooth away his distress, of that she was confident. But there was disappointment immediate and keen in the realization that she must leave and return home without delay. It filled her with keen regret to be leaving Reisbaden – a place so full of new, interesting, intellectual people – of meeting James Conroy again, perhaps even alone, at the Greek chapel in the forests. The invitation that had been exercising her thoughts and passions all night long, it was no longer within her power to accept. All that it might have been, remained conjecture. And now she was quite certain that she would have gone to meet him.

Lady Faversham came to Arabella's room and said : 'I have such good news for you, my dear.' Arabella's heart lifted in hope of she knew not what. But the good news was only that Lady Faversham had been successful in finding a companion for Arabella's journey. The Honourable Mrs Proctor, it seemed, was returning to England but she was leaving by the midday train. Arabella was advised to make all haste. Lady Faversham's Molly would come and pack her clothes for her.

43

Sir Hugo so organized matters that he succeeded in getting Arabella to the station at least half an hour before she needed to be there. There was a constraint of manner throughout her departure that made Arabella feel that she was returning home in disgrace rather than in response to an emergency, for the Favershams were put out by her departure, and it had the effect of disapproval. The Honourable Mrs Proctor in no way helped matters. A granite-faced griffin, pious and unbending, she had taken the waters of Reisbaden most assiduously. Not for her the diversions of the roulette table and the gossip and the balls. But the waters had done her little good. She was returning to England as sour and grey as she had come.

And she made it clear that she did not approve of young women who spent the greater part of their time gazing dreamily from the window as the train sped across Europe, or who read from a book with a kind of rapture and seemed at times to be almost stroking the pages.

CHAPTER THREE

Arabella completed her long and wearisome journey, her spirits low and her anxieties about her father increasing with every mile. When she arrived at Bishop's Linden station, there was only a growler available to convey her to the house in Lansdowne Road. It was a vehicle she always disliked for it had a gloomy interior and a funereal pace. The leaves of all the lime trees hung limply in a light persistent rain. It seemed to her that the low skies over England were weeping with her, and when she reached the house she found that even the aspidistra which had stood in its Grecian urn beside the window for as long as she could remember, had drooped and died.

As she had feared, she found her mother prostrated with helpless grief, and her sisters full of useless agitation and alarm. Her Uncle Edward had moved in. Her mother had turned instinctively to her only male relative, her bachelor brother, and he had come at once. Edward Couchman was a Government clerk, but his main concern was with the church where he was a sidesman and his one remedy to all problems was to bow to God's will, to submit in humility to one's fate.

Her mother was almost incoherent in her distress. 'I'm so thankful you've come, Bella. It's been so terrible – and I don't understand – and he won't speak – only your name.'

'Did my father suffer some kind of stroke?' Arabella asked, unable to escape from her mother's clinging arms even to remove her mantle or to go upstairs to her father.

'A stroke? Yes, from the shock, the doctor said. As soon as you left your poor dear father felt unwell and seemed to give up, to lie on his bed without moving. I thought to send word after you and reach you at Dover before the party left for the Continent, but you know how often he has suffered cruelly with his stomach and then there was the disappointment of your refusing to marry Mr Rossiter.'

Arabella flinched and was filled with remorse.

'He had set his heart on your marrying brilliantly and I thought it was just all these things. But then we had callers from London. They were most rude and disagreeable and I couldn't understand why they should be so unpleasant and when they talked with your father he fell down in some kind of coma and he has not moved from his bed since then.'

Arabella hastened to her father's bedside and was shocked by the change in him. The stillness of the figure lying propped up with pillows, the greyness of his skin, the shrunken look about him, even his face seemed to have changed. At first she was too shaken by her dismay to do more than sit at his side, taking his hand from the coverlet to hold it in hers. It felt so cold, inanimate.

'Father,' she said with hopelessness in her heart. 'It's Arabella, Father.'

Then she saw the line of his eyelids lift and that his eyes in deep caves were alert and painfully aware. 'Arabella. At last.' It didn't seem possible that a voice could come from the cracked lips, and the voice was so hoarse and rasping that at once she had to beg him not to try to speak. But he seemed desperate to speak at however great the cost, to speak to her. His hands clawed at the covers in agitation. Arabella must fetch the ledger from his study, locked in the desk. With

45

enormous difficulty he indicated the key to unlock the drawer and she went down to his study to fetch the ledger, feeling at once the strangeness of opening drawers she had never opened and taking out a book that she had never seen.

The ledger when she brought it was far too heavy for him to hold. He kept pointing at the pages, telling her she must look and understand. Arabella looked at page after page of columns of figures entered in her father's precise hand and it conveyed nothing to her.

'Grandison and Fergus,' her father said. 'Failed. All the railway shares – worthless. The bank foreclosing. The mortgage, bills –'

Arabella stared, strained to hear, baffled and struggling to comprehend. He was telling her there was no money, that he faced financial ruin and her mind reeled away from the shock.

He must be confused in his mind, it must be a delusion, some nightmare of sickness.

'There is no more money,' William Curtis said and his voice was so hollow it seemed like a voice from the grave, forcing her to believe its truth. 'No money to pay the servants – for the house – the food. No money for poor, poor Hester and all your sisters. Only debts, Arabella.'

'Don't, Father, don't try to sit up. Don't try to talk. There is nothing you can do –' Arabella said filled with compassion for the frail figure, the cold hands clutching at her arm, the hoarse whisper urgently telling its sorry tale.

'Nothing,' her father's last effort seemed to collapse under the strain. 'Nothing. And there is no one, not Hester, no one. You are the only one, Arabella, only you – you.'

'I shall take care of everything, Father. Please don't distress yourself so. It will all be all right again, now I am here.'

'You are here,' William Curtis said. 'Now you are here.' He seemed to take some comfort from that and for a moment his eyes closed. Then painfully the eyelids lifted again to reveal the tormented eyes that flickered to and fro like some hunted animal in its last retreat. 'But I have failed and left you destitute.'

It was the last word he spoke and it seemed to echo on and on in Arabella's head during the succeeding days while her father sunk deeper and deeper into his coma of unconsciousness. He passed almost imperceptibly from there into death and a sombre cloud of mourning descended upon the house. The heavy fringed and tasselled curtains were drawn across the windows, shutting out the obtrusive spring sunlight and the door knocker was draped in crape. Her mother lay moaning upon her bed and her sisters, very young and white-faced in their black dresses scuttled about the house like frightened spiders.

Paying her last respects to her father, Arabella felt most of all a remorseful sadness. She had taken his favour, affection and indulgence of herself completely as her right, utterly for granted. He had delighted in her existence, she could do no wrong in his eyes. She stood looking down at her father's face, more relaxed than she had ever known it, and was filled with regret for the way she had scarcely troubled to show him the strong affection she felt for him.

Awareness of her shortcomings towards him and regrets for what she could never do for him now, mingled with Arabella's grief. In accordance with his last wishes, she studied with care the long closely-figured pages of the ledger and became as she did so more and more baffled. For there appeared to be no income at all, there was no way in which the figures could be made to balance.

'There must be some mistake,' Arabella cried. She sat now, in her turn, at her father's desk in his study, trying to comprehend something she had never thought about before. She was as ignorant as her mother of the business details of their resources. They lived in comfort. They had a cook and a maid and a slavey to help in the house and a man to do the garden. They didn't own a carriage, but they didn't want for ordinary things. If her father had looked tight-lipped sometimes when she had wanted a better horse to ride, a new gown for the ball at the Assembly Rooms, or the money for her trip to Reisbaden, she had thought it was just his way.

He had always produced the money; he had always indulged her generously, as he had with the magnificent necklace he had bought her for her birthday. William Curtis had succeeded in sheltering his wife and daughters from the financial

47

realities of life; he had given them the happiness of complete security, taking all the acute anxieties of doing so upon himself. It had turned into acid poison in his body.

Ruin stared Arabella in the face from the pages of the ledger. Not only had the income from the shares ceased completely, there was a long list of debts and mortgages and bills not paid. The word that had been haunting her sleeping and waking, became a reality – they were joining the ranks of the destitute.

This wasn't as intended at all: she had grown up with a conviction that she was to shine in the world with brilliance like a star. It wasn't intended that she should be ground down by the fortunes of fate, subdued by poverty and distress. She had often thought it was her misfortune to have been born into a modest background with a very limited scope and income. Now it seemed even those modest supports were to be denied her.

How could such things happen? Who could advise her? Her father's lawyer came to the house. He was a very small man who spoke in such a discreet whisper she could scarcely hear what he said. She couldn't believe that such a diminutive individual could be of any help to her. 'We will talk again after the deceased is laid to rest,' he said.

Hester Curtis, anguished and ill, was quite set upon attending the funeral. It was the one thing she was determined upon, the one act she would carry out at all cost. She rose from her bed, shaky and tremulous, and her daughters dressed her in sooty-black paramatta covered with crape and coiled her hair into the old-fashioned loops over her ears that made her look like a pathetic spaniel.

Supported by her brother Edward on one side and Arabella on the other, she descended to the funeral carriage. The cortege began its slow and painful progress through the town; hats were doffed and heads were bowed as it proceeded. William Curtis's journey beneath a black pall crowned with wreaths and black ostrich feathers was more impressive than any journey he had made in life.

Half-swooning, Hester sat cowed in the awesome Gothic vastness of Holy Trinity, listening to Canon Gore-Stanley speak with the evangelical fervour that had made him famous and attracted Christians from far and wide to come and live in Bishop's Linden under his ministry. Clinging desperately to Arabella she followed the hearse out into the cemetery where the keen spring winds and bright intermittent sunshine and racing clouds were incongruously full of life and movement. The wind unabashed tossed the jet plumes and tails of the funeral horses and disarrayed the black draperies of the veiled women, as freely as it tossed the blossom on the trees.

Hester Curtis kept to her feet, right to the last. It was her great achievement. Then she gave in to her affliction, retired to her bedroom and collapsed completely. Below her the small drawing room was dark with people in mourning talking in hushed tones. Relations Arabella had never seen before arrived and played their parts with due solemnity and left and she never saw them again. Uncle Edward during those days remained with his head permanently bowed.

Arabella sat with the little solicitor and listened to what he had to say, and watched him turning over books and papers in hopelessness. Everything was in perfect order, meticulously recorded and painstakingly correct. But she was quite right in her understanding of their financial situation. There was no money at all.

How unlucky her father had been, Arabella thought, her heart aching for him. So many had made handsome fortunes out of railway shares; but he had put his money into a line that was never built. He had been badly abused by his advisers, but more than anything else luck had been against him and he had been the victim of chance.

There were so many bills and liabilities. The mortgage on the house in Lansdowne Road could only be settled by putting it up for sale. They must find some very modest rented home; the estate would claim everything of value to pay off the debts. It was all worse than she had imagined it could be. It was clearly essential for her to earn her living, to support the household. She must at once give notice to the cook and the parlour maid and make arrangements for her horse to be sold. Already it had been found acutely difficult to pay for the black gowns they must all wear. She must explain, as best she could, to her prostrated mother and her helpless sisters the disastrous state of their fortunes.

Poor Hester Curtis wrung her hands and moaned pitifully. How was she ever to face people in Bishop's Linden again? 'Lady Darnley,' she wailed. 'Mrs Mansard. Mrs Worthington-Smyth. Mrs Hamilton.' Each name was more agonizing than the last.

Her sisters talked of taking in sewing to earn a little money.

'That will not be necessary,' Arabella said. 'I shall take care of everything.' But she had only vague ideas of how she was going to do it.

She sat beside her mother's bed, comforting her. 'You are not to worry, Mama. There is nothing for you to worry about. Now I am here I shall take care of everything.'

'Oh I am so thankful you are here, dearest Bella. You were so far away when I needed you. Oh, if we had known Bella if we had known. I cannot help wishing – if it had been possible for you to accept Mr Rossiter.'

Arabella broke from her mother's clinging arms and sat upright, her head held very high. 'Mama, do not speak to me of Mr Rossiter. I told you, I never want to hear of him again.'

Hester's tears flowed afresh. 'How can I help but want the best for you, Bella. It would have been such a brilliant match, it would have meant the future secured for you. And I thought you liked him, Bella,' she added wistfully.

'Why should you think that?' Arabella asked harshly. 'Just because I danced with him.'

'Five times,' her mother said. 'Five times, Bella.'

Arabella couldn't begin to explain. The five dances had been a challenge. He had dared her to accept. She thought of his arrogance and his condescension here in her home and was infuriated my him all over again. I think I hate him, she thought suddenly. I think I have never hated anyone so much ever before.

When the cook and the parlour maid departed the family were reduced to the rough ministrations of the slavey, a little creature called Lil who had a lop-sided look as though always cowering away expecting a blow to be aimed at her. It never had been at Lansdowne Road, but she hadn't managed to straighten up in two years there. Arabella gave instructions for the running of the household and her sisters in their clumsy amateur way and Lil in her simple-minded way, struggled to carry them out. Arabella herself never stayed long in the kitchen.

The meals were not up to standard, but neither Hester lying in the darkened room with her smelling salts nor the girls gathered round the dining table had any appetite. Only Uncle Edward ate slowly and steadily through everything. He was a dried-up bony man with a great capacity for food. Arabella found the steady chomping of his jaws intensely irritating.

'I feel sure you must be needed at your office, Uncle Edward,' she said. 'Now that I have returned, I feel we should not keep you here.'

'It is my duty to stay,' said Edward Couchman, his head bowed low now over the mutton. 'Greatly as I would wish to be back at my desk. I must stay until I can feel I have instilled God's will into your understanding. And until some alternative accommodation has been found for you.'

He always looked at Arabella as if her earthly radiance offended him. A few days later he announced that he had been successful in finding an alternative home for them in Bishop's Linden. In Quarry Road, he said, with a kind of satisfaction.

Hester, who had begun to feel just a little stronger, gave a shriek of horror when he told her. Bishop's Linden had its area of slums, as every town had. Hester had never been there. Neither, in fact, had Arabella. The slums began at the end of Quarry Road.

'What number Quarry Road? Is that at the top or the bottom?'

'It is Number 22 – that's about half way,' her brother told her. 'It is not a slum property. It is a respectable artisan's dwelling.'

Arabella listened to them arguing whether 22 was nearer the top or the bottom and through her mother's horror and dismay, she could sense her meek acceptance of the inevitable.

'This is intolerable,' she said. 'How can my mother possibly live there?'

'With humility –' Edward Couchman began, but Arabella wouldn't let him continue.

'No. You are not to move Mama. You are not to consider this respectable artisan's dwelling for a moment. I shall make other arrangements.'

'What will you do, Bella?' Hester asked, looking up fearfully at her daughter.

'I have my own plans,' she said. 'Don't ask me now. I shall tell you when matters are arranged.'

Arabella went first of all to call upon her friends the Favershams, who had now returned from Reisbaden.

Lady Faversham spoke kindly. 'We were so sad to lose your company in Reisbaden,' she said.

Arabella responded, warmed by the note of sympathy.

'At least I was in time to speak with my father before he died. But these are very sad times for my family. My father's income has ceased altogether and we face financial ruin, indeed we must leave Lansdowne Road at once and I must seek employment.'

She didn't seek pity or compassion. She didn't get it. Sir Hugo and Lady Faversham refused to accept the possibility of anything so disturbingly inconvenient and upsetting. It must all be a mistake.

Lady Faversham laid a gentle hand on Arabella's. 'Don't be too distressed, my dear. Everything appears very black at the time of bereavement. Your father's business affairs are naturally thrown into some confusion.'

Sir Hugo seized upon that as the best and most comfortable explanation. 'You have to be patient, d'you see. These legal fellows always take a deuce of a time to sort things out. No doubt you'll find it will all be all right in the end.'

As to the prospect of her finding employment, Sir Hugo didn't think that was advisable. 'I don't think you would find it at all agreeable, you know. And what could you do?'

Arabella had been thinking about that. 'I could perhaps became an actress,' she said. Arabella's experience of the theatre was limited, but Public Rooms for entertainment had been opened in Bishop's Linden only the year before and she had attended to hear Mrs Scott Siddon give readings from

Dickens and Shakespeare and a certain Miss Enriquez give a dramatic performance of The Caliph's Daughter. Arabella considered that she could perform quite as well as Miss Enriquez who was not even particularly beautiful.

Sir Hugo dismissed that idea very quickly. 'You can have no idea I think, my dear, of the lives these people lead. Artists they call themselves, but they are mostly Bohemian riff-raff with no decorum. Behind the performance that you see on the stage there is squalid struggle for existence without payment or praise.'

'You would not care for that at all,' Lady Faversham said and Arabella was forced to agree that it did not accord with her idea of what her role in life should be.

The Favershams refused to believe in her problems, offered no guidance, gave her no hope and said they were leaving Bishop's Linden to spend a few weeks of the season in London. Sir Hugo felt in need of a little diversion, Bishop's Linden could be so very dull at this time of year, wouldn't she agree, and there was a dampness in the air, something enervating in the atmosphere of the town, they were not at all certain that it was good for his constitution.

Arabella left their urbane company with her spirits very low. Their reactions had given her a cold foretaste of what lay in store for her now in her changed circumstances.

The following week she found herself assisting, in a very humble capacity, at a board School. Uncle Edward had been assiduous in his efforts and he had persuaded — 'with some difficulty' – he said, a leading member of the Committee of the Town Mission Ragged and Industrial Schools to give employment to Arabella. Her task was to attend the church school and to instruct the girls in the rudiments of writing.

'It is a great boon to these poor girls,' said Mr Clough, he was a man exuding good conscience, deeply aware of his own benevolence. 'I am happy, with Divine blessing, to render a satisfactory account. There has been no falling off in the female classes. As some leave to go into service, others take their places.'

The boys attended tailoring and shoemaking classes and habits of industry and good order were promoted by the school. 'Not only moral good is effected,' said Mr Clough with an air of worthiness and complacency Arabella had never seen equalled, 'but good of a spiritual kind also. You must understand that while their hands are busily employed, they are listening to the Word of God being read and explained to them.' This was a task which Mr Clough took upon himself.

For two days Arabella presented herself at the school at the appointed time and submitted to its routine. The curriculum for the girls, she discovered consisted of learning collections of facts parrot fashion and copying copperplate writing. The girls were docile, servile; they seemed cowed and apprehensive. 'Your predecessor, Miss Sharp, had a strong sense of discipline. She was a most devout lady,' Mr Clough added. He had his doubts about Arabella's fitness for the post. He had been persuaded, as ever, by his Christian principles, but he found her too young, too spirited, too womanly, too disturbing. He had grave misgivings.

On the third day, Mr Clough had a report to prepare for the committee and as none of the team of pious ladies who assisted him in the work of Bible reading to the industrious children was available, Arabella was called upon to undertake the task. The Book of Ezekiel was laid before her.

When Mr Clough had completed his work, with Divine Blessing, he returned to the classroom and was aghast at what he heard – Arabella's voice, clear and bell-like reading of towered Camelot:

'And sometimes thro' the mirror blue The knights came riding two and two: She hath no loyal knight and true, The Lady of Shalott.'

Arabella had quickly wearied of Ezekiel and turned to Tennyson instead.

'This is no place for poetry,' Mr Clough said in a voice like thunder.

'I see no reason why not,' Arabella said, 'It is not sinful.'

'It is not suitable,' Mr Clough said. 'These poor children have to earn a living. By the grace of God they are fortunate enough to be allowed to come here to receive some rudimentary education and to receive spiritual guidance. There is no room for poetry in their lives. I will not have it.'

'Then this is no place for me,' Arabella said.

'I thought this was how it would be,' Mr Clough concluded, all his doubts thoroughly realized to his satisfaction.

Arabella left the board school without a backward glance, but she left behind some regrets in the half-formed minds of the repressed children and one child at least was left wondering what became of The Lady of Shalott.

Hester Curtis stared fearfully at Arabella when she swept into the house with her head held high.

'I have left the school, it is not tolerable,' she said.

'What is to become of us?' Hester said and she took to her bed again.

'I have decided upon another course of action,' Arabella said. 'I intend to take a position as a governess.' To be such a Miss Humble was a future she would not have considered a few weeks ago, but now it compared with some favour in her mind after the Board School. At least she could teach the children as she saw fit, read Tennyson to them, and not be subservient to the obnoxious piety of such as Mr Clough.

Every morning for the next week Arabella sat in the drawing room reading the advertisements in the newspapers. Outside the spring sunlight was brilliant and it came into the room in slanting bands between the pendulous draperies at the window to lie across the wreath-pattern on the Brussels carpet and the faded plush of the over-stuffed furniture and the solid mahogany that was now filmed with dust. On every surface, in carved glass-fronted cabinets and all over the piano, there were displays of china and ornamental vases and family photographs. Scattered about the room there were cushions and runners, bell-ropes and firescreens, stools and antimacassars all patiently embroidered by the daughters of the house other than Arabella, who had no time for such things.

All the knick-knacks had taken on a pathetic look of doomed neglect now. She thought how she had always hated this room with its crowding furniture and oppressive atmosphere, but now that it must be dismantled, the room had a sweetness it had never possessed before. She looked round its solid security and plush comfort and thought of the utilitarian depths of Quarry Road to which, it seemed, they must now after all descend. There would be no place for her mother's beloved treasures there, not even the ormolu clock on the mantelshelf or the shell flowers under the glass case. She could cheerfully have consigned them one and all to the rubbish tip but she felt outraged to have them denied her by Fate.

The advertisements she read were no comfort to her. The most it seemed she could earn as a governess was thirty pounds a year. Arabella thought with vexation of the piles of money she had seen put down and raked away on the gaming tables of Reisbaden, so much more than a year's salary changing hands on the spin of a wheel.

Some of the advertisers even expected the applicant to pay fifty pounds for the privilege of having a comfortable home, the money to be repaid out of salary, which would take years and years, Arabella thought, dismayed. Another advertisement in *The Times* requested a lady to undertake the education of two children for no payment at all, a comfortable home in a Gentleman's family being considered equivalent to a salary. One advertisement in the local Gazette offered a salary of seven shillings a week to a daily governess 'able to teach English, French, Music, Needlework and perhaps Drawing'.

'And perhaps drawing,' Arabella said slamming the newspaper down in unladylike fashion. Her English and French were adequate if somewhat erratic, her abilities in music were distinctly modest, she was far too impatient to devote herself to Needlework for long, and she could not draw at all. The more she read the advertisements, the more forcibly it was borne in upon her, that she was not by nature or by temperament cut out to be a governess. The problem was not only would she be able to bear to apply herself to the post, but also would any employer consider her?

'To be reduced to this,' Arabella said, starting to her feet and walking about the room. It had all become like a bad dream and one from which she couldn't wake. Life, which she had confidently expected to open out before her, was closing in alarmingly. A pattern of drudgery and unpleasantness was taking shape. The prospect was mean and grey and depressed. To be a governess, to live out her days in the obscurity of some back bedroom and school-room, to have her meals brought to her there by servants who would despise her, to be surrounded every day by the giggles and taunts of obnoxious children – she could think of nothing she had done to deserve such a Fate.

Interruption came with the sound of carriage wheels in the drive. It was such a rare occurrence, particularly in these latter days, that she was even moved to walk to the window to catch a glimpse of so dignified an arrival, but she had no need to peep from the window. Loud and peremptory tones had already warned her that the Dowager Lady Darnley, her old adversary, was about to descend upon them.

With her mother still confining herself to her bed, Arabella received the lady, in all her splendour of peacock blue and ostrich feathers, quickly moving an occasional table, a vase and two miniatures out of the way of the massive circumference of her skirts as Lady Darnley advanced into the cramped and crowded room. Edward Couchman retreated backward before her, bowing. His devout humility extended not only to the Deity but to all personages of quality such as Lady Darnley.

'This will teach you to spurn proposals of marriage from gentlemen of high estate far above you,' Lady Darnley said, without preamble to Arabella. 'After the effrontery of the five dances at the Assembly Rooms, I see no reason why Bishop's Linden society should concern itself with your troubles. But your father was a quiet and much respected man in this town, even if your mother ... Yes. Well, it's quite clear you must take a situation and the sooner the better. I have heard of two possible positions among my acquaintance for which you might be suitable.'

'How exceptionally kind,' Edward Couchman said. 'How extraordinarily generous of your ladyship to concern yourself with our misfortunes.'

Lady Darnley looked at him with a moment's mild astonishment and then ignored him completely. She described the two situations and they sounded to Arabella equally disagreeable. One was as paid companion to a rich widow, a lady Arabella knew well enough to know that attending to her melancholy grumbles for an hour was unendurable, to do so every day was not a fate to be contemplated. The other lady was unknown to her. A Mrs Bayliss of Maidstone with three children was in need of the services of a governess.

'She doesn't seem able to keep her governesses very long. She would have preferred someone with experience but I told her she was in no position to be choosey. Her children, in my opinion, are spoilt and out of hand. They are in need of correction as much as instruction. I told her that you had the character for it, so she is prepared to consider you.'

'Since it seems I must find a situation as quickly as possible, I am much obliged to your ladyship,' Arabella said with an effort.

'Quite right. You go and see her. I've told her your circumstances. Told her you have my recommendation. But try to look and act like a governess. You should wear a grey holland pinafore, in my opinion.' Arabella's main disadvantage for the position, Lady Darnley knew, was that her looks would alarm Mrs Bayliss. She had an errant husband to contend with and she might not be prepared to run the risk of the lovely Arabella under her roof even to please Lady Darnley.

'I want to provide for my mother and my sisters. I am doing everything I can.' Arabella looked Lady Darnley straight in the eye with the kind of spirited determination that the dowager lady recognized.

'What you don't seem to have understood, child, is that it is essential for a young unmarried woman to give the impression of being gentle, yielding, submissive and passive. Whether she remains so after marriage is another matter. I most certainly did not. But you, Arabella, are not conveying the right impression at all. An air of submissiveness would be altogether more becoming.'

Edward Couchman joined in. 'This is what I have been saying to Arabella. In her present circumstances –'

But Lady Darnley never listened to anyone else's opinion. She swept towards the door, ignoring him as completely as the occasional tables and the what-nots that lay in her path.

When the splendour of Lady Darnley's carriage had withdrawn from the drive, Arabella was left with the prospect of an interview with Mrs Bayliss. One of the most pressing problems was lack of money. When she talked to her uncle about the matter of the money which she would need for her journey to Maidstone to see Mrs Bayliss he addressed her in words St Paul might have used.

Arabella left the room and went up to her bedroom. The 2nd class fare on the train to Maidstone was six shillings return. Where was she to find six shillings? It was possible to travel third class for only three shillings and fourpence return, but Arabella could not countenance that; she would sooner walk.

She was not permitted to sell any of the family possessions as they were being claimed by the estate. She took out her jewellery case. At least it was permitted for her to sell her own jewellery, but sadly it would not raise much. Only the necklace with the amethyst star was of any great value, the other pieces – a bracelet and a brooch and some beads – would raise only a little.

The sight of the necklace with the amethyst star on the velvet ribbon turned her thoughts back to the last time she had worn it – at the casino in Reisbaden. Then she had sat like a princess in her dress of crimson velvet, she had played roulette with such style and how successful she had been! All that money she had won so easily.

She sat stroking the velvet ribbon of the necklace and dreaming of a man with dark eyes and an ardent voice who had been so quick to come to her aid at the casino, who had looked into her face and had seemed to understand everything about her.

She said his name aloud, softly, to herself. James Conroy. It was a noble name. He was a man she could admire. A man of intellectual power and lofty idealism who cared nothing for the petty restrictions of polite conventions. A man who had admired her and invited her to meet him.

She sighed deeply and laid the crimson velvet against her cheek. He was far away and she would probably never see him again. She must sell the necklace and do her best to obtain a position as governess to the spoilt children of Mrs Bayliss of Maidstone, but she would remember him, and she would keep the book he had inscribed to her, she would keep it for ever.

CHAPTER FOUR

While Arabella went forth in search of a situation, Neville Rossiter journeyed southward through Europe. It was a raffish, hell-driven progress. He stopped off wherever a casino or a racecourse took his fancy, at Baden Baden, at Marienbad and at Longchamps. While in Paris he went to a party that lasted for three days. By the time his friend, Charles Sankey, had caught up with him his aggressively dissipated travels had reduced him to a kind of torpor. He sat on a terrace shaded by palm trees and oleanders with a bottle of absinth on the table before him. The girl who sat on his right side was exceedingly fair and the girl on his left side was duskily dark and in front of him the Mediterranean was so blue it hurt his eyes. His thoughts went no further than trying to decide whether he should spend the afternoon sailing that blue sea or whether he should just continue to sit and look at it.

In his dormant state Rossiter found the ebullience of Charles Sankey's greetings rather unnecessary. Sankey expressed his utter boredom with life, London and marriage true to the languid style then prevailing in Society, but his exuberant way of doing so was all his own. He had also acquired a mannered lisp and affected not to pronounce his Rs. He described at great length for Rossiter's benefit how he had come from Westwood where his wife had kept up continual fretting and complaining about his absences for three days and succeeded in driving him right out of the country.

'She's always saying she's not well. It's such a bore. It's all caused by reading French novels while wearing tight corsets — she will do it.'

Charles Sankey was always full of goodwill and he was highly pleased to see Rossiter. 'You're doing very well here, my old friend,' he said. 'You're doing the right thing here.' Sankey slapped him on the back with excessive enthusiasm. 'This is how life should be lived. The only problem that concerns me now is, which is the prettiest?'

He sat looking with benign consideration from the fair girl

to the dark girl and back again. The fair girl never said a word; she sat, statuesque in her pose, slowly moving a white fan up and down. The dark girl talked vivaciously, a stream of voluble animated French with a lot of pretty gestures with the hands, rolling of the eyes and shrugging of the shoulders.

Sankey looked and listened and slowly a happy smile spread across his bland face. 'I can't understand a word she says,' he observed with complete contentment. 'Not a single word.'

He patted her hand and put his arm around her shoulders and called for the waiter to refill the glasses.

'I am very glad to find you so happily established here, my old friend,' Sankey continued in due course. 'Upon my word, you had a lucky escape from the marriage stakes in Bishop's Linden. Upon my word, yes.'

Rossiter turned his gaze from the blue horizon to look at him. 'How's that then?'

'The girl you were hell bent on marrying in your madness – Miss Arabella Curtis. Just as well you didn't get yourself caught there. The family income is gone for nothing. The father has died and there's heaven knows how many daughters and the mother does nothing but shriek and moan from all accounts.'

'And what of Arabella?' Rossiter asked.

Charles Sankey puffed out a great cloud of tobacco smoke. 'Well that's the best of it. You know the way she always walked around Bishop's Linden like a duchess, like royalty in exile? Well now it seems she must become a Miss Humble to pay the rent of a slum cottage for the mother and daughters. Just think what an escape you've had? If you'd have married her, you'd have had to do the handsome for the whole brood of them. As it is, she's got the task, and a fine task she'll find it, of governess to some odious children, pursued by dishonourable proposals and insulting attentions.'

Neville Rossiter stood up so suddenly he knocked over his chair and upset the equilibrium of the fair girl who let out a faint shriek. The dark girl burst into another spate of excited French. Rossiter still didn't say anything, but before he strode away, he picked up a full glass and absinth and poured it with deliberation over Sankey's stupid, unsuspecting head, making it quite clear how deeply Sankey had offended him with his unheeding remarks about Arabella and how completely he had finished with the South of France and all that it had to offer him.

Arabella was at last successful in obtaining a post as a governess, but not with Mrs Bayliss of Maidstone. Over several weeks a series of unpleasant and unsuccessful interviews merged in her mind into one long lesson in humiliation. She was kept waiting, she was left standing, she was told to use the side door – 'never the front door, who do you think you are?'

Mrs Bayliss said: 'You don't look like a governess' and her fear of the effect Arabella's looks would have on her susceptible husband was greater than her fear of displeasing Lady Darnley. She said: 'I was thinking of someone altogether more – homely. I don't think you'll do.'

Other interviews followed. A Mrs Morris with a mean and condescending manner said: 'You wouldn't last long. I know your sort.' A Mrs Black said coldly: 'What makes you think you could teach my children anything?' and she proceeded to cross-question Arabella on dates of the English kings and battles Arabella had never known or long forgotten.

The house where she finally managed to obtain a situation was the gloomiest house she had ever encountered. Bleak and comfortless, it was ruled with rigid Protestant discipline by a dour and miserly Scot, Mr McCabe. His wife was a bed-ridden invalid and his main aim, it seemed, was to employ a governess who would keep their two daughters out of sight and mind so he could forget their very existence. Arabella for this interview had borrowed a bonnet from her mother and tucked every strand of hair away inside it and worn the drabbest shawl she could find over her black dress. Mr McCabe was mostly concerned about whether a governess would eat a lot, but his eyes were furtive. Shown round the tall dark house by the housekeeper, Arabella discovered that behind the spare gentility of the front rooms, there was a mean dinginess. There were bare boards and curtainless windows. Every potato was counted and the candles were marked off in half-inches. Her own bedroom was like a cell with the most spartan bed

62

coverings possible, a wash stand with a jug and bowl, and just two pegs on the wall to hang her clothes. The daughters were pale to the point of anaemia and inclined to whine and snivel when they spoke.

'You can start on Monday. No need for you to be here all day Sunday for meals,' Mr McCabe said.

Arabella scarcely lifted her eyes to speak to him. If she must have a job then it must be; it was so odious a fate that no matter where it was she would hate it, but she would endure it. Thirty pounds a year paid quarterly. Her mother and sisters were assured of a roof over their heads, even if it was only in Quarry Road.

'It distresses me so, to think of you shut away in some backroom as a governess,' Hester repeated over and over and Arabella herself could only agree it was a penitential life she had done nothing to deserve.

Edward Couchman, now satisfied that the household had been subdued to an acceptance of God's will, prepared himself to leave. He stood in the doorway to deliver his last words of advice and then broke off his discourse to remark that the same young man had walked past the house three times in as many minutes.

'Why it's dear George Hetherington,' Hester exclaimed, and had Arabella not restrained her she would have rushed outside to bring him in.

George Hetherington needed little encouragement to approach, and as he did so Arabella, who had quite forgotten that he existed, remembered with a depression of spirits how kind he was, how tedious and how wearingly slow.

'You will take some tea, Mr Hetherington?' Hester said eagerly, and then transparently arranged that Arabella should be left alone with George Hetherington, giving him every opportunity to renew his offer of marriage. This he did – but not promptly. He was a slow moving, slow thinking man and as he commenced his long preamble she looked at his big, red roast-beef face, and listened to his loud breathing, and tried to think well of him.

He was not, he told her, a wealthy man, in the sense that some are wealthy (meaning Rossiter), but his father and his grandfather before him had been careful men, no overnight collapse of shares would reduce them to penury (meaning her father), their families would always feel secure and be well-cared for (meaning herself).

'You have heard that we have lost our income completely? Then you will know that we must move from here, that I have taken a situation as a governess,' Arabella said crisply.

'I cannot express my regret strongly enough. But I am a plain man, Miss Curtis, and you know me well enough to know that I speak plainly. I have made to you an offer of marriage on more than one occasion before and I want to repeat that offer now. In doing so I am also offering to provide for your mother and your sisters. Will you do me the honour to consider that?'

Arabella bent her head, unable to bring herself to look at that big honest red face that like a full moon beamed kindness at her. Was this what she should do? Agree to be the wife of George Hetherington, for his sake, for her mother's sake and her sisters? Was this the path it was her duty to take?

'I cannot think you wish to be a governess,' George Hetherington observed and it was a telling observation, for to attend the McCabe house in that capacity felt like banishment and exile. But not imprisonment. There was some element of freedom in being a governess, she remained in charge of her own fate, gloomy though it was. Marriage had a finality about it, an enclosure, a restriction, a subjection of will that had always dismayed her. George Hetherington could not reconcile her to that, the very sight of him made her ache with boredom. The thought of seeing his bland round face across a thousand breakfast tables was like a sentence of living death. She thought of the disturbing, exulting excitement produced in her by the nearness of Neville Rossiter or the cloquent dark eyes of James Conroy, and knew that she could not commit herself to George Hetherington.

When Hester Curtis came back into the room, hopefully, eager to dispense tea and congratulations, she found that George Hetherington had remembered an urgent appointment.

'Thirty pounds a year paid quarterly,' Arabella reminded

herself when she presented herself at the McCabe household at an extremely early hour on Monday morning. It was the only fact that made her mode of life endurable, and it was a grim enough fact.

She installed her belongings in the spartan bedroom high up under the roof and found her charges waiting for her in the schoolroom.

She had to remind herself of necessity again, when she discovered how hopelessly depressed they were, without it seemed a spark of character or originality or curiosity or enthusiasm. She found it impossible to comprehend such children.

Thirty pounds a year is very important, she thought with some desperation when she met Mrs McCabe for the first time. The lady was an invalid reduced to a state of being resembling a peevish jelly fish. She was vastly, shapelessly large, overflowing the pillows and coverings of the bed in which she lay, complaining, ringing her bell night and day for someone to draw the curtains, smooth the pillows, fetch her hand mirror, refill her glass, even – on an occasion when Arabella was summoned – to straighten the doormat.

A meagre luncheon was served to Arabella on a tray in the schoolroom and it was so unappetizing she could eat none of it. A plain supper was served in the dining room and she found she was expected to join Mr McCabe for this meal, while he kept a watchful eye on every morsel of food she ate. Lights were unnecessary at this time of year, he told her, so as the daylight faded she could but retire to bed.

Uneasy, unhappy and also hungry, she took the precaution of locking the door. In the morning the key was taken away from her.

'Servant's doors are never locked,' Mr McCabe said.

And that was the last straw. No salary was enough to compensate for such a dismal and humiliating existence.

'I shall not stay in this house a moment longer,' she said, and gave herself the satisfaction of telling him what she thought of his employment. She didn't wait to listen to what he had to say. She packed her belongings together, and walked out of the house.

She had no choice but to walk home, for she had no money

to travel by coach or by train.

As she walked she had plenty of time to review the situation in which she found herself. It had been her proud determination to support her mother and her sisters and it had been her promise to her father, and now after a series of arrogant rejections, she had failed. She felt more chastened and dispirited than she had ever been in her life and her feet dragged wearily. After seven miles her thin shoes not designed for such unladylike use, were worn right through.

Her footsteps trailed through the outskirts of Bishop's Linden, where carriages passed and re-passed under the sweet honey-flowered lime trees. They moved in a world to which she no longer belonged, a world of fashion and servants and comfort and independent means. She felt, as she climbed the last hill to Lansdowne Road, like a ghost of herself, and two of her former girl friends passed her without recognizing her in her drab shawl and bonnet.

At the square grey house there were signs of activity. A strange vehicle in the drive and the front door stood open. Arabella's spirits quailed before another blow; this time the carriage did not belong to Lady Darnley delivering the benefits of her opinion. This time the vultures had descended; the broker's men were working their way through the house preparing what they were to remove.

Arabella ran the last few steps into the drawing room.

'My poor dear Mama,' she cried running to embrace her, her heart full of sadness for her mother. 'Oh Mama, I have failed you. I wanted to spare you this. I was so sure that I could find a way —'

They clung together, mother and daughter, for once reduced to the same state of helplessness.

The arrival of another carriage in the drive, the sound of the doorbell, and a commanding masculine voice outside in the hall did not reach them in their misery. Lil came shambling into the room and Hester turned to her distractedly as she said: 'If you please, Ma'am, there's a gentleman wishes to speak with Miss Arabella.'

It was the name on the embossed card that made Arabella turn pale and stand very still. 'Mr Rossiter?' Hester said in awe. 'He has come again to see you.'

'Gentleman said to tell you he had just come back from abroad . . .' Lil said.

Arabella turned away, pressing her hands to her mouth as though to suppress the intensity of her reaction, the confusion of surprise, triumph, dismay, something like fear.

If he had been abroad, she thought quickly, her mind racing and alert now, it was likely that he knew nothing of their straightened circumstances. Her pride came back to her, flowing like wine through her veins. She could not bear that he, of all people, should know of the straits to which she had been reduced, the humiliation of recent months. Could it be possible for her to keep it from him, even though she could hear the footsteps of the broker's men on the floor above?

'Lil would you ask Mr Rossiter to – to wait, if he would be so kind, in the garden, and I will join him in a moment,' Arabella said with all the calmness at her command.

She clasped her hands together for they seemed to be shaking. She looked quickly out of the window into the garden – and looked away. The sight of the lean, well-dressed, well-remembered figure pacing along the gravel path disconcerted her; producing a warm and startling sense of gladness that she could not control.

She said in a flat voice, almost talking to herself: 'He said he would not come again. I said I would not see him. How can I –'

She broke off to look again at the pacing figure. As before she was struck by the animal-like movements; he was like a caged tiger out there, hedged in with rhododendrons. At that moment she felt a strong reluctance to go out and face him.

She crossed quickly to the mirror and was startled at the reflection there – pale, sad, wan and dull, she seemed a stranger to herself. This would not do at all. With all haste, she untied the drab bonnet and shawl and laid them aside, quickly she re-arranged some strands of hair and seemed then by an effort of will to summon the beauty back into her countenance. Suddenly it shone forth, gloriously, and with it the confidence that she needed. Hester said: 'I see Mr Rossiter is keeping the hired fly from the station waiting in the drive. I think he must have come straight to call upon you on his return from abroad. It is strong proof of his attachment to you. Dearest, try to be – reasonable.'

'Reasonable, Mama? You know that is not in my nature. I cannot promise that,' Arabella said. But Hester saw that the brilliance was back in her eyes, the proud tilt was back in the way she held her head, the spring was back in her step as she went out into the garden to face Rossiter.

Rossiter hated waiting for anything or anyone, and the narrow confines of an urban garden were not to his taste under any circumstances. His character was a strong combination of resolution with impatience. He had come a long way to speak with Arabella and speak with her he would come what may. But he was impatient.

Beneath the arrogant, tight-lipped manner, Rossiter was concealing a weakness he had discovered in himself, a deep unremitting need of Arabella. Her name, the thought of her, the picture of her clear in his mind, were set apart from all others. For him she had a special radiance surrounding her and he wanted to be within the orbit of that radiance. That he was there at all was witness to the greatness of his need, for he was there in defiance of his own powerful pride.

The sight of Arabella, as she appeared at the top of the steps leading down from the house, pale and upright in her black dress, stopped him abruptly in his tense pacing. She was there, as he remembered her, dramatic in mourning and she seemed to be a mile away from him still, remote and untouchable.

They advanced, to meet each other half way down the garden, stiffly, like two players on a stage.

'I must apologize for asking you to wait in the garden, Mr Rossiter.'

'It's no matter.'

'My mother is having some furniture re-arranged.'

'Quite so.' There was a pause, and then Rossiter went on: 'We met here once before. And then you ran away.'

'I did not run –' Arabella said, at once haughty and cross at the very idea.

'You departed very quickly.'

'The arrangements had already been made for our travelling to Reisbaden. Sadly, my stay there was cut short because I received news that my father was gravely ill.'

Rossiter said: 'I was most grieved to hear of your father's death. Please accept my condolences.' Arabella thanked him and changed the subject.

'You have been travelling on the Continent also, Mr Rossiter? Was that enjoyable?' she enquired with a polite distance in her tone.

'I found it tedious. It was a way of passing the time – and I wanted some time to elapse.' Rossiter's clipped reserved formality matched her own.

'Indeed? How very strange. Usually one wishes time to stand still, it is so agreeable –'

'You are fortunate that is so,' he said stiffly. 'But on occasion time reconciles one to circumstances and on other occasions brings about a change of heart and a different determination. You will allow this to be true?'

'Oh, I will allow that it so,' Arabella agreed warily.

'Now that two months have passed since our last meeting, I wished to satisfy myself of your resolution on the subject of marriage. Whether it is a subject still abhorrent to you in general and to myself in particular. I ask you again to consent to be my wife.'

There was a rigid ferocity in the formality of his tones, almost as if he hated her, Arabella thought. She could not look at him. The tension was unbearable and she moved away from him down the path. Her mother watching back at the house held her breath in fearful dismay.

Rossiter followed her and his words followed her. 'I want you to marry me. I think you should explain to me why you will not agree.'

Why would she not agree? Arabella asked herself the same vital question. At his coming she had stepped from the gloom of bitter poverty into a sunlit garden, full of the sweet scents of summer and a radiant future was being placed before her. Yet her contrary nature held her in check. Something was wrong.

'I must ask you then, is there someone else?' Rossiter asked, his voice very cold, very hard.

'Someone else?' Startled, for a moment Arabella thought he must know of James Conroy of the single brief meeting in Reisbaden and the proposed assignation. Fleetingly she thought of dark eyes intent upon her, of an encounter that was more of a dream than reality. Conroy had gone on his way into his life and she into hers. 'No,' she said. 'That is not the case.'

'Then is it marriage in itself that you dislike, or just the idea of marriage to me?' Rossiter looked into her face, determined upon his answer, and as she looked away from him he said quickly: 'Do you want me to go?'

'No,' Arabella said. She spoke so impulsively then it was quite involuntary, as though instinct took over and spoke for her. The thought of his going away filled her with great alarm. She was forced to the acknowledgement that her life would be very grey and dreary if he had no part in it.

In her confusion, she moved aside on the gravel path and caught her foot on the grass verge. Her light shoes in which she had walked all the way from the McCabe house had finally fallen to pieces. Seeing her difficulty Rossiter bent to replace the shoe upon her foot, and it came apart in his hands. In that moment his fingers touched her instep and lightly brushed her ankle. His touch seemed to connect with a deep inner core of unexplored emotion and aroused a brilliant rainbow of sensation. When he looked into her eyes then her emotions became locked with his and she couldn't move or speak or look away. That moment was suspended on a high arc of discovery.

Then with a quick, graceful movement Arabella tossed both her shoes aside and walked without shoes on the grass, looking at Rossiter as if daring him to allude to the incident. And as if he refrained from drawing attention to the strange state of her footwear or the heightened state of her emotions, Rossiter turned aside to a shrub of roses that was filling the garden with deep fragrance and with a decisive movement he broke off the stem or a crimson rose, a bud just opening to the moment of perfection before it becomes a flower. He put it into her hands, then his own hands closed round hers.

'Will you tear this to pieces in your fingers too?' he asked her and she knew he was recalling the pale green leaves she had shredded in her agitation at their last meeting here in the garden.

The rose lay fragile and deep red, glowing like a jewel in the whiteness of her hands and she could feel the velvety softness of the petals. She looked down at the flower and at Rossiter's lean brown hands enclosing hers – strong hands, and there were freckles, she noticed, on the backs of them.

She knew a strange contentment, a sudden irrational feel of utter safety and excited exultation at one and the same time. It was an emotion that was almost more than she could bear – a seducing sweetness that seemed to rob her of her will and wash away her resistance. She wanted to stay within that firm and gentle grasp. The moment trembled.

Rossiter said: 'Arabella,' and she looked up at his face so close to hers in time to see the naked pleading in his eyes that she didn't recognize as desire.

'Yes,' she said, in a quiet and tentative tone.

'You will marry me?'

'Yes,' she said it with more confidence.

'You will be my wife?'

'Yes,' Arabella said with a kind of triumph and a little toss of her head. And he smiled at her in a way she had never seen him smile before. He clasped his hands about her's with fervour, then seeing he was crushing the rose between them, he rescued it and tucked it instead into the neckline of her black dress. He took her hands both together and pressed them to his lips.

'It will be good,' he said softly. 'Believe me. It will be good, you'll see.' There was a vibrant excitement in his voice that thrilled her almost to the point of fear. Her thoughts were incoherent; she had spoken instinctively, her emotions had taken over completely. Her feelings told her that she could accept the closeness of this man, arrogant and forceful and demanding as she knew him to be; she could accept the grasp of his lean brown hands, she could accept the touch of his lips. She couldn't think beyond that. Couldn't resist or stand on her dignity or tell him to go. Couldn't impose the negative

71

of a refusal on the positive pleasure of his presence. She gave no thought at all to her state of destitution or the fate of her mother and her sisters.

'So,' Rossiter said with a deep satisfaction in his voice. 'We will be married very soon.'

'Yes,' Arabella said – and then, suddenly, laughing up at him, laughing at herself. 'I don't seem to be able to say anything else, but yes.'

'It's a beautiful word – beautiful,' Rossiter said. 'Will you let me hear you say it again? Will you allow me the privilege of dismissing those insufferable broker's men from your house? I have been wanting to do it ever since I arrived.'

Arabella caught her breath in dismay and the colour rushed to her face. Caught out in her deception, she could only stare at him, and then she took heart for she saw unmistakeably, the quick gleam of his amusement. A feeling of well-being and amazing happiness swept over her.

When she ran indoors to find her mother, she could hear as she did so, triumphantly, Rossiter ordering the broker's men out of the house with curt relish.

'Oh Mama,' she said running to her. 'It is all arranged. I am to marry Mr Rossiter and you must be happy for me.'

Hester Curtis could only weep yet again, this time with relief and joy; 'Oh I am happy for you, dearest Bella. It was my dearest wish for you. And your poor father would have been so happy.'

She wept on and on and then, persuaded by Arabella, she came downstairs to see Rossiter and wept all over the drawing room.

'And you will not be so very far away from us, when you are married, Bella dear. Goodwood is not so very far away across the county,' Hester said.

'But we shall not be there all the time,' Rossiter said. His tone had changed from the gentle, persuasive persistence in the garden. Now it was crisp and very decisive.

There was a new voice of command in the house. Arabella listened to him instructing the broker's men – 'Bring that back – leave that alone – put that back – at once!' It was a tone of voice that had them running to his bidding, a tone that allowed no argument whatsoever. It was also the voice of unquestioned male dominance and authority and it made Arabella think, for the very first time, what marriage to Rossiter might mean.

CHAPTER FIVE

Society in Bishop's Linden found it difficult to adjust to the rapid changes in the fortunes of Arabella Curtis. The news that she was after all to become the wife of Neville Rossiter startled the ladies meeting over their scandal-broth in a score of polite drawing rooms in the town; they were still shaking their heads over her fate as a menial governess, considered by most to be just reward for her wilful flouting of convention and her proud and supercilious airs. Now they were left momentarily speechless; at a stroke she had been lifted into a sphere of society far above them.

Then Lady Darnley decided that she approved. She had always been of the opinion, loudly voiced, that the best thing for all concerned would be for Arabella to be married off as soon as possible. Many took their cue from her. Elizabeth Mansard was one of the few to offer Arabella genuine congratulations.

'I am happy for you,' she said with honesty. Her mother may have schemed with Lady Darnley to attract Neville Rossiter's attentions to her. 'But I could never have held him,' Elizabeth said, embracing Arabella. 'You will be a match for him.'

Uncle Edward could only think that God moved in a mysterious way that Arabella's outstanding lack of humility had been so richly rewarded on this earth. He was too unworldly to know much of Rossiter's reputation, but he did know that Rossiter directed his main energies towards gambling, horse racing and women. He could not approve, but neither could he bring himself to voice his disapproval. Who could tell what benefits Rossiter might have at his disposal? Uncle Edward bowed his head and said he hoped he could be of service.

Hester was in a very confused state. The grief of bereavement mingled with her relief when she learned that their home and financial security was generously assured by Rossiter, and that, combined with her excitement at the prospect of Arabella's splendid marriage, increased the fluster Rossiter always reduced her to. She wanted Arabella to have a fine wedding, she wanted everyone in Bishop's Linden to be aware of the magnificence of the match, but she was desperately anxious not to offend the proprieties. Theirs was a house of mourning. She and all the girls wore total black – must Arabella have a black wedding dress and a muted ceremony?

Rossiter made his wishes in the matter very plain. He gave instructions that the marriage should take place simply and above all speedily. Having made his wishes known he was absent from the preparatory proceedings. There were no courtesy calls on friends and relatives, no long discussions of the arrangements and the future. Arabella scarcely saw him for several weeks.

'He has business to attend to,' she told all those who asked, 'in Newmarket.'

'Oh? And will the Prince of Wales be there?' They asked her with eager curiosity.

Arabella had no idea. She felt herself during those weeks at the still centre of a swirling sea of decisions and problems, excited speculation and preparation and she, having made her own decision, seemed almost to have no part in it.

The problem of how the wedding was to be arranged at a time of mourning, which had been keeping her mother sleepless for nights on end, was smoothly solved by the intervention of Sir Hugo and Lady Faversham. They were wholly delighted to discover the good fortune that had overtaken their favourite and the minor problems that were exercising Hester's anxieties were the kind they could solve without any trouble to themselves. They said Sir Hugo must give Arabella away at the church, and the wedding guests could be received at Ashley House where there was room to spare and every facility. It was a pleasing suggestion received with relief by everyone.

'We are both so happy for you,' Lady Faversham said patting Arabella's hand. 'What a secret you were keeping to yourself. And I thought you had lost your heart to the intellectual Mr Conroy.'

'Did you see him again in Reisbaden?' Arabella asked.

'He enquired after you, of course. But we told him the reason for your sudden return to England. He travelled on to Berlin next day, I believe. An interesting man. But not, let it be said, in the same category as Mr Rossiter.'

'Do you and Sir Hugo know much about Mr Rossiter?' Arabella enquired.

Lady Faversham hesitated. 'A little. He is well-known. But Sir Hugo is of the opinion, and I am sure he is right, that marriage will have a settling effect upon him.'

The wedding was fixed for the 1st August. 'You will miss Cowes,' Charles Sankey said to Rossiter.

'But I shall be here for Goodwood,' Rossiter said and Sankey acknowledged that was the more important fixture.

Sankey had returned from the Riviera to find his friend so set upon a course of matrimony that, recalling the absinth poured over his head, he refrained from endeavouring to prevent or at least not all the time.

'Daughters get like their mothers. Has that thought struck you, old friend? Look at that mother! Imagine yourself married to that in twenty or thirty years time.'

Rossiter coldly refused to imagine anything of the sort. He stayed with Charles Sankey at Westwood when he paid his brief visits to Bishop's Linden. He endured the irritations and the tedium of the events like a man stoically ignoring the midges and mosquitoes of a fine summer evening. The chosen goal was in sight and he was set upon it.

The day of the first of August dawned beautifully blue and gold.

'The Queen's weather,' Hester said. Queen Victoria had always enjoyed the good fortune of fine weather for special events and important State occasions; Hester felt it was only right that Arabella should enjoy the same privilege.

Arabella sat before the looking glass in her bedroom while her mother stood behind her brushing her hair.

'When you are Mrs Neville Rossiter, you will have a maid to do this for you,' Hester said contentedly.

'But no one could dress my hair so well as you, Mama,' Arabella said and the sadness for the passing girlhood days came over her then. The secure privacy of this little bedroom, muslin hung and ribbon patterned; the garlands of flowers on the wallpaper she had so often counted as she lay in bed, the volume of Tennyson's poems bound in crimson leather by the bedside, her mother coming to wake her every morning. Suddenly the pattern of her days and nights took on the sweetness of familiarity. Would she ever know that kind of affectionate security again?

She pushed the thoughts aside as she moved about the room taking up the clothes she needed – the white silk stockings, the white satin slippers. Tomorrow she would embark upon the adventure of her marriage. She felt quite equal to it.

She caught sight then of her reflection in the long glass, in the underpinnings of the bustled shape, lacy chemise and frilly drawers and over them the corset tightly laced that enriched the curves of nature and gave her a handspan waist. It was a very seductive and flattering state of deshabille and instinctively she knew it.

'I think I shall go to the church like this, Mama,' Arabella said, turning and twisting a little to admire her reflection at its best. 'I don't think I shall wear the petticoats and the wedding gown at all.'

Hester turned pale and stared at her open-mouthed with shock, too overcome to say a word. 'Oh Mama,' Arabella said, full of remorse. 'Don't look like that. I was only teasing. And please, will you lace the corset a little tighter for me. My waist must measure no more than 20 inches, the same as my years. Pull it more tightly still. Tighter. Tighter.'

There was pleasure in the tight pull of the laces, pleasure in the sight of the effect it had. 'But not so tightly that you will faint at the altar,' Hester protested.

'No,' Arabella said more soberly. 'I would not want to faint at his feet.'

Hester seeing the clouded look on Arabella's face, had then her own misgivings. 'You are – you are marrying him because you want to, Bella, aren't you?' she asked piteously. 'I could not bear to think that you agreed to marry him to save us all from poverty. I could not bear to think that—' Her voice shook and her pale and bulging eyes filled up with yet more tears.

'You must not think that, Mama. Not for a moment. It is

not true. I agreed to marry him because that was what I wanted to do.'

She thought: I agreed to marry him, selfishly, because it was a far more pleasant prospect than being a governess and enduring a poverty-stricken existence. I agreed to marry him, because he made it easy for me to accept with dignity and I was grateful to him for that. But also, Arabella had thought about it a lot, probing deeper into her motives, she had agreed to marry him because he threatened to go away and she did not want him to walk out of her life. And why was that? Was it because the very thought of him had its own excitement? That his close awareness, the sound of his voice and the touch of his hand, produced wholly new and desirable sensations and she wanted to know more of them? Was that it? She found it difficult to be honest, difficult to clarify her thoughts.

'I have no doubts of his attachment to you,' Hester said. 'I think he has proved that without doubt. But I do have doubts about your feelings for him.'

'Oh Mama, he is a fine gentleman. Quite the finest I have ever met. You are not to have any fears for me, Mama. I shall marry Mr Rossiter and live in a grand house and be happy ever after, you will see.'

Hester still looked tight-lipped, aware of the sharp note in Arabella's voice, concerned with the nature of her anxieties, and guessing at the reason for her apprehension.

'There is something else I should say to you. Today you are to be married. Tonight – every night now – you will be a wife to your husband.'

'Mama,' Arabella protested. 'I know I have had a very sheltered upbringing, but I know what marriage means.'

'How can you know? How can you?' Hester said. She pulled at the delicate material of an embroidered petticoat, pulling it this way and that as her own recollections of twenty-three years welled up in her mind. So much she had had to endure. How could anyone possibly know what she had to put up with in the long and turgid hours of darkness, how she had suffered and endured. The demands, the passive resistance, the ordeal, the tight distaste. 'There is a price to be paid for the privilege of being a wife, for the security of a home and status. A husband has rights. He will – he will assert his rights.'

She sat down on the edge of Arabella's narrow bed, feeling weak at the recollection, pressing her hands to her cheeks. 'Your poor dear father was a man like any other. When we were first married it was really too much, on and on. It was more than my health could stand. And then, it seemed, every time, another birth, another daughter.' In the confusion of her memories she wasn't sure which had been the most hateful experience.

'Poor Mama,' Arabella said, putting her hand gently on her mother's shoulder. 'I'm so sorry.'

With an effort Hester recollected that she was supposed to be advising her daughter. 'This is all I can say to you. It is the price that has to be paid. Try to think of something else, something pleasant. Lie quite still. And with good fortune, it does not last so very long.'

At her wedding Arabella wore a white satin gown with a long train, lavishly trimmed with Alencon lace. She wore long white kid gloves, a string of pearls, a knot of white flowers at her breast and a fine tulle veil. All brides look radiant, but for most it is the demure and virginal purity of the snowdrop as they walk down the aisle. Arabella was quite unlike a modest snowdrop; more like an arum lily, proud and erect and queenly in her white satin, shining in the gothic gloom of Holy Trinity, glowing in her own radiance as she walked, stately and with fine grace down the long aisle on Sir Hugo Faversham's arm, her head held high on her long neck. She was taking her rightful place now in the centre of the stage.

Neville Rossiter looked at her and felt deep familiar pleasure. Charles Sankey looked at her and said: 'By George, she is a beauty. When you take her to London for the season, they will be standing on chairs to see her.'

'I know,' Rossiter said. 'I know that.'

Canon Gore-Stanley conducting the service, assisted in a minor capacity by Uncle Edward, boomed forth in his famous stentorian style: 'Wilt thou, Neville Richard Guy ... keep thee only unto her? ... Wilt thou, Arabella Mary ... take this man ... to love, honour and obey?' He looked down then with condescension at the bride and found her looking boldly back at him.

The general opinion of the wedding guests was that Arabella didn't look in the least like a destitute girl rescued from dire straights and a dim future as an underpaid governess. As for Neville Rossiter he moved through the whole ceremony with a kind of suppressing calm, but as though at any moment he might break through the civilizing restraints.

Seeing them walk together for the first time as they walked out of the church into the brilliance of the sunshine, Charles Sankey said: 'The tiger and the lily,' and then he kept saying it, delighted with his own inspiration. When Rossiter scowled at him he chortled with still greater pleasure as the name became even more apt.

Nearly everyone Arabella knew in Bishop's Linden was at the church and many went on afterwards to Ashley House. But Neville Rossiter was not supported by friends and relatives. He said he had no family.

'I am so sorry your uncle, Lord Helvyn, was unable to come,' Hester said, liking to say the name. Was she not related to an earl by marriage now? He might not be here, but it gave her the right to say the name loud enough for people to hear.

'He never goes anywhere,' Rossiter said, always abrupt in speaking to Hester. His words gave her more pleasure than he knew. She immediately imagined Lord Helvyn very elderly, fragile, bed-ridden. Soon no doubt then, Neville Rossiter would inherit the title and Arabella would be a titled lady. That would mean she was very closely related to the nobility. Hester gave a little sigh of complete contentment. That made the day perfect, quite perfect. She talked to the assembled company, even to Lady Darnley, with a newfound assurance; like a spaniel still but an eager optimistic spaniel, wagging its tail.

The Helvyn family owned large estates in Sussex. The family residence was Copper Down, a manor house set in extensive parkland and surrounded by its own farms as far as the eye could see. Neville Rossiter himself had a house there, Copper Down Grange, built in 1830, he had a London house in Curzon Street, he also owned a castle in Wales and it was there, first of all, that he took his bride.

From the railway station at Bishop's Linden they began a

golden journey. First to London and then departure from Paddington, then westward to Reading, on and on, mile after mile in high summer through rich farming lands where the corn was ripe in the fields, a tide of waving shining gold at that moment of fullness before the harvesting begins. Elm trees between the fields of wheat and rye and barley were glazed in a heat haze. The smoke from the engine trailed away over the corn fields pursued by its more substantial shadow. The lanes they saw were dry and white between the hedgerows, the sky was a perfect arc of blue.

At first Arabella enjoyed the luxury and privacy of the first class compartment on the Great Western Railway and she watched the passing fields of gold with dreamy contentment. But repeatedly they had to change trains, wait tediously to proceed again, and each succeeding train was less luxurious and comfortable than the last.

When darkness fell over Gloucestershire there was only the dim, smoky, smelly oil lamp in the compartment to light them on their way, and a meal of mangled cold beef to revive them at yet another station refreshment room. All night she sat straight-backed in the compartment, her snatches of sleep shattered by the clanking of engines and rattling of wheels and Rossiter sat apart, a man of iron, with no words of encouragement or concern.

In the pale dawn light they arrived at Hereford and she found to her dismay that they had still only accomplished a part of their journey.

'The easiest part,' Rossiter said.

The private family coach awaited them, painted sombrely with the Helvyn crest on the door panels, with the flyman, sturdily deferential, but speaking nothing but Welsh. Allowing no delay Rossiter gave the order to depart. The ostlers snatched away the cloths from the horses, and they were under the archway, out into the street and away into the Welsh hills, into a wild land that the railways had not invaded yet.

The old-fashioned balanced spring carriage was excellently built, the seats were large and deep couches. It was airless and hot though, and if the windows were opened it became full of the dust from the road. The roads were potholed and rutted to a knife edge by dry weather. The horses, changed at every ten miles laboured fearfully at the high ridges and rugged hills. Across the Black Mountains, then north of the Brecon Beacons, it was a journey of forty miles so rough and so steep that it took them all day.

In his impatience to reach their destination Rossiter set a furious pace and allowed no respite. When they stopped at the stages, she was scarcely allowed time to get out of the carriage and ease her cramped limbs, the change of horses was effected in two minutes.

At one staging post she protested at the fierce pace. 'And the horses,' she said. 'I think you should spare them.'

'Do you?' Rossiter said, and that was all.

They stopped just once for a meal at a roadside inn, demanded food immediately. The food was served in a dark low wainscotted room, pigeon pie and kidneys and steak and rashers and poached eggs brought forth in haste and served with tea and coffee that was too hot to drink in the time, and then they were off again.

As they journeyed on, the land became steeper and stonier and seemed to be inhabited only by sheep. She glimpsed tumbling streams and waterfalls and forested mountain tops. The landscape was wilder and seemed more strangely foreign than the Europe she had seen from the train on her journey to Reisbaden.

Her body ached with the roughness of the ride and when she dozed it was to dream uneasily, fearfully. She woke feeling feverishly hot and found that still they travelled – on, on. They seemed to have been travelling for ever. All the poise and radiance of her wedding day drained away on the long, long journey. Her head ached, her eyes burned, her mouth was dry and Rossiter seemed a silent, relentless stranger she couldn't understand.

Then at dusk on the second day, they came to an idyllic place. She had an impression of a lake still glimmering with light, and hills around it, of ivied castle walls and stone stairways and deepset windows.

When she got out of the carriage at last, her legs trembled under her and she heard voices, sing-song voices without knowing to whom they belonged. She was conscious of being carried inside, upstairs, of gentle hands unlacing her from the cage of her corsets, unpinning her hair and letting it flow free, conscious of the relief at last of being able to lie down and ease her aching body between cool sheets that smelled of lavender. At last the thundering of hooves and the rattle of the carriage had ceased, at last she had escaped from the captivity of the journey, at last there was peace and she felt herself falling into a deep well of sleep, down and down into greater depths, so deep that it seemed she could never come to the surface again.

And yet, part of the deep sleep, part of the dreamlessness, she had the sensation of being drawn into a soft embrace, upgathered into arms of gentleness. A hand caressed her, almost like a child. Kisses were light as a breath on her eyelids, on her lips. She moved with pleasure, warm and half asleep, to meet a tide of sensuousness washing over her. Stretched out her arms like a flower in the sun, wanting to give, to receive. Feeling herself brought up from the great well of sleep, from the great depths, up to unimagined heights to discover such passion, such joy, sweeter than anything on earth.

She heard a voice, very close to her ear, saying: 'Beautiful, beautiful, beautiful.' And then the tide rolled back, leaving her washed up on the shore, utterly content. She could fall back with happiness, smiling to herself, into her deep and dreamless sleep again.

Morning broke over the Welsh hills lifting the mist from the lake, and the sunlight reflected from the water dappled on to the ceiling of the room where Arabella lay. She opened her eyes and watched the play of the light, bemused, memories returning to her of the hours of the night. She turned her head. Neville lay sleeping beside her and she found he was holding her hand in his against her thigh.

So it was not a dream, she thought, recollecting in wonder. It was real. It was a revelation. She had never imagined such feelings existed, that such fierce passion could combine with such sweet tenderness, that such pain could be at once such joy.

Nothing had prepared her for this experience. No one had

spoken of it. In all the books she had read, delighting in tales of star-crossed lovers and intrigues and happily united husband and wife in the last chapter, the story had stopped short discreetly at the bedroom door. Only in poetry she had sensed something of a greater joy possible somewhere, somehow, for the chosen ones, a joy that once experienced it was so terrible to lose.

A lot of things she understood now, a lot of things suddenly made sense. Love – this was what it was all about then. Love, she thought, triumphant because she had found it. No one had mentioned love. She had not mentioned it herself. Rossiter hadn't mentioned it when he had offered marriage. Her mother hadn't mentioned it when she had tried to prepare her for what to expect of her wedding night. Arabella thought of her mother's words, the chilling glimpse they had given her of a married life that had been bleak and painful endurance, and she thought of her own experience.

Poor Mama, Arabella thought. Never to have known, never to have discovered, never to have loved and been loved like this. Poor, poor Mama.

She looked at Rossiter's sleeping face, its strong lines relaxed. He looked younger, kinder, quite different. She wanted to touch his cheek, smooth his hair. As she moved he opened his eyes and looked at her. Not a muscle of his face moved, yet his eyes were smiling at her.

'Good morning, Mrs Rossiter.'

The name made her smile. 'Good morning. How good it is.'

'You slept well?' he asked with a mock politeness.

'Oh very well. I've – never slept better.'

'I'm very glad to hear it.'

Smiling still he drew her into such a close embrace it seemed that they could never be taken apart. 'How I am going to love you, Mrs Rossiter. How I am going to love you.'

Gradually during the slow sweet hours of the nights that followed and the sunlit, carefree days, the tension between them eased away. Layers of constraint and reticence and pride and doubt, stripped away one by one like the silken petticoats Arabella stepped out of as she undressed. She discovered the man she had married and revealed her own self to him. Mr

83

Rossiter, the proud and reserved stranger, became Neville, her lover and her husband.

No one disturbed them. Castell y Bryder seemed to be a castle fortified against the rest of the world, guarding its lake valley intact against intruders. Waters cascaded from the lake, tumbling over rocks down a deep ravine and the castle windows commanded views one way across the still waters of the lake and the other direction down the valley with its folding lines of hills.

It was a castle out of a fairy tale, its towers hung about with ivy, its battlements mossy and lichen grown. Inside, the floors were of oak so highly polished and slippery that walking on it was quite hazardous and in the hall a tiger skin lay so life-like that Arabella kept her distance.

There were noble rooms hung with portraits of the Helvyn family, one of the most illustrious and historic families in Wales. The castle had been held by the feudal lords, and the original Baron of Bryder had accompanied Richard I on his crusades. It had seen much violence during its long history. In the time of the civil war, hoisting the banner of the king, it had been under siege and held out in brave defence against a parliamentary army, with the result later that the Baron of Bryder became Earl of Helvyn.

Arabella discovered a little about the family from the portraits, a little from Neville himself, but more from the housekeeper, Mrs Owen Williams, who was guardian of Castell y Bryder.

'When we return to Copper Down you must have a maid and engage some more staff,' Neville said. 'But while we are here, there is just Mrs Williams.'

Owen Williams spoke only his native Welsh. Mrs Williams spoke English in a lilting sing-song voice and she was a kindly, friendly person with plenty to say for herself and many stories to tell. She was so happy Mr Neville had married, so happy that he had found such a beautiful bride, so pleased to see them at Castell y Bryder.

'Everything goes well for the family when they are at Bryder. It is their rightful place, you see? It is when they go back to England that things go wrong for them – and then they never return here.'

They were an unlucky family, she told Arabella, tragedies and misfortunes had befallen them over the years; they seemed marked down by Fate.

'The troubles began long ago when the sixth Earl of Helvyn became ambitious for lands and title in England. He deserted Bryder and brought ill-luck down on the family. But things never go wrong for the family here,' Mrs Williams insisted, fiercely partisan. 'Here in Bryder all is well for them.'

Neville's father had brought his bride to the castle and Mrs Williams remembered the day. Her own mother had been housekeeper then and she described Neville's mother as: 'Such a sweet, shy girl, very tiny, like a bird.'

His mother had died when he was born, Neville told Arabella, and his father had mourned her for the rest of his life. A scholarly man, something of a mystic, he became more and more a recluse, alone with his books at Copper Down, studying dead languages.

'It was at Copper Down she died,' Mrs Williams said. 'He never returned here. Never.'

Neville, an only child, had spent a great deal of his childhood in Wales, cared for by the Williams, ignored by his father for great stretches of time.

'Oh he was a wild one,' Mrs Williams said, describing him as a small boy riding horses too strong for him to control, without saddle or bridle, and racing barefoot around the ramparts, balancing at the top of the towers and making her heart stop with his daring. But he had learnt something. He studied with an old Welsh pedagogue who was hard of hearing, and read his father's books before he was sent away to school.

His father's older brother, Guy, was the present Earl of Helvyn. He never came to Bryder. Mrs Williams' voice as she told the tales was full of dark portent when she mentioned him. 'He'll never come back here now,' she declared with heavy significance.

'Why does she say that?' Arabella asked Neville. 'She's most insistent that he'll never come back to Bryder.'

'He never goes anywhere,' Neville said dismissively. 'Don't take too much notice of all she says. She's like an old Welsh

85

witch sometimes, all soothsaying and omens.'

But Arabella was fascinated and wanted to discover all she could of Neville before she knew him. She had discovered that when his father died Neville had come into considerable estate.

' 'Lots and lots of money – and how he spent it,' Mrs Williams said. 'Oh he was shocking with it. Supposed to be studying at Oxford. More gambling than studying. Then what a life he led in London. But that's not for your ears, is it? He'll have turned over a new leaf now.'

From Mrs Williams Arabella learned that Neville was on good terms with his uncle – 'and no one else is, I can tell you' – and had been made heir to the title.

'There are never enough children in the Helvyn family, you see. It has been such a great family in the past, but ill-fated, so many tragedies, and now so few left.'

'And Lord Helvyn's wife?' Arabella asked.

'Poor soul. She died of a fever many years ago. Some say she didn't want to live. But I don't know the truth of it. I don't know what goes on at Copper Down. I only know the Earl never comes here. He should come. It's his castle and his lands. He's denying his birthright and his Welsh blood.'

Clearly Mrs Williams thought if the Helvyn family had stayed in Wales, in their rightful place, they would have thrived and prospered and brought forth many children.

'But now, now everything will be different. Now Neville has married. Now there is you,' she said.

Neville and Arabella walked often by the lake, Arabella in dresses of lilac voile and lavender muslin that she wore in deference to her state of mourning. On one side the hills were gentle, with glades of oak trees and mossy banks edging the water. On the other side the mountains towered and dark crags were threaded with tassels of silver where the streams cascaded down from the heights into the lake. The sun rose behind the hills dappling the ceiling of the bedroom where Arabella lay content in the brass bedstead; all day the mid-summer sun was mellow on the valley and the lake was tranquil and there were always, whenever Arabella looked from the window, two black swans coming towards her over the water; in the evening the sun set between the two mountains Mynydd Maw and Mynydd Bach and then the August moon rose full and splendid and so beautiful that she felt it couldn't be real.

Sometimes they rode off across the hills, through the oak glades, startling the white horned deer, and setting them bounding and glancing in the sunshine. And all the time they spent in each other's company they came closer together in spirit and body and mind, so close that Arabella felt she could say anything to him and yet constantly he surprised her.

Once standing beside him on the terrace, watching the last light fade from the lake and one bright star appear over Mynydd Bach, Arabella said it was all like a poem by Tennyson.

'Which poem?' Neville asked her.

She repeated the lines she loved from The Princess: 'The splendour falls on castle walls, And snowy summits old in story; The long light shakes across the lakes, And the wild cataract leaps in glory.'

'I think it is more like the land of the Lotus-Eaters,' Neville said. 'There is sweet music here that softer falls Than petals from blown roses on the grass, Or night-dews on still waters between walls of shadowy granite, in a gleaming pass; Music that gentlier on the spirit lies, Than tir'd eyelids upon tir'd eyes; Music that brings sweet sleep down from the blissful skies.' It is lotus land. One would wish to stay for ever. Shall we do that?'

Arabella smiled at him, her eyes full of tenderness. 'I would like to stay here with you for ever. And I never guessed, I never thought that you would like poetry.'

'Did you think I could only read the form of a race horse and the numbers on the playing cards? Yes, there is poetry. And there is a lot about me for you to discover yet, may heaven help you.'

'Why should I need heaven to help me?' Arabella said, laughing. 'I think I am in heaven. I think you are right, this is lotus land, this is paradise. And do you know something strange, whenever I look out at the lake there are always, always, two black swans coming towards me over the water.'

'That is a good omen,' Neville said. 'It is a sign of good fortune, believe me. You don't believe me? All right – ask Mrs Williams. She will tell you.'

He seemed extraordinarily pleased. So too was Mrs Williams when Arabella asked her, her sing-song lilt going higher and higher at the end of her sentences.

'Always two, are there? Always coming towards you, are they? Oh that's good fortune, isn't it?' She told Arabella how in times of misfortune the swans were never seen and when Neville's father had brought his bride to Castell y Bryder the swans had turned their backs and sailed away from her.

Arabella mimicked Mrs Williams' Welsh accent when she told Neville about it: 'Oh that's good fortune, isn't it?' He smiled at her with great indulgence.

'So now you are lucky as well as beautiful, brilliant and passionate, Mrs Rossiter.'

She felt lucky. She felt a great sense of well-being. Contentment seemed to flow in her veins like wine or like the wind on the Welsh hills racing through her hair when they galloped together through the sheep strewn land. It was another world, a very different world from Bishop's Linden with its cramping constraints and genteel anxieties, another world to Reisbaden where the avid gamblers gathered under the gaslight to win and lose.

She could feel that it was a good place. The farms looked well kept and cared for; life was hard there, tending the sheep on the hills in the wild winters, but the country people they met, the sheep farmers and labourers and the innkeeper and his wife, greeted Neville with deferential pleasure that was almost affectionate, and though they were shy and many of them spoke only Welsh or very little English, they seemed pleased to see her and made her welcome. She liked to hear the lilting sound of their Welsh speech, the rise and the fall of it had a musical sound like the wind in the trees. Once they rode away up into the hills to find the source of the river that cascaded down into the lake and gave the castle its name. It was a long ride up a steep and stony track and towards the end of it they had to leave the horses and continue up over the rocks and sheep trails on foot.

'About a mile further,' Neville said. 'Can you walk?'

'Yes,' she said, keeping up with him.

'It's only a small spring starting from the ground, when we get there,' Neville said. 'But it's right in the centre of the hills. You feel when you reach there as if you have got to the heart of everything.'

The sun was warm and the sky far above them a hazy blue. There were no trees, just the stone sheep walls and the green hills folding about them up the valley. Beyond the last ridge in the very heart of the hills they found where the clear water sprang from the earth – so beautifully clear and eager, so fast-running over the bright stones into the covert of grasses. Arabella wanted to be a part of it, she knelt down to plunge her hands into the sparkle of the water and splashed its bright freshness into her face.

For a second she closed her eyes – and next moment the sky filled her vision and the hills spun round her and the short turf was a pillow beneath her head. Her skirts were tossed and tumbled like a country wench. She was part of a force that was one with the earth itself, with the arch of the sky and the encircling hills. It was a simple elemental force, direct, uncomplicated, joyous.

She looked up at the lightly bearded face above her, the amber eyes. This was no Victorian man of property taking possession, exercising his rights. This was more a triumphant satyr and she joined in his triumph.

When she had breath enough to speak, she said: 'And at the heart of everything, there is love.'

'There is love,' Neville said and he got to his feet and shouted it to the hills, spreading his arms wide as though he was conducting great music, the climax of the greatest symphony on earth. 'And more love. And more love. Love, love, love ...'

The hills echoed his voice around and around, and then her voice – 'Love, love, love.' They were surrounded with it, gloriously.

All the time they were at Castell y Bryder within the quiet world of the valley, they had intact their private world, an inner world they shared. It was a communion not only of the

89

senses, but of their whole natures, intellectual, imaginative and sensitive, a complete and perfect sympathy. Night after beautiful night, she sank into Neville's arms in the high brass bedstead. The only sounds they heard were the waters tumbling over the rocks and the occasional hooting of owls. They were locked into the fastness of their own passions.

Arabella, who had delighted in the excitement exhilaration of riding a horse at full gallop in the fever of the hunting chase, whose heart had beat fast and joyously with the daring of the five dances that had shocked Bishop's Linden, and who had exulted in gambling with all the money she possessed at Reisbaden, found in their shared passion a richness of sensation so much greater that it made those past experiences seem as nothing at all. With all her heart she embraced a transportation of delight – again, again and yet again – until it seemed there could be no end to the mountain-peaks of passion.

'We stood tranced in long embraces Mixt with kisses sweeter sweeter Than any thing on earth,' Neville said. 'And that too is Tennyson.'

'Sweeter sweeter Than any thing on earth,' Arabella said in complete agreement.

In the mornings when she woke she found him awake before her, gazing into her face.

'Grey eyes,' he said once, making an announcement of the fact. Her long dark lashes flickered under the finely arched brows. 'Grey eyes are the most beautiful of all. Blue eyes can be too bright, too hard, superficial, unfeeling. Grey eyes are warm and passionate and deep. I can see myself in your grey eyes. I can lose myself in them for ever.' With one finger he traced a line across her wide brow, down the curve of her cheek and pressed it to her lips with tenderness.

Sometimes the effervescent wine in their veins spilled over like sparkling champagne into wild high spirits. Once Neville snatched up the tiger-skin from the floor and draped himself in it, chasing her up stairs and down, while the old stone-walled castle resounded with racing footsteps and the happiness of their laughter. Arabella picked up her skirts and ran from the tiger in pursuit, but she kept looking back over her shoulder, amazed that this too was Neville Rossiter.

It seemed as if the rest of the world had ceased to exist. But the time had to come when they had to leave.

CHAPTER SIX

The high walls with spikes on the top of them were the first thing Arabella noticed about Copper Down. The Jacobean manor house, where she was going to meet Neville's uncle, was surrounded by acres of parkland at the foot of the South Downs and all around the park the wall was ten feet high.

'Is your uncle wanting to keep people out, or keep people in?' Arabella asked as they waited while tall iron gates were opened for them, clanging as they closed.

'He likes building things,' Neville said.

The manor house itself was massive and impressive, built of flint and brick with towers and arches, and though it was not a fortified manor it looked as though it could well withstand attack or siege. It was at the centre of a community of attendant buildings, cottages and farms. The Grange a mile away, where Neville and Arabella were to reside, had been built by Neville's uncle. His initials were carved in brick and stone on buildings erected on his estates spread over a fair portion of Sussex, from the South Downs nearly to the sea.

'When he'd built enough houses and cottages, he took to building gothic gazebos and such,' Neville said. 'Once he built a tower a hundred feet high, because he wanted to see the sea from Copper Down. He's just built an extra wing at the side of the house because he's got a great collection of old guns and firing pieces and he wanted to display them. But he wouldn't allow a railway line to be built anywhere on his land, says he won't have those infernal machines anywhere near him. That's why there isn't a railway station within so many miles of Copper Down.'

They had been met at Chichester station by the family coachman with the dog-cart that was used for station work. Lord Helvyn found no inconvenience in the distance of the station, Neville told her, because he never went anywhere. If he needed to travel about his own estates he rode, always, a huge black horse with a shotgun strapped to the saddle.

'He still thinks he's living in the Regency,' Neville observed.

The interior of the manor was plain and dark with panelled walls and dark ceilings, windows high and small and mullioned. The daylight was excluded. Footsteps sounded heavily on creaking wooden floors before Neville's uncle became visible in the gloom.

Lord Helvyn contrasted strongly with the picture of him that had formed in Hester's mind as an elderly invalid. Guy Helvyn was a man entering his sixties with enormous vigour; a big man with powerful sloping shoulders, iron grey hair and beard, fierce moustache and eyebrows, wearing an old-fashioned stock and frock coat and monumental trousers. He spoke abruptly and had a way of laughing, an agressive snort of laughter, by way of comment.

'Well, here I am then, the wicked uncle. Keeping the young man from his inheritance by living to be a hundred. Every intention of doing so. You'll have to make the best of it.' He laughed and Arabella wondered if she was supposed to. 'So this is your bride, your beauty.' He stared hard at Arabella. 'The future Countess. Well I hope, young lady, you are not too much of a lily-lass to produce children.'

Prudery in Bishop's Linden would never have permitted such a direct statement; Lord Helvyn had the aristocrat's contempt for bourgeoise proprieties. Arabella was only momentarily taken aback. She tossed her head a little.

'I see no reason why I should not achieve that. In my observation it seems to be managed by the meanest intelligence.'

Lord Helvyn gave another loud bark of laughter and Arabella saw that Neville was smiling at her, that flash of a smile she had discovered during the weeks in Wales, such a rare smile it seemed to be for her alone. Lord Helvyn took her hand then and held on to it. 'So I must call you Arabella, and you must call me Uncle. That's what I'd like. I've never had a niece to call me Uncle before. Next best thing to a daughter, isn't it?' Arabella braced herself and then placed a daughterly kiss on the forbidding cheek. 'Very nice. Yes, very nice. I think you'll do.'

They talked briefly of the journey and of Bryder. 'I'm sure it is the most beautiful place in the world,' Arabella said, her voice soft with her experience of the place.

The Uncle wasn't interested in Bryder; he was preoccupied with events at Copper Down, the harvest on the farms, a stable block he was planning to build, trouble he'd been having with one of the tenants.

'You'd best take a look now you're here, Neville. Well, tomorrow, then. But now you are back, now you've got yourself married, oblige me by staying here for once. Make him stay,' he said to Arabella, then gave a fierce bark of laughter. 'What does he need to go off for now. He'll have quite enough to keep him busy here, one way and another.'

Arabella was glad when the time came for them to leave. The house with its lowering beams seemed full of dark secrets. She thought of the stories Mrs Williams had told her of the ill-luck of the family, the accidents, the misfortunes, the wife who was said to have died of a fever because she didn't want to live. The spirit of the unhappy past seemed to have seeped into the dark grain of the house. If there were brooding spirits at the manor, Lord Helvyn was not the man to dispel them, living in the great empty house alone with his servants, barking his orders and his comments, laughing his humourless laugh. He evidently led a very solitary life.

'He's not lonely,' Neville said. 'He's forgotten any need for company. He never sets foot outside Copper Down estates, doesn't know or care what happens outside them. He's always active, always building something, enjoys shooting. Spends most evenings with a bottle of port.'

They left him in his splendid isolation and the dog-cart took them on across the park to Copper Down Grange. This had been built by Lord Helvyn in Georgian style and the first impression of its grey stone facade was uniform formality and dignity, well set about with cedar trees on sweeping lawns.

The entire household staff lined up for them and as Neville introduced the servants to her one by one and as the men's heads bowed and the women's dipped in curtsies, Arabella was actually conscious of her new status.

For a moment they seemed an intimidating line of people; they were so entrenched in the Grange and she was so new to it; they were grey-haired, elderly, experienced and she was young and new to everything. Within moments of the introductions Neville had them all running around. There weren't enough lights, he said, there weren't enough fires. Why wasn't there a fire lit in the bedroom? In fact the September evening had only just, suddenly, turned chilly after a warm and sunny day. Fires were lit, the luggage was taken from the carriage, the horses were snorting and crunching on the gravel of the drive and there was a great bustle of coming and going.

Neville showed her round the house, and she saw that here too there was a lack of charm and comfort. It was a house that had lacked a woman's touch for a long time and Neville's prolonged absences had let the household organization deteriorate. She would soon do something about that, right away, Arabella said to herself, taking pleasure in the prospect.

One room was completely walled with books, and they were piled all over the floor, dusty ancient volumes. Arabella had never seen so many books. 'My father lived here,' Neville explained. 'He lived in this room with his books for most of his life.'

'I shall read them,' Arabella said, seized by immediate enthusiasm.

'You won't find any novels,' Neville warned her. 'And any romantic poetry will be in a dead language.'

'They were very different, weren't they, as brothers?' Arabella said. 'Your father so withdrawn and scholarly. Your uncle so energetic and – and bold.'

'Bold, yes,' Neville said. 'And a law unto himself.'

Neville seemed unlike either of them. Yet she thought she could see something of Neville in the Uncle's quick vigorous movements, the formidable autocratic air.

They completed their tour of the Grange at the master bedroom where now a fire was flickering brightly and more lamps had been lit and the room glowed with light, reflected in old mahogany making it gleam. It was a room with grandeur, a large four-poster bed, a dressing room adjoining. It was all on a far grander scale than Castell y Bryder, but it too had a faded, neglected feeling to it. Pale blue brocades, Arabella thought, would look well at the casement windows.

'So, Mrs Rossiter, this is your home. What do you think of it?' Neville put his arms about her and the feeling of pleasure that was her immediate, familiar response to his touch warmed her with delight.

Everything felt good to her. There was really nothing she could think she wanted. 'There is just one thing –' Arabella said.

'Anything,' Neville said. 'Anything.' He kissed the line of her eyebrows and then the curve of her neck at her shoulder. 'Your every wish –'

'Then I would like the bed round the other way,' Arabella said. 'I am always happiest when I can open by eyes to the sunshine in the morning. I would like the bed to face the window.'

'At once. At once, my lady.' Neville summoned servants to undertake the removal immediately. It was done while they dined, with much effort, disturbing the dust of long years. Arabella had a sense of satisfaction. Things would be different now she was here.

But later, when the elderly housekeeper was in the bedroom unpacking for her, as she had no maid, Arabella looked at her, so frail and grey, her brown speckled hands shaking as she struggled with fastenings, and she felt stricken with remorse. Suddenly she had a sense of what it must be like, after a lifetime in service to the family, to have a new young wife arrive and change everything. If things had been different she could so easily have been in service as a governess herself, standing in line, docile and deferential.

'You've worked here a long time, Mrs Baker?' Arabella asked.

'Miss Baker,' the prim correction increased Arabella's sadness for her. 'Yes, ma'am, I've been here forty-five years. I can manage. It's just the stiffness in my hands –'

Arabella could see the anxious, nervous, need to please. 'We'll have to get you a strong young assistant – that'll make it easier for you.' Tears sprang into the old, colourless eyes and Arabella had to look away.

Neville stayed on at Copper Down. It was his plan, he said, to stay in Sussex for the winter and then take Arabella up to London for the season. Regularly he went over to his racing stables at Bassetts near Goodwood a few miles away where he had horses in training, and he spent a good deal of time on the estates with his Uncle. There were problems. Too many of the most valuable agricultural workers were leaving the farms for work in the factories.

'But why should they want to leave?' Arabella asked. This was such a rich and pleasant land, good farming country. She had seen the cottages of the farm workers; they were trim and well-built and each had a bit of ground with vegetables growing and a pig fattening. 'Surely there's dreadful hardship in the industrial towns, slums, overcrowding and children working terrible hours in factories? Why do they want to go?'

'They are fools,' Neville said.

Sometimes there were dramas. In one of the villages a man had been sacked, and his family had to be turned out of the tied cottage. Arabella had seen them walking along the lane, bedraggled and forlorn, carrying all their possessions with them.

'He was a trouble maker,' Neville said. 'He had to go.'

Lord Helvyn was undisputed lord of the manor, the squire of three villages, a tyrant who ignored or bullied his tenants and his word was law. Arabella was surprised to discover just how much power he had over the countryside; the ministers in the churches, the landlords of the inns, the farmers, the craftsmen, the farm workers, the labourers – their livelihood was in his hands and effectively he ruled their lives. The countryside seemed feudal to her in its gentry and peasantry divisions; the strong middle-class society that she had known in Bishop's Linden scarcely seemed to exist. Lord Helvyn did just exactly as he liked. Neville was the only man who had any influence with him, as far as she could see, he was the only one not in awe of him.

Whenever she went with Neville to Copper Down Manor, Arabella found her uneasy dislike of the house increased. Each time she stepped through the front door she had the sense of the dark beams pressing down on her with the weight of the past, of the dark walls closing in. It was a house full of narrow stairs and dark passages, and unexpected doors in the panelling of the walls, countless unused rooms. She never explored it fully and felt no desire to. Something about the house seemed impenetrable, but she had the feeling that there were ghosts of the past there, listening, waiting, watching.

'I shouldn't want to live there. Ever,' she said with great feeling to Neville.

Neville shrugged his shoulders. 'We'll see.'

Arabella wondered, thinking about it, if it was simply that the manor was a house of men. Her own home had been in a houseful of women; bustled skirts for ever rustling up and down the stairs, feminine voices shrill in all the rooms, a feminine hand upon the flounces and the flowers, and her father retreating from that female domestic world to his study.

At Copper Down she had only seen men. Lord Helvyn's servants seemed few in number; one gloomy, silent man-servant was always on hand, and occasionally an old man bent over the bottles he carried, and a young boy who didn't look normal. She thought there must be some women there – a housekeeper, a cook, a parlour maid or two hidden away in the servants' quarters somewhere, but she enquired and found there were not. It could be simply the lack of feminity that gave the house its plainness and comfortless, forbidding atmosphere.

Arabella seemed to gain Lord Helvyn's approval because she spoke up and spoke her mind, but she couldn't warm to him and she couldn't bring herself to address him as anything but 'Uncle'. She always thought of him as 'the Uncle', never as anything more friendly like Uncle Guy.

The Uncle was certainly unpredictable. His hermit existence seemed to admit no social contact at all, and then suddenly he announced that he had decided to invite local society to meet them at a dinner party. Neville couldn't remember the last time such an event had occurred.

'You are greatly honoured,' he said to Arabella. 'Quite right too.'

Duly pleased, Arabella felt nevertheless it was going to be

an odd occasion. 'Who will be there?' she asked.

'People,' Neville said vaguely. 'They will all want to come to meet you and see what you are like. You will not object to being on show, will you?'

On the evening of the dinner Arabella wore a dress of dove-grey silk, still being in half-mourning for her father. The dress was slender and clinging; she had had it made for her in the latest narrow style, the high neckline edged with ruffles of tulle. It was a graceful, romantic dress but the radiance of her appearance was in her face. Her happiness shone there with a glow as though her marriage had lit a candle within.

She had been right in thinking that it would be a curious sort of evening. The ways of hospitality were as creaky with disuse at the Manor as the floorboards underfoot. Lord Helvyn dominated the gathering, his fierce laugh disconcerting the small talk of his guests, and they – an oddly assorted group – seemed uneasy, rather surprised to find themselves there and deeply deferential to their host. There was a retired Army man, Major Knowles, upright and rather handsome, with a wife who seemed much older than him; the Rev. Lacey, Vicar of Copper Down church whose wife giggled nervously; and a Mr Browning, a neighbouring landowner, who made pompous pronouncements that his wife devotedly repeated after him.

The lady who seemed most at ease and in her element at the dinner table was a Mrs Catherine Becket who wore a gown of turquoise blue that matched her eyes, a very fine choker of pearls that Arabella noted, admired and rather coveted, and a daringly deep decolleté. As she leant forward, warmly fulsome and smiling to each of the men at the table, the magnificence of her bosom was repeatedly revealed and Arabella was made to feel glad she had elected to wear her high-necked dress. She was so slender that no amount of pressure from her stays could push her bosom up into competition with Mrs Becket's display.

The meal took a long time in the gloomy dining room of the Manor; in the flickering, guttering candlelight, dark shadows stood around them deepened by the heavy panelling of the walls, and the food was cold when it reached the table from kitchens a long distance away down draughty corridors.

The ubiquitous, ever-silent manservant served the meal. He had also cooked and prepared the Southdown mutton, so Lord Helvyn informed the company; he had been doing it to his lordship's satisfaction for thirty years, but that seemed to be the extent of his skill. The rest of the meal was unappetizing, though the wine was superior and plentiful. The Uncle talked with some pride of his cellar of claret.

After the meal the men lingered over their port for more than an hour and Arabella was restless, left to the company of the four ladies. Mrs Knowles, wife of the retired Army man, was too old to find anything to say for herself that late in the evening. Mrs Lacey, the vicar's wife replied to any remark with a high pitched nervous giggle and Mrs Browning, when apart from her husband, confined herself to the subject of her health.

Mrs Becket didn't trouble herself to charm or make conversation with these ladies and they, pointedly, did not address themselves to her.

'The Queen allows the gentlemen five minutes only, to collect themselves after dinner before joining the ladies,' old Mrs Knowles remarked as time passed.

Arabella decided that she would impose the same regulations as the Queen when she came to entertain in her own house. In this house she didn't know her way about well enough even to lead the ladies to the right room to tidy themselves.

'I'll lead the way,' Mrs Becket said. 'It doesn't do to open the wrong door in this house.' Arabella heard behind her, Mrs Lacey's giggling rise to a higher pitch of nervousness.

In an unused bedroom with a musty smell about it, Arabella found there was a large oval mirror above a washstand. She could never refrain from looking into a mirror; not that she was in need of reassurance, just confirmation. As she was standing there in silent acknowledgement of her own serene reflection, Mrs Becket's image suddenly appeared, almost ghostly in the dim lamplight.

For a moment they both contemplated the images side by

side, the one so young, with clear grey eyes and a tender glow about her face framed with cloudy grey tulle; the other blue-eyed and golden-haired with a full and peach-like bloom.

'You see the difference that ten years can make,' Mrs Becket said. There was no regret or envy in her voice, simply an amused confidence.

'Ten years?' Arabella said, her finely arched eyebrows rising with just sufficient emphasis, she hoped, to make it quite clear she thought it was more like twenty.

'What do you know of me?' Mrs Becket asked, with a composed smile, still addressing Arabella's reflection.

'Nothing at all,' Arabella said. She herself thought it was odd that knowing nothing at all, she should have unsheathed her claws. She felt a strong instinctive dislike of this woman, with no apparent reason. She had all the advantages over her surely. All possible advantages – except in the matter of bosoms.

When at last the men appeared and conversation became general, Arabella said to Neville: 'I am glad to see you. What is to happen now?'

'We are going to play baccarat,' Neville said.

'The Queen has banned baccarat,' Mrs Knowles said. 'It is illegal to play it now.'

'That doesn't stop the Prince of Wales,' said the Uncle. 'And it's not going to stop me in my own house. Why should it? What do you say, Arabella?'

'Arabella has the temperament for gambling, I'm sure of that,' Neville said smiling at her. But Arabella felt quite differently about roulette at which she had enjoyed some success, to baccarat from which she was excluded.

'This is one of the things you will have to learn,' Mrs Becket said, smiling too, as she seated herself in queenly fashion at the baccarat table with Neville and the Uncle and the handsome Army man. Arabella was left to the tedium of playing whist with the Vicar and the pompous Mr Browning and Mrs Lacey giggling.

Observing Catherine Becket, Arabella could see she was a woman who understood men; she was worldly with a kind of worldliness Arabella had not known anyone to possess in Bishop's Linden, with a sharp and hostile wit far more dangerous than the offensive broadsides of such as Lady Darnley.

She knew she must be wary in matching herself against her, for in Catherine Becket she guessed she had an enemy, a sweet-smiling, angel-faced enemy.

'Tell me about Mrs Becket,' Arabella said, after the party, alone with Neville in their bedroom at the Grange.

'My Uncle invited her this evening,' Neville said and he looked displeased about it. 'What would you have me tell you? She is a woman with a past – with more past than future. But a woman more sinned against than sinning.'

'I didn't care for her.'

'Yet she spoke of you with admiration.'

Arabella shrugged her shoulders and looked coldly. She was not going to ask Neville what had been said.

'This fastening is very difficult to manage,' she said, arching her neck a little, her arms raised to the back of the grey dress, looking like some Athenian goddess. 'If you would be so kind –' Neville was across the room before she had finished speaking.

People were on the outer circumference of their lives and their happiness. They had at the centre of their being a private world within a world and it was here in this room, in the curtained privacy of the four-poster, dark canopied, ornately carved, gold fringed and velvet draped, a shrine of voluptuousness. Love had been a revelation to Arabella at Bryder, now it was a kingdom, a kingdom in which she was gloriously content.

Neville said, a few days after the dinner party, that it was unfortunately essential for him to travel to London on business. He would only take two days to settle some boring but urgent business matters and be quickly back again. Arabella hated the thought of being parted even for such a little while and the Uncle was extremely put out.

'Well, come back, damn you. Oblige me by coming back, when you say you will. I will not believe any explanations for a delay.'

'Will it be possible for you to exist for two days without me?' Neville asked Arabella with great tenderness as he prepared to depart.

'Undoubtedly' Arabella said: 'I shall devote myself to my

correspondence. In fact as it looks to be an exceptionally fine day I shall sit in the garden undisturbed by your presence and write to Mama.'

'Reporting on your experience as a much married lady? What will you tell her?'

'That in my experience marriage is truly remarkable, but that I do not recommend it to my sisters.'

'No?'

'Decidedly not. Unless, that is, they can find husbands of the unique calibre and quality of mine – and that is extremely unlikely.'

Neville kissed her, lingeringly, saying: 'I have such love for you. It is extraordinary,' and making her promise to look for his return on Thursday, and then the dog-cart bearing him to the station drove away.

It was an October day as blue as midsummer, with the leaves falling slowly down the windless air. Beech leaves and chestnut leaves in rich and colourful abundance spread over the grass and the gravel paths of the Grange gardens, despite the constant besom-sweeping of a small army of gardeners.

The brilliant displays of carpet bedding that were the head gardener's greatest pride were over now, the geometrical beds had been scrupulously cleared of plants and their immaculately turned earth was a bare brown shape on the impeccable lawns. But there was one long border that stretched the length of a high wall of weathered local stone and the hardy herbacious perennials sunned themselves there still, flowering as though they thought the summer would never cease. Michaelmas daisies crowding with golden rod, pale japanese anemones mingling with black-eyed susans, a happy untidy mixture of catmint, lacy filigree rue, dark polished acanthus. There were bees and butterflies clustered about the dusky rose heads of the sedum as if it was still August. Behind the wall, in the kitchen gardens, the smoke rose from a bonfire, straight and white and smelling of autumn. It was a day when the year seemed to hold its breath in still perfection before it crumbled into decay.

Arabella walking there took pleasure in the landscape of the garden and the background of the South Downs, in the richness of the autumn day and the fragrance of chrysanthemums. The scenery of her own life pleased her too – to love, to be loved, to live in such style, to enjoy a sequence of days that were pleasing. She felt richly content, and Neville's reluctant absence was so brief a parting it only added piquancy.

'Dearest Mama.' How far away she seemed, Arabella thought as she sat writing her letter in the gazebo, her pen held aside and her thoughts wandering. How far away the quiet world of Bishop's Linden where she had lived in such ignorance of life's riches and joy. She thought there was no way in which she could convey to her mother her own perfect happiness, her ideal love. Her mind was full of the images of joy, of a fairy tale castle by a waterfall and two black swans coming towards her over the water; friendly sing-song Welsh voices and a brass bedstead in a cool stone room; the spring at the heart of the hills and a voice very close to her ear saying: 'Beautiful, beautiful, beautiful.'

Impossible to describe her love, but her pen ran on with prosaic details of her happiness that her mother would appreciate; the maid she had engaged called Becky – a funny, bright-eyed little girl, the curtains she was having made for the bedroom in palest blue brocade.

' ... And it is such a very lovely day, dear Mama. Neville has gone to London and I am sitting in the garden to write to you. Now you are not to worry about anything, Mama. Any doubts and anxieties you had about my accepting Neville Rossiter, any doubts I had myself are to be forgotten. He is the best and kindest of men –'

The best and kindest, she thought, ceasing to write, leaning back and smiling at her thoughts – that didn't sound like him at all. How inadequate the words were. He was the most ardent and exciting lover, the most tender husband, a man to love and trust and admire, a man so quick to amaze her.

'I am so very fortunate,' she wrote, her pen racing on in her delight, carried away with the warmth of her own affections. 'I feel sure I have the prospect of great happiness before me.'

A movement across the grass caught her eye then, a shadow darkened the doorway. She looked up and found Catherine

Becket standing there.

Smiling and serene Catherine came into the gazebo and sat down uninvited, folding her hands in the lap of her powder blue dress. In the small enclosed space of the little summer-house they were sitting very close together and Arabella could see in the clear sunlight the lines of her face, the downward lines about the mouth, the blurring of the angle of the chin, the shadows under the bright blue eyes. She noticed again most particularly the fine choker of pearls Catherine wore and that it looked a little tight around the neck.

'I thought I should come to have a talk with you,' Catherine said. Her voice was breathy and rather husky.

'Do you live near?' Arabella asked with cool politeness, and her tone was clear and bell-like in contrast. She sat straight; she felt young, slender, superior.

'Oh yes. Didn't you know? I live just a walk across the park, at Bassetts. Haven't you been told anything about me, even now?'

'What is there to know?' Arabella asked coldly, dismissively. Curiosity had made her ask Neville about Catherine Becket. His answers had told her nothing at all. 'What should I be told about you?'

Catherine appeared to hesitate. 'Well perhaps, for reasons of his own, Neville could not bring himself to tell you. He is very sensitive about his generosity and likes to pretend he never acts out of the kindness of his heart. But he is most generous. I want for nothing, the cottage at Bassetts is quite charming and – I see you have been admiring my pearls – they are another example of his exquisite taste and spontaneous generosity.'

The sweet and husky voice ceased and Arabella found herself speechless. Her mind was spinning with speculation, suspicion, sudden doubt. A host of unanswered questions reared up at her.

'Have you – have you been living there long?' Arabella asked and the bell-like assurance had gone from her voice completely.

Catherine sat stroking a fold of her pale dress. 'Let me see – it must be four years now. I was there when Ralph was born and he is nearly five. I brought him with me today – he is playing in the garden somewhere. He is so fond of this garden, hiding in the dark under the cedar trees is his favourite game.' She smiled again and looked vaguely out at the sunlit garden, but not seeing the boy, turned back to Arabella. 'You see, I feel it is best that you and I should understand each other. You are here – and I am here – and neither of us is going to go away.'

With a great effort Arabella said. 'I don't think I quite understand what you are saying.'

'Then you will have to to ask Neville yourself,' Catherine said, with an air of calm triumph. 'He should have told you. Ask him – if you don't believe me. Let him tell you the whole story. It began eight years ago when I left my husband.'

'Are you divorced from your husband?' Arabella asked. Such things happened, she had heard of them.

'I could never get a divorce,' Catherine said. 'He is in India, he has an Army career, divorce was not to be considered. And that, you may think, is one of the reasons you are Mrs Neville Rossiter and I am not.'

At that moment there was a rush of footsteps and a small boy came hurtling in and flung himself at Catherine. Arabella could only stare at him. There was no mistaking that quick and tawny look, fiercely alert, like a small tiger. Catherine smiled as she saw the expression on Arabella's face. 'This is my Ralph. There is a strong resemblance, is there not?' Arabella couldn't speak. Suddenly, appallingly she knew the truth. All the hints and insinuations that Catherine Becket had made were suddenly clear. Neville had a son by this woman. The child, the beautiful, darting child was evidence of that.

Catherine stood up, her arm about the boy, pressing him to her. 'And there is something else you should know – if you have not been told. Ralph is to inherit a large part of the estates after Neville. Did you know that? It is only right, don't you agree?'

'What do you mean?' Arabella said faintly.

'What do I mean?' Catherine said husky and mocking. 'You'll have to ask him, won't you? That's something else you'll have to ask him.'

She went away with the child close beside her, and Arabella was left bereft of speech and thought and the power of movement. This couldn't be true – any of it – it was like some bad dream that she would wake from and dismiss as fantasy. Confused with the incoherent thoughts of what Catherine had been saying came a kind of confirmation. She knew nothing of Neville's life before she met him. He had dismissed it in an off-hand tone: 'Wasted years,' he had said. 'Meaningless. Unimportant. This is what matters – you.' She had not thought deeply about it; she had been so trusting, child-like, naïve.

Words he had spoken to her came into her mind and took on new meaning, different implications. 'Grey eyes,' he had said on waking beside her – surprised that they were not blue? 'I have such love for you – it is extraordinary,' he had said, amazed at his own emotion. 'Beautiful, beautiful, beautiful,' he had murmured, and now it was a comparison.

And his great skill as a lover. In her stupid ignorance, Arabella thought now with fury, she had not realized that such a lover must be practised and experienced. I am a fool, she thought, an agony of wounding jealousy twisting her heart with pain. And he has a son.

She looked down at the letter she had been writing and the words seemed to leap out of the page at her ... 'a man to love and trust and honour and admire ... I am sure I have the prospect of great happiness before me ...'

She snatched up the paper and tore it through and let it fall. She gave a cry of pain that no one heard, and then she ran, like a hurt child, to the house.

CHAPTER SEVEN

As well as estates in Sussex and Wales, the Helvyn family owned extensive mining and marketing rights with frequent disputes and claims to be settled. Lord Helvyn settled everything by ignoring it, but Neville taking over from his Uncle believed in enforcing all legal rights to the full. After a series of meetings in London, when everything had been settled entirely to his satisfaction, he spent some time in a Bond

Street jeweller buying a necklace for Arabella, trying to decide what gem could match such a woman. Should it be diamonds, rubies, sapphires, or amethysts? Or a choker of creamy pearls to clasp about her graceful neck? A difficult decision, an enjoyable one.

But London could be a very tedious place, Neville decided. Boredom was the chronic ailment of Society these days in his view. The young men about town had plenty of money, a great deal of leisure, and few duties. They occupied their mornings leaning over the iron railings of Rotten Row watching the riders, their afternoon gossiping languidly with ladies in high class drawing rooms, and their evenings were passed at dinner parties and balls. It was little wonder people in Society had to manufacture excitement with elaborate practical jokes.

Charles Sankey was turning into a bit of a joke himself, with his Dundreary whiskers straggling down in wispy waves and his mannered lisp drawled out with such exaggerated weariness now as to be virtually incomprehensible.

Neville met all the old high-flying set he used to know at Lady Despencer's and felt himself alienated from them. They seemed to him caricatures of people leading ineffectual lives.

'Why didn't you bring the pretty creature with you?' Sankey wanted to know.

'Why don't you join the Army – or go into politics. There must be something you can do,' Neville said.

Sankey looked surprised and vaguely affronted. 'I'm waiting to inherit. I've got all sorts of things to do.'

'Oh yes, of course,' Neville said.

The ladies reproved Neville for marrying so quickly and quietly and to someone outside their charmed circle, but they admired the boldness of the action. 'So spontaneous, so unexpected, so romantic.'

'Everyone loves a lord,' they said. 'How did she catch you?'

'She is an exceptional person ...'

'A respectable girl, from what I hear,' Lady Despencer said. 'But of a rather lower order.'

'I find that irrelevant,' Neville said.

Lady Despencer had grown old and grey in the service of

Society and knew its fickle ways better than anyone.

'Yes. I think you may. You get more and more like your Uncle and he always was an independent old reprobate. There are always exceptions, like you, to prove the rules.'

'Let us see for ourselves your exceptional person,' the ladies said to him. 'Don't keep her hidden down there in Sussex.'

The men found it frankly impossible to believe that Neville had so changed his nature as to devote himself solely to one woman. 'You've got a long way to go to prove that,' they said. 'As likely to happen to the Prince of Wales, as to you.'

He left them tossing the joke to and fro like a frayed ball. Had the conversation always been so banal, the jokes so predictable, the gossip so tedious? He felt infinitely superior to these people, with all their flirtations and ther coquetry, their running in and out of bedrooms on country house weekends, the mistresses they set up for themselves in St John's Wood, their conquests and their lovers – they had no idea how glorious love could be. 'No idea,' he said aloud. 'They simply do not know.'

And as the thought of Arabella and the image he had of her in the bedroom at Copper Down Grange came vividly into his mind, he decided that there was nothing here to keep him from her a moment longer.

He cancelled the dinner invitation, the party he had promised to attend. If he left at once he would be in time for the last train of the evening leaving Victoria Station for Chichester.

Thoughts of Arabella went with him. Twice before he had travelled to find her; to her home at Bishop's Linden after and five dances at the Assembly Rooms; then back from the Riviera to find her again and win her. He reflected that he had fallen in love with her beauty first of all, then with her candour and her vibrant spirit, then perhaps with her proud independence when she refused to marry him. But since they were married his love for her had grown and strengthened and deepened immeasurably, enriched above all by her glorious sensuality. It never ceased to amaze him. This was the glory of it, the amazing good fortune. He had never expected to find himself in this position, where one woman mattered so much to him that all the rest were insignificant. Arabella had won him completely with the warm and passionate sensuousness she had revealed to him.

How, in heaven's name, had she come to be the woman she was? He knew that her upbringing had been in the tight propriety of the bourgeoise. Like most middle-class daughters she had been protected like a caged canary, with curtains of respectability drawn round her and veils of prudery obscuring the real world.

He could not guess from where Arabella had inherited her passionate, generous spirit, perhaps from some primitive forbear. How had she become a woman who could respond to the pleasures of the flesh with such delight, revelling in it with such a robust sensuality? She would talk of their love on a high, pure plane and at the same time she would be stepping out of her silken petticoats with a delicious wantonness that inflamed and thrilled his senses.

It struck him as even more amazing because there was such widespread disharmony between the sexes. The upper classes might still pursue their pleasures with gusto and only occasional panic when the newspapers got too close, but the majority of Queen Victoria's subjects were set upon proving their upright purity by completely repressing the animal in man. Indeed there were people, he knew, who considered relationships outside marriage should be made a crime. And he knew that the sexual law was all the more powerful for being unwritten.

Neville had a shrewd idea of the nature of most marriages; of the domestic duties performed in darkness and distaste, of how the majority of wives had become child-bearing vegetables and taken refuge in invalidism and prudery, and the majority of husbands made use of the vast army of prostitutes.

He knew something too, of the contrasting world of the professional; how she cultivated to a fine art the erotic attraction of removing her underclothes; judging just how to fascinate and delight. By what amazing grace had Arabella acquired that art? It was a constant astonishment to him.

When she prepared for bed she never called her maid to assist her. When he went into the bedroom he would find her standing before the long glass unlacing her ribboned corsets, or sitting at her dressing-table in her lacy chemise and frilly drawers languorously brushing out her hair, and she would smile at him in the glass, tossing her head a little, with such a desirable innocence that his senses burned.

Young gently-nurtured brides had fainted before now at the experience of being seen in their petticoats by their husbands for the first time or at the shock of first seeing their husband's nakedness. How had she survived the strait-jacket of her upbringing to blossom like the glorious lily she was, in sweet desire and the fullness of love, reaching out her arms to embrace it and crying out in a soft ecstasy?

Neville swore violently when he reached Chichester station and found that there were no cabs for hire, cursing his Uncle's stubbornness that had left Copper Down so isolated. It took him some time to knock up Wm. Powell, livery stable keeper, fly and job master, whose advertisements all over the station declared his willingness to hire out carriages for parties to drive themselves, but who went to bed at ten each night regardless of who wished to travel.

Woken by an irate and impatient Rossiter, Wm. Powell nearly found himself out of business, and was much berated for his tardiness and incompetence, but he produced placatingly a fine horse that would, he said, cover the remaining miles to Copper Down with no difficuly at all.

The action suited Neville's mood, riding through the night, a velvety autumnal darkness with no one abroad it seemed in all of Sussex and the road to the Downs empty under the stars. He shouted her name – Arabella, Arabella, Arabella – for all heaven to hear the glory of it. The passionate urgency in him communicated to the horse under him and the magnificent animal galloped through the night as if there was a race to win.

Arabella would be sleeping by this time, but she would wake up quickly, surprised, pleased, warm and full of love for him. He could see her as she would look when he woke her, wearing one of her pink trousseau nightgowns made of a delicate fabric that had worried her mother because it was almost transparent.

When he reached the Grange there were no lights. But lights appeared in answer to his shouts, as he took the horse to the stables himself, shouting for the groom, throwing the reins to the sleepy youth, then without pausing, racing up the stairs to the room where Arabella slept.

To Arabella, waking in the downy depths of the four-poster which seemed to swallow her up when she slept there alone, he looked like an apparition of the night in his black riding cloak, the candlelight making his eyes gleam, the cold air and the urgency of the feverish ride still about him.

She sat up, staring at him, her eyes wide and startled. He paused only for a moment to take in the sight of her, the reality of the image he had been riding towards, then he moved very quickly to her, putting down the candle to take a packet from his cape.

'This is for you. Let me put it on. Now.' He took it from the wrapping papers and held it out to her. Not diamonds. He had decided after all to choose a choker of milk-white pearls to go about her throat. He bent over her with the pearls held out towards her.

At the sight of the pearls, Arabella startled into full wakefulness, reacted with sudden violence as if he was about to choke her. She drew back, across the bed, crouching out of his reach, her eyes wide, hunted, outraged, the pale pink nightgown clinging to her, and she screamed at him again and again:

'No. Never. Go away. Don't touch me.'

The shock of her reaction made Neville act instantly. He seemed to leap at her, snatching hold of her shoulders, pulling her forward to him so that she was pressed against the serge of his cape and flinched at the pressure of his hands. The fury of an animal was in his eyes. 'What are you talking about? What's the matter with you?'

'Let go of me. Leave me alone.'

With a kind of baffled amazement he let her go and Arabella drew back from him again, to stand the other side of the bed away from him. As she moved away she pulled a covering from the bed to wrap round herself and that covering movement, the first that had ever come between them, struck him like a stinging blow with acute pain.

'What has happened to you? What's wrong?' Neville asked her.

'Catherine Becket,' Arabella said and the name sounded like a knell in her own ears. 'I now know a lot of things I should have been told before.'

She knew? She assumed. She dared to accuse and demand. Neville's immediate reaction was anger. Why should he justify any of his actions at any time, to her or anyone else? He found her behaviour incomprehensible, outrageous and unforgivable. Not for a moment did he consider explaining himself.

'What should you have been told, do you consider?' There was cold contemptuous fury in his voice.

'Are you going to deny that you know her?' Arabella demanded. She couldn't get her thoughts in any kind of order or keep her reactions under control. His arrival in the middle of the night had so startled her, and she was frightened by the violence of her own feelings. She hadn't planned her actions; she was swept along by the force of her overwhelming, right-minded indignation. At the very least she wanted his denial and his explanation. At the very least –

'Yes, I know the lady. I know many such. Do you want a list?' Neville was standing very still, very upright now, across the bed from her. She could see the whiteness of his face in the light of the single candle and the harsh lines in it, but she couldn't guess how the overwhelming desire, that had ridden with him through the night, had turned to icy wrath. The words came twisted out of suppressed rage. 'What did you think? To marry a man as pure as your virginal self? I know your upbringing was sheltered in the extreme, but did you never imagine –'

'I never imagined that you would have a mistress installed here, almost on the premises, flaunting herself and her gifts from you and her child –' The extremes of Arabella's sense of outrage made her gasp for words. She was beside herself now with passionate, righteous fury. She hardly knew what she was saying. She only knew her pain and her hatred.

Neville's voice was cold, quiet and lethal. 'And if I have – if I have – what are you going to do about it?'

If at that moment Arabella had crumpled, helplessly, into tears, weakened, softened, let him see her hurt, he would have said or done anything she wanted. But her furious pride kept her upright and inexorable, clutching her blanket to her breast. Whereas a few moments ago she had been as desirable as Juliet crouched startled and lovely on the bed, now she was Lady Macbeth, hostile and untouchable.

Neville in his anger, having infuriated her to breaking point with his lofty, icy refusal to defend or deny, completed her destruction by laughing. He laughed, as his Uncle laughed, fierce and humourless, and the laugh killed the last tender hope Arabella had been clinging to that magically he might be able to say or do something that would put everything right again.

He laughed, and then he said: 'There isn't anything you can do, is there?'

Arabella didn't answer him. She acted so quickly, with such sudden violent force that he didn't realize what was happening. In one movement she dropped the blanket, and rushing round the bed, hurled herself against him, putting all her strength into pushing him bodily through the open doorway behind him. Then she slammed the door and locked it.

'I can keep you out of my room' she screamed at him through the door. 'Tonight and every night.'

Neville regained his balance in utter amazement and a power of pent-up fury gathered itself for an onslaught on the door. He gave one mighty shout that reverberated through the house and wrenched at the door handle, which came off in his hand. He turned to ram his shoulder against the door, but as he did so he caught sight of a small face looking down on him through the banister rails. From above in the servants quarters, Becky, Arabella's new maid, was peering down at him, saucer-eyed.

Suddenly, above all other feeling, he felt a fool. Standing there, locked out of his own bedroom, with the door handle useless in his hand, bellowing at his wife to let him in – it was a farcical situation to be in. He had an acute sense of all the other servants sitting up in their beds with their ears flapping to hear what was going on. He had no intention of giving them a theatrical treat. He swore with violence and threw the door handle to the ground. Arabella heard it roll along the floor; she heard Neville's rushing footsteps furious on the stairs and then nothing more. She went on standing there, sustained by the throbbing indignation that possessed her, the unbearable hurt pride, the sense of deepest outrage. He had treated her so badly that anything she did was justified in her own estimation and her only regret was that she hadn't been able to inflict a more visible revenge.

She was in no state to analyse her impetuous action, but even so, obscurely, she realized she hadn't screamed at Neville or pushed him from the room and locked the door against him, because Catherine Becket was his mistress, because Ralph was his child and destined to inherit much of his estates, nor because he had brought her so dramatically in the middle of the night a necklace that was just like the one he had given to Catherine. Her emotions were in a turmoil of outrage for those reasons, but her violent action had been triggered because he laughed.

Once before he had had the same effect on her. Once, walking in the garden in Bishop's Linden he had proposed marriage and she had considered what he had to say with sweet reason – until he smiled. That arrogant, lordly, superior smile had infuriated her so much she had refused him, impetuously, before she realized what she had done.

Now it had happened again. He had laughed, like his Uncle, that hard, contemptuous laugh. 'What are you going to do about it? There is nothing you can do, is there?'

There had to be, there had to be.

For the rest of the night Arabella remained sleepless, stoking the fires of her hatred. She was up on a high plane of emotion, as intense and vivid as the excitement she had once sought so daringly, hunting, gambling and dancing. The same kind of pounding in her temples and racing quicksilver in her veins, the precarious elation and exultation, the dangerous recklessness, careless of caution. They had called her impetuous, self-willed and headstrong, but it wasn't her head that ruled her actions; her mind didn't plan what she was going to say or do, her brain never reckoned up the results of her actions, the future effect for her and for others. She acted entirely from the heart, from an instinctive upsurge of feeling, from the great power of the love that he had created in her and then shattered so cruelly.

She paced the bedroom, wrapped in her fierce pride, determined above all that she would not be crushed by the way he had treated her, addressing him in his absence with well-chosen words of scorn and fury.

In the morning she heard one of the servants come and quietly repair the broken door handle. By the time Becky came to draw her curtains, Arabella was sitting up in bed, propped up regally with pillows, his as well as hers. Let him come now, she thought, and start apologizing and give me some explanation.

'Mr Rossiter left a message, Ma'am,' Becky said. She was looking down at the floor. 'He said he would return in a matter of days.'

'In a matter of days.' It sounded like a sentence. Did he think he would punish her by his absence? A whole new wave of fury swept through her. His absence enraged her. Above all else she wanted to see him and let him know the state of her feelings; she needed to discover the facts, to know – above all to know. With everything left in suspense, unresolved and confused, the vacuum filled up with festering hatred.

What kind of a man have I married? she asked herself, walking alone in the gardens, sitting alone in the house in the days that followed, attended by the servants in her solitary state. She had no one to talk to, and all her thoughts, fears and suspicions turned inward. Endlessly she tried to reconcile her love for him with her hatred of him, and his love for her that she had believed in so totally, with the way he had behaved towards her. Endlessly she failed. She couldn't believe in him now or in anything he had said to her.

Only one thing gave her any purpose and satisfaction. She wasn't going to let him triumph over her. He couldn't treat her like this, because she had no intention of putting up with it. She was no meek little bride, docile and submissive to her lot. She thought of Charles Sankey's neglected wife, she thought of her own mother and how she had let her life be ruled by her father's irritability; of Lady Emily, utterly devoted and submissive to Sir Hugo's every whim – that way of life was not for her. She had discovered during the few months she had been married to Neville, that they were equally matched in their love – that had been the great glory of it.

Now she began to see how it was that for so many wives their most intense passions turned instead to their homes and their children and their domestic duties. Perhaps it was treatment like this that had turned their love away from the ecstatic passionate heights she had known, into the flat meadows of domesticity.

But if Neville thought that he could do as he pleased and treat her with casual arrogance, certain that she would put up with it because she was his wife – then he should prepare himself for a shock. He was going to be surprised – very surprised, Arabella thought, as she walked the gravel paths of the Grange gardens, sustained by her hatred and planning her actions and holding furious long conversations with him in his absence. Never at any time did she shed a tear.

After three such days, Lord Helvyn came over to the Grange – an unprecedented event in itself.

'Where is he, then? Where is he?' Lord Helvyn demanded storming into the house. 'Why isn't he back from London? Why isn't he here?'

When Arabella said that Neville had been detained on a matter of business and would return in a few days, Lord Helvyn was aggressively disbelieving.

'Rubbish. Rubbish. Matter of business? Nothing of the sort. He's back in with that fast set, gambling his life away and frittering his time with wine and women. He's going the pace, d'you think I don't know?' He laughed abruptly and Arabella winced. 'It takes an old reprobate to tell a young one. I wasted half my life that way – and it's about time he called a halt to it. And what are you doing about it?' He rounded on Arabella. 'You're his wife – I'd have thought you could keep him here if anyone could. What kind of a milksop wife are you that you let him go off like this?'

Arabella was too deeply concerned with her own state of outrage and unhappiness to be affected by the Uncle's tirade of angry abuse. Then it struck her suddenly that Lord Helvyn might be the person who could tell her one of the things she badly needed to know.

She interrupted what he was saying, completely disregarding his anger. 'Uncle, will you tell me something? I must ask you this, is Catherine Becket's son, heir to a large part of the estates after Neville?' Of all the questions she wanted answered, that was one she felt she could ask him. Surely he could give her a straight answer to that question at least.

Stopped short in the middle of his outburst, Lord Helvyn frowned and hit the side of his head with the flat of his hand several times. He walked away from her to the window and stared out at the cedar trees and sighed deeply and noisily in a way that made her think of a volcano.

'Is that what she's been saying to you then? Women – malicious creatures.'

'But is it true?' Arabella persisted. 'I just want to know that.'

'Well I can't tell you. Neville inherits everything from me, that's as far as I go. After that, it's up to him to decide what is to happen. He can do absolutely as he pleases with the estates. You'll have to ask him. Why don't you ask him?'

'I will do,' Arabella said, with an effort, for the confirmation in his words had filled her with a bleak hopelessness.

The Uncle seemed disturbed and confused, frowning and muttering, more to himself than to her. 'People – always problems – difficulties – no way out. You'll have children, lots of them, I wouldn't be surprised. Then what will happen? How can I decide what's for the best?' He went on mumbling incoherently to himself and she could scarcely hear. Suddenly he spoke up, looking at her. 'Not frightened of me though, are you? Most people are. Most people.'

Arabella shook her head and he went out of the house still muttering. 'Well that's how it is. That's the way it is.'

He seemed old and she realized as she looked at him that he was an old man, for all his strength and his energy. He didn't frighten her, but she could very well comprehend the fear he inspired in others. The aristocracy were allowed to be eccentric but allied to his lordly arrogance there was a fierce air of unpredictable violence about him; he created an acute uneasiness because no one could be sure what he was going to say or do next. His words, his manner and the things he hadn't said, all left her feeling chilled and desolate.

'He can do absolutely as he pleases with the estates,' the Uncle had said. Neville could do absolutely as he pleased. What about her?

She made a sudden decision the next day and rode across the park towards Bassetts, purposefully, to see for herself. By the direct route across the park, the cottage was only a mile distant. It was almost dusk and she sat on her chestnut horse in the shelter of a copse of hazel trees, staring and staring at the cottage windows as if she would read some explanation in their blankness. She had no idea why she had come. She had no wish to confront Catherine, nothing to say to her. There was little point in knocking on Catherine's door to tell her how much she had come to hate her and what damage she had done.

Then as the dusk deepened and Arabella was about to ride away, Catherine appeared in the doorway and walked to the gate to look up the lane and call for the boy. He came at once from the paddock, riding bareback a tough little pony, riding it with such assurance that Arabella was astonished. He was just a scrap of a boy and yet he rode like that, bareback. Immediately she thought of Mrs Williams' words to her at Castell y Bryder telling of Neville's childhood there and how daringly he rode horses too strong for him to control.

She gave a kind of groan. There was no comfort anyway she turned. She rode back to the Grange with no sense of purpose now, feeling at a loss. And later when she looked from the windows of the first-floor at the back of the Grange, she realized that now the trees were losing their leaves she could see the roof of Catherine Becket's cottage at Bassetts. She could actually see the smoke from her chimney. Each time she saw it it offended her and increased her sense of outrage.

There was nothing for her to do but wait for Neville's return and when he came, when she heard the sound of carriage wheels on the gravel and looked from the window in time to see him leap out, then she felt suddenly alarmed. Now what would happen? The strength of her feelings made her heart beat with a furious apprehension. She couldn't think how she was to face him, yet she wanted to face him more than anything in the world.

They came slowly towards each other, Neville advancing across the hall from the front door and Arabella descending the curving staircase. At the foot of the stairs where they met, Neville gave a slight formal bow, his eyes watchfully on her face then she led the way into the drawing room.

'What have you to say to me,' she asked him with all her dignity mustered.

'What would you have me say?' The question was polite, but the tone was immediately aggressive.

'I would like to be made fully aware of the facts of the situation regarding Catherine Becket – and her son. She tells me you established her in the cottage at Bassetts, that you support her and the child. Is that right? She implies that the child is yours. Is that right? Furthermore she insists that the child is to inherit –'

'Furthermore!' Neville's tight control broke quickly into rage. 'How dare you cross question me?'

Arabella seemed to hear Catherine's voice in mocking challenge: 'Ask him. Why don't you ask him?' She had known very well how it would infuriate him.

'I have a right to know these things,' Arabella said, her voice very hard, demanding and obdurate.

'No,' Neville's voice in return was like a lash. 'You have no rights. I decide. It is up to me. I do exactly as I wish and you have no claim on me for any explanations. Do you understand?' He took hold of her arm, then both arms in a fierce grip. The touch of his hands was an insult not to be borne and Arabella wrenched herself free.

'Then don't touch me. Don't come near me.'

They stood staring at each other, and kept several yards apart.

'You locked your door against me,' Neville said, dangerously quiet.

'I have every intention of continuing to do so,' Arabella said, fighting with the only weapon she had. 'Until –'

'Oh you have terms, do you? And what are they?' It was a snarl of sarcasm.

Arabella drew a deep breath. 'Until such time as you can assure me that you will have no further association of any kind with Catherine Becket – and her child.'

Even as she spoke the words in her proud certainty they gave her a feeling of power, of triumph. As though she was determined to give him no possible way of acceding. Let him apologize, plead, promise abjectly. She was almost enjoying the moment – almost.

Neville could hear the note of triumph in her voice and his own brooding pride set rock-like into position. 'If those are your terms, then we have nothing to discuss.'

Yet the talk went on, during the days that followed, at meals, as the servants came and went, and they came together repeatedly because they couldn't leave the battle undecided and because each in turn found things they were determined to say.

'I thought you impulsively warm, gentle, loving,' Neville said to her. 'Now I find I have married a prig of a woman whose fire blasts my soul. You should, after all, have become a governess. You are most suited to that.'

'I thought you a man I could trust and admire, a man of most generous spirit, capable of great love. Now I find your power is not in love, but in love-making and comes not from great sensibility but from great practise.'

'I have known other women. Many women. I never gave you to understand otherwise.'

'That I accept. A husband is fully entitled to his adventures before marriage.' Arabella spoke with haughty certainty, as though she alone laid down the rules in marriage and decided what was acceptable. Were there not vows? They had made vows to each other – 'to love and to cherish ... to keep thee only unto her ... until death do us part.'

As they battled on, tearing at each other's emotions, each became more deeply entrenched in position, hoisting banners of hatred and resentment.

On the subject of the locked bedroom door, though, they never exchanged another word. It was tacitly agreed. Each night Arabella walked up the curving staircase with her head high, and locked the door with cold deliberation. Neville was too proud even to follow her or check that the door was locked.

As Arabella pulled the blankets about her, lonely but resolute in the wide space of the four-poster, she did not acknowledge her secret thoughts. This will not last long. He will not let a mere locked door stand between us for long.

Neville as he prepared himself to sleep in a room apart had parallel thoughts, deep down and unacknowledged. She will not be able to sustain this. It is not in her nature.

Also without discussion they both agreed, out of their mutual pride, to keep up appearances in public. No one guessed, seeing them together, how far apart they were in private. Certainly, the Uncle did not guess, and on the occasions when they mingled with local society, no one realized they were estranged. They were the young couple, the newly weds, a handsome pair: Neville with his position and background, his thoroughbred elegance and quick vigorous style and at his side his beautiful bride, matching him in elegance, slender and lovely from the top of her darkly chestnut head to the soles of her buttoned boots.

Apart or together in a room full of people, whether they spoke to each other or not, there was a vibration of tension between them. Arabella was aware of him at all times, thinking how much she hated him. And as she sparkled against the dull backcloth of stolid Sussex society, Neville would watch her with quick darting watchfulness.

At these gatherings Catherine Becket was never to be seen. Arabella was always expecting to see her, and each room she entered her glance checked over the assembled ladies, seeking her. But Catherine, it seemed, was not accepted in local society. The Uncle's invitation to her had been an exceptional one.

On Sundays, though, when they attended matins at the little village church, any devotion Arabella might have been feeling was dissipated by the occasional sight of Catherine Becket with the boy, Ralph at her side. Arabella sat beside Neville in the place of honour that was due to the Helvyn family. The Uncle never came to the church, but he had rebuilt it some years before, replacing the simple Norman structure with an elaborate facade and an amazingly high spire and the interior was full of memorials to past generations of the family.

Arabella would never see Catherine arrive, but she would become suddenly acutely aware of her presence and then glancing round she would find her. It must have been a trick of the strange light through the stained glass windows, but Catherine's hair always seemed to gleam like gold, and with her soft-pink and white serenity and the blue mantle she always wore, she had a look of the madonna. Arabella's thoughts on these occasions were far from saintly.

It became a winter of some severity, the ground too hard-frozen for hunting. Neville went about his business on the estates, working in partnership with his Uncle, and sometimes, she knew, he must have gone to Bassetts, though whether to attend to the racing stables or to wait upon Mrs Becket, she had no way of knowing.

She occupied her time with the refurbishing of the Grange; she supervised the modern improvements that were being made to its amenities and travelled to Chichester to buy new gowns and hats.

Pride made them keep up appearances in public and pride kept them from making the first move towards each other. With the passing of time and chasm that had formed between them widened and widened so that bridging it became more and more formidable. Each began to exult in their own staying power.

Arabella thought, as she drew the curtains round her solitary bed: see, I scarcely miss him now. I sleep so soundly alone.

Neville thought as he himself prepared to sleep: I am very unkind to her to leave her alone for so long. But she must learn – she must realize who holds the reins.

Only gradually, imperceptibly, the fierce brooding pride and the righteous indignation changed to sorrow. Arabella didn't realize it had happened, until one day she was turning the tissue-thin pages of the little crimson-bound volume of Tennyson, reading the sweet familiar lines – and she was back again at Castell y Bryder, back again in the delighted discovery of love.

The enchanted images of a medieval castle in Wales, where the casements in the ivied tower looked down on the tumbled waters cascading over the rocks and two black swans came for ever towards her across the mirror surface of the lake, were images of lost joy, of a kingdom from which she was exiled.

A wave of pain and love and despair swept over her. The lines seemed to be arranged on the page to speak to her, and they spoke of grief: 'Tears from the depth of some divine despair Rise in the heart, and gather to the eyes, In looking on the happy Autumn-fields, And thinking of the days that are no more ... O Death in Life, the days that are no more.'

At that moment she was crushed by the realization that she had let life's greatest treasure slip away from her grasp perhaps irretrievably. Grief welled up in her heart and she found the tears pouring down her cheeks. She let the tears fall, unchecked, feeling sick at heart.

It was then she said impulsively to Neville: 'I want to go back to Castell y Bryder. I want to go now.' It was the nearest she came to a reconciliatory move. Everything would be all right again if they could escape to their enchanted Castle, their secret, private world. Hadn't Mrs Williams told her the misfortunes of the family engulfed them at Copper Down, but at Bryder all was well? If they went back there now – even now in the depths of the winter – if they once again slipped into the spell of that idyllic place, they would come together. How could they help it?

'That is quite impossible,' Neville said impatiently, and without explanation.

But later he surprised her by saying stiffly: 'If you wish – we will pay a visit to Bishop's Linden, so that you may see your family and friends at Christmas.'

She had thought he had determined to keep completely aloof from her family, it was almost as if he was making a conciliatory gesture of his own.

They sat silent and apart in the railway carriage, as they crossed the county to Bishop's Linden by way of Horsham and Three Bridges. His constrained manner inhibited her; it seemed as if there was always to be such constraint between them now. Yet in the confined privacy of the first class compartment they were closer together than they had been for a long time and the thoughts of each were concerned entirely with the other.

Arabella's hands were snug in a muff resting demurely on the lap of her quilted skirt, but her attention was held by Neville's hand that lay negligently on the carriage seat between them, only a few inches away from her. It was a strong, lean, brown hand with tapering aristocratic fingers and the plain heavy ring with the crest of the Helvyn family engraved on it. She was shaken by a sudden longing to seize hold of his hand and press it to her cheek.

Neville's attention was drawn by the way long ringlets of hair straying over Arabella's shoulder brushed against her neck and her cheek with the movement of the train. This morning she was wearing her hair loose; it escaped from the small hat she wore tipped forward and vagrant curls hung past her collar. The white skin of her neck was partly revealed, partly obscured by the swing of the curls.

She was so muffled up, covered from head to toe in her layers of fashionable winter clothes. There was only that half-revealed glimpse of pale skin to remind him of the beautiful body he had known so well, but the very primness of her attire, allied to the sight of her perfect profile and her long neck was enough to set the pulse of sweet desire remembered, pounding painfully. So often he had kissed her neck, to begin with. There was a soft vitality to her skin, a clear, pale, translucent smoothness. There were blue veins down the inside of her arms, that he remembered and brooded upon.

At the station at Bishop's Linden there were hansom cabs and growlers lined up for hire and Arabella was pleased that he selected a hansom to convey them stylishly to her old home. Growlers were used by the elderly and those with much luggage. There was something more dashing about a hansom, something more romantic, more intimate.

She looked out at the familiar roadways of Bishop's Linden, muddy with melting snow under the bare lime trees, the pedestrians backing away from the slush and spray of the flying hooves. It was strange to return and remember her own immaturity, her own aspiring emotions. Since she had left her girlhood, she had known in a few months such unimagined happiness, and such pain.

The cab swung into the semi-circular drive of the house in Lansdowne Road, a drive too modest for the horse to manage with ease and the sudden turn past the familiar, sooty laurels threw Arabella off-balance against Neville. Her hair brushed his cheek, his hand went out to support her – and at once the momentary touch produced the arching radiance of the rainbow. For an extraordinary moment Arabella thought he was going to press his lips to her neck. Deep inside her, she felt a well of sensation spring to life.

They looked at each other with wild surmising amazement, recognition, appeal. And even as they looked, it was too late, the flyman was opening the door for them.

Taking a deep breath, Arabella straightened her hat and together they went into the house. Disturbingly the memory came back to her of once before when accidentally his hand had brushed her ankle on the occasion when her shoes had fallen to pieces in the garden. That was long ago, before they were lovers. Now it seemed they were strangers to each other again and a passing touch was danger.

The front sitting room of her home had always been a cramped and excessively over-furnished place. Now with Neville and Arabella, her mother and all her sisters there, it was ridiculous. She ran to embrace her mother and each of her sisters in turn and they backed and dodged between the what-nots set with framed photographs and the tiny stools specially designed to trip up the unwary ankle and precarious displays of china ornaments on occasional tables ideal for being knocked down by the swish of skirts and draperies.

The room was also extremely hot. Hester Curtis had been anxiously ordering more and more coals to be piled on the fire to warm them after their long cold journey and now the heat was overpowering. In her excitement she nearly backed into the roaring blaze and set light to her precarious bustle. Her daughters pulled her away, giggling and embarrassed for her, but nothing stopped her talking or damped the effusive warmth of her welcome.

'How amazing to see you – how amazing. Such a journey – in such weather. How tired you must be – what can I get for you? What can I do for you?'

'I know what you can do,' Neville said frostily. 'Give away two or three of these what-nots. Give them to the poor.'

His manner disconcerted Hester completely. 'Give away? Would the poor ... ? Should I? Is that what I should do?'

It was a chaos of a welcome and hot drinks were produced with great palaver. Hester twittered and fluttered and when the sisters didn't know what to say they giggled and simpered together and when the excess of women was increased with the arrival of Lady Darnley in full feather, Mrs Mansard and her daughter Elizabeth, still Neville managed, even in that overcrowded room to stand apart, aloof, detached and disdainful.

Arabella looked at him as he stood stonily regarding an illuminated text on the wall that called on him to Repent, and she thought, that is how they have always known him. She herself on his first visits to Bishop's Linden, had been struck by his insolently contemptuous, supercillious air. What had amazed her was the other side to his nature she had discovered after she married him. There is another side to him that they do not know, she thought, tender, gentle of speech, remembering romantic poetry, loving. Now she could scarcely believe that other side existed.

The ladies swooped and shrieked over Arabella.

'How well she is looking,' Lady Darnley boomed. 'It was always my opinion that marriage would agree with her.' She leant massively towards Neville with a creaking of her stays. 'Though it isn't a meek and docile wife you've got yourself, as I expect you've found.'

She got no satisfaction. Neville raised his eyebrows and looked down his nose. 'She is quite docile enough for me,' he said and made Arabella sound like a mettlesome horse he had curbed and trained.

Lady Darnley had not the perception to discover their estrangement, nor had Hester. When she talked to Arabella apart, she had nothing but praise for her noble son-in-law.

'Such generosity. I have never known so much kindness. I am to have six hundred pounds a year. With that I can have two servants and live in comfort and never have to worry about another tradesman's bill. What an extraordinarily kind and generous man, Bella. Such devotion to you.'

Happiness, Arabella thought, for her mother, was six hundred pounds a year. He had been kind. His actions were more generous than his words. He had acted generously towards her mother and she must acknowledge that. But her thoughts were confused and unhappy because he had been kind and generous also to Catherine Becket and how could she live with both and accept it?

Elizabeth Mansard was more shrewd and observant, but she was a little preoccupied with her own affairs.

'My mother gets very anxious that I am not married yet, but even more anxious that I may marry someone without money. To ease her misery, I have agreed to marry George Hetherington.'

'Not George,' Arabella cried, remembering his red roast-beef face and his loud breathing, and how at one time she had thought it might be her duty to accept his offer of marriage. She hated to think of her nice, sensible friend Elizabeth married to him. 'Will it not be a little – dull for you?'

Elizabeth smiled. 'Probably. But I think I am suited to a dull life. I could not live everyday with the kind of excitement that you and Neville know.'

And I cannot live with it, Arabella thought.

Because of the severity of the weather Sir Hugo and Lady Emily Faversham could not venture out, so Neville and Arabella paid them a visit at Ashley Court.

Lady Emily, at her most gracious, patted Arabella's hand and was happy to hear the good news. She would always insist that all was well, all was for the best, no matter what evidence was produced to the contrary and Arabella had no intention of producing any such evidence.

Neville and Sir Hugo talked of politics, from which Sir Hugo had retired but never lost interest. 'You should stand for Parliament,' he told Neville. 'The Tories need men like you from the old landowning families – the great families that have played their part in England's history through the centuries. After all, one of your ancestors was Lord High Chancellor of England. There should be a constituency there for you in West Sussex soon, a safe seat.'

Neville did not dismiss the idea. 'I have listened to Randolph Churchill talking a good deal of rubbish lately, I have though it about time someone contradicted him.'

'High time, yes. High time. He's brilliant but he'll destroy himself, d'you see, that's what will happen to him. You should be taking a hand in events. And you'd support him on the platforms very prettily, Arabella, my dear, would you not?'

Immediately Arabella saw herself at Neville's side on platforms and balconies, smiling, acknowledging the cheers as the electorate threw their hats in the air. It was a turn of events she hadn't considered at all, but she was always happy to take on a leading role of any kind.

On the return journey to Copper Down Arabella framed her thanks and her gratitude to Neville for his generosity to her mother. 'The allowance you have made to her is very kind and I am most grateful. You have made her very happy.'

Neville was stiff and seemed indifferent to her thanks. 'It is only money. I have plenty.'

They were as far apart as ever.

The severe weather continued into the new year, but as soon as the iron grip of frost was out of the ground, the hunting began. The meet of the local hunt, a few miles from Copper Down, was held on a bright cold day with an icy wind slicing into the pale sunshine. Arabella was set upon taking part. Neville had none of the narrow-minded Bishop's Linden disapproval of ladies riding to hounds and made no objections, but as the riders assembled on the village green Arabella noted that she was the only woman with that intention. The other women were preparing to follow in pony carts, with the gentlemen too elderly or infirm to ride.

The flinty clatter of hooves along the roadway, the vapour clouds of the horses' breath in the cold air, the hounds surging and scrambling, the forceful voices of the men all around her, the interest and admiration she aroused, revived for Arabella all the elation she had felt when she had ridden to hounds near her home at Bishop's Linden.

She had the additional pleasure of wearing a new tight-waisted riding jacket and knew it to be highly becoming. Bold bright feathers were waving on her black hat set at a confident angle. She felt eager for the excitement of the chase; in her present mood it appealed to her strongly.

'You will not attempt to keep up with the leaders, I trust,' Major Knowles, the retired Army man, said to her.

'Oh yes, she will,' Neville said. 'She may come to grief, but she's always to the fore – that's Arabella.'

Arabella's confidence was a little shaken by an uneasiness about her mount that was increasing minute by minute. The dark chestnut that had been Neville's gift to her was a joy to ride, but a minor lameness had made that impossible today. The big grey she was riding instead had an impetuous look and pulled strongly.

Neville had praised her riding, approved of the way she mounted a horse unaided; he had said she was the only woman he had ever seen who could mount without two or three men holding on to the horse's head, and she was reluctant to betray her anxiety to him.

Major Knowles said to her: 'Neville must have great faith in your ability to let you ride that champion. The fence isn't made that he can't jump.'

I just hope I jump with him, Arabella thought.

The hunt was preparing to move off and she felt the remembered tingling in the blood, the fever of anticipation. The hounds were yelping and running on all sides and being shouted at by the huntsman. He cracked his whip with an echoing report that had her grey twitching and pawing.

Then just at the last moment, she realized that she was not the only woman riding with the hunt. Catherine Becket had arrived. She had a curious way of just being there suddenly; she was never to be seen approaching. Arabella felt the grip of immediate resentment and hostility and her pleasure in the occasion poisoned.

Catherine too was stylishly turned out, in beige and blue,

with her hair in a gold chignon. Arabella watched her talking and smiling to the huntsmen. She's always smiling, she thought, and it offended her that Catherine had so much to smile about. Catherine, secure and serene on a very manageable-looking roan, came up beside Neville, but Arabella couldn't hear what she was saying.

She pulled the grey's head round and urged it into a position between Neville and Catherine.

Catherine looked as poised and calm as though she sat holding court in her own drawing room. 'You seem to be having some trouble,' she said, soft-voiced and sweetly solicitous. 'Is the mount too spirited for you?'

Arabella was prevented from replying at that moment by the efforts needed to keep her seat.

She heard Neville say: 'A spirited horse for a spirited rider. I chose the grey for her myself. They are well matched.'

He rode forward to speak to the Master of the Hunt. It was as though he had thrown her a challenge and immediately Arabella took fire from the thought and regained her customary assurance. She could overlook Catherine's presence in her determination to meet his challenge.

Catherine sat idly swinging her hunting crop, flicking it to and fro. Arabella didn't notice that the crop had an unusually long lash and was unaware when, no doubt accidentally, it flicked the hindquarters of her own horse. The grey, restive and eager, kicked and then bolted, with Arabella clinging and gripping hard. It took her a distance of a hundred yards before she could bring the horse to a halt. Several gentlemen of the party came quickly to her aid, but by the time they reached her she was able to hide her discomfiture, to assure them she was unhurt and determined upon her intention to ride.

The hunt moved off. It was a good day and the hounds did not take long to find. Horns were blowing and the company spilling across the brown fields in a vivid quick-changing pattern of colour, action and noise. Arabella on the eager grey was up among the leaders, whether she liked it or not. There was a great gallop through leafless woodland rides to the open country, the wind was keen and cold in her face and the proud feather in her rakish hat blew like a flag of defiance. Her heart was pounding and the hot smell of horses and hounds thrilled her senses. Ahead of her the hounds streaked towards the bare woods looming purple on the downland.

Then at the edge of a covert, the riders drew to a halt and waited. Hounds and huntsman disappeared into the oaks and undergrowth. There was tension and anticipation in the waiting, a muttering of oaths that the fox had gone to ground. The horses shook their heads about with flecks of foam flying.

Neville came up to Arabella. 'Splendid,' he said. 'Well done.'

She looked at him, her eyes sprakling with exhileration and triumph, breathless and careless of mud-splashing and disarray.

Then Catherine Becket caught up with them. 'Oh, such a pace. And this cold wind has such an unfortunate effect on the complexion. I do believe, Mrs Rossiter, you have mud on your face. Actually on your nose – allow me –'

But Arabella had no intention of allowing Catherine anywhere near her. Haughtily she jerked the horse's head away. There was a shrill halloa from the far side of the covert, the fox had been found again, the hunt was away, the hounds racing downhill. Her bold grey was immediately in pursuit, hell for leather with galloping hooves, racing on across firm pasture land, taking a small hedge in its stride as if it wasn't there. All Arabella could do was to cling on, but there was something like ecstacy in the speed and the excitement, the old thrills she had known once in the passions of loving, a joyous fever, a sensation of glory.

Then at the foot of the hill she saw the stream. Saw how wide it was. Saw the leaders shoot over and other riders drawing aside, heard voices close to her shouting warnings: 'Hold there. Hold hard.'

I can't hold this horse, I can't turn him, I can't stop him, Arabella wanted to cry out with rising panic as all her attempts to avoid the stream had no effect at all. I am going to fall – now – now – I know it.

But the grey horse soared over the stream blithe as a swallow and Arabella stayed firmly in the saddle.

It was Catherine who fell. From the far side of the stream

Arabella saw the undignified clutching at the air, the humiliating crash to the ground, the unladylike sprawl on the muddy bank, and there was no denying her moment of malicious pleasure. Several occasions of her own discomfiture were repaid then. But it was a brief moment. She saw Neville go to Catherine's aid, reaching her far quicker than anyone else, lift her from the ground and carry her to a nearby cottage.

For a long time afterwards the picture that remained in Arabella's mind was the picture of Neville carrying the inert form of Catherine in his arms, effortlessly, as if she was no weight at all, the skirts of her blue riding habit falling about his arms and her hair released from the chignon trailing gold against his shoulder.

CHAPTER EIGHT

Streetlamps formed haloes of light in the London springtime dusk. Hyde Park which an hour before had seen the brilliant equipages of the fashionable and the famous parading between Cumberland Gate and Albert Gate, had become a shadowy place where the young green leaves stirred in the soft air. Now even the sparrows had disappeared and only the ghostly shapes of poverty-stricken lovers wandered across the grass.

Society had moved indoors into the fine houses in squares, crescents and streets around the Park and a bevy of fine ladies and elegant gentlemen were making impressive entrances into glittering rooms. Victorias and broughams, hansoms and phaetons passed and re-passed along the fashionable streets of London delivering the right people to the right functions.

One notable phaeton left Curzon Street at nine p.m. heading for Stratford Place, a large cul-de-sac of elegant houses. There Lady Despencer was entertaining and there Arabella was to make her debut in Society. She sat beside Neville in the enclosed security of their carriage and she could forget her unhappy situation for the moment in excited anticipation.

She had been eager to know this fashionable world, eager to play her part in Society, confident that she was equal to it,

Neville had made it possible for her, coldly and remotely, but as if it pleased him to spoil her and to show her off. They were proudly separate still. They were preparing to play their parts merely, as the young couple – strikingly attractive, and well-to-do, newly married and proud of each other – Neville the heir to an earldom and great estates in Sussex and Wales and a considerable fortune, and the unknown girl he had married from the obscurity of middle-class Bishop's Linden, who made up in beauty what she lacked in social distinction.

And if Society, curious, looked to see if they were in love – what would it see? That they looked at each other frequently, that there seemed to be a tense invisible wire stretched between them that vibrated at a touch or a glance from an intruding outsider, that each spoke softly and warily of the other. Society drew its conclusions from that, being unable to follow the couple home at night to their separate bedrooms and see the fierce and lonely pride that kept them there.

Neville had introduced Arabella to Lady Despencer, doyenne of the London Society hostesses. She had known Neville through all his Society days, and his uncle before him. Indeed, she had known everyone of consequence during her long life. News of Neville's marriage to a girl from a distinctly lower order had not met with her approval and her obvious appraisal with a cold shrewd stare reminded Arabella of the matrons of Bishop's Linden passing their provincial judgements on social performances and standards. But Lady Despencer moved in a wider world and conveyed a sense of regal power as she assessed Arabella's qualifications to walk the drawing rooms of Society.

'The stance is good,' she observed. Her voice was a flat monotone, as if to show expression was ill-bred. 'The position of the head – excellent. General deportment – admirable. Now your parents, my dear, their residence was in the country?'

'Bishop's Linden,' Arabella said.

'Hmmm. A middle class town. I don't think we'll specify then. We'll just refer to the county. And your father?'

'Was of independent means,' Arabella said firmly. It was no concern of Lady Despencer's that his means had proved so disastrously inadequate. 'He died last year.'

'Ah. A modest background is so much more easily overcome with a parent deceased –'

'No doubt my father would have been relieved to learn that,' Arabella said with a dry note of her own as Lady Despencer continued.

'Of course, as the wife of Neville Rossiter, you have every prospect of success in Society.'

'And on my own account, I have every intention of enjoying it,' Arabella said.

Lady Despencer nodded. 'I think you may do quite well. Society is fickle and quickly tires of the familiar. Yours is a new face, and a beautiful new face; a new voice – speaking out, I note, with quite refreshing candour – well suited to amuse the jaded spirits. And yours is a new marriage to one of Society's favourite sons and the new alliance will, I predict, be found intriguing. There are great possibilities to be considered. We will begin with a reception here.'

For the occasion of her debut in Society Arabella had chosen to wear a white velvet dress, classically severe in line, embroidered with pearls. Every line of the dress showed off her slender shape, the handspan of her waist, the gracefulness of her movements. Her hair was piled high and proud, gleaming with a rich shine and scattered with pearls. About her neck she should have worn the choker of pearls in three strands that Neville had given her. She had resolutely refused to wear it, ever, for Catherine Becket had just such a necklace.

The carriage drew up at a tall, Italianate house with a sculptured portico and shallow stepped staircase of stone, beautifully balustraded in curved wrought iron. As Arabella stepped out of the carriage, the brilliance of lights and the warm murmur of conversation within seemed to reach out to her. This was a dazzling new world she was stepping into; this time there was a real red carpet spread before her.

Footmen whose house livery, silken stockings and powdered heads proclaimed the exalted position of their mistress, led them through a dark pillared hall up the stairs to an open landing, passing them on to a butler who announced their names to the glittering reception. Arabella moved, with all the proud grace at her command, into the fashionable throng of women in lavish and luxurious fashions and men with stiff white shirt fronts, into the rich babble of conversation that sounded to her so superior and sophisticated. Lady Despencer advanced to receive them.

'Very nice, my dear. You look most charming. Now let me see –'

Arabella's eyes were filled with stars as she heard some of the distinguished names that were presented to her. Not only the butterflies of Society were present; great names from the political arena mingled with famous names from the world of the arts and well-known names from the theatre. Lady Despencer had no match as a lion hunter.

'Introduce me – This instant ...'

'I want to be the first to capture your exceptional beauty on canvas...'

'Such grace, like a goddess ...'

'A man would risk anything for a word or a glance ...'

'Permit me, Mrs Rossiter, to sit at your feet for ever ...'

Some of the compliments and the flattery were so flowery and outrageous that she laughed outright at their absurdity. Neville heard her laughing and watched her from across the room as they heaped bouquets of praise about her.

'You'll be the talk of London tomorrow...'

'You'll take Society by storm ...'

'Wherever you go, people will be standing on chairs to look at you ...'

'The world will be your oyster,' they said to her.

'Then the world must be a much smaller place than I realized.' Delighted as she was to find herself so immediately the centre of attraction, Arabella's voice remained crisp and cool and calm, no matter how they elbowed each other to fill her glass, or fell over each other to sing her praises.

She looked at the circle of faces around her, brilliant, famous, wealthy, aristocratic, and her gaze going from face to face, she was surprised suddenly to see a face she knew, to feel a dark gaze intent upon her. In a moment she was back at Reisbaden, back at the gaming tables, winning spectacularly at roulette and feeling the intense regard of dark eyes.

James Conroy. The name came back to her and the meeting in Reisbaden, his talk of socialism, his idealism, how deeply he had impressed her. Seeing him again, she was impressed again. She looked at the dark, strong, dramatic face and thought this was a man she could turn to, who would understand everything.

She felt immediately confident of his sympathy and sensibility. He was the man who had come to her rescue at the roulette table, who expressed his admiration for her, and extended such a daring invitation to her. She had reason to be grateful to him, and to think well of him.

James Conroy had been watching her for some time and at the same time he had been engaged in conversation with others interested in her. One was Charles Sankey who was taking a proprietorial interest in Arabella's Society debut and the other was a foppish gentleman of the fourth estate, known as Latimer.

'She's a real beauty. One must say that. I've always said that.' Sankey said congratulating himself on his discernment.

'Arabella Curtis,' James Conroy said nodding. 'I met her in Reisbaden last year.'

'Ha, then she was Arabella Curtis, now she is Mrs Rossiter.'

Sankey's lisp and drooping whiskers made nonsense of the name and Conroy frowned, baffled.

'Rossiter, Neville Rossiter,' Latimer said immediately. He made it his business to know everything and everyone. All kinds of information, snippets of facts, a hint of scandal, a nugget of gossip – it was meat and drink to him. He sold what he knew to *Reynolds News* or *The Sporting Times*, whenever the detail was salacious and colourful. Latimer's independent means had run out long ago, but his aristocratic connections and deliberate charm still gave him entry to all the best places. 'In other words she's married a villain,' he added with a languid airiness.

'You can't say that, Latimer. He's an old friend of mine,' Sankey protested. 'Rubbish anyway. He's married the girl and done the handsome by a penniless family and there's God knows how many sisters.'

James Conroy considered what he knew of Rossiter. Only his inherited wealth and his reactionary Tory attitudes and he didn't approve of either. He kept silent.

'Done the handsome has he? And what about Mrs Catherine Becket?' Latimer threw the name down to see what effect it had. He had come across some interesting information of Catherine Becket's whereabouts from a drunken groom dismissed from the Rossiter racing stables at Bassetts, and now, seeing how much attention Arabella was attracting, he had the feeling he was on to something that might prove valuable.

The effect of the name on Charles Sankey was quite considerable. He was so startled he forgot to lisp. 'Catherine Becket? That was years ago. Looked as if it was going to explode into the Divorce Courts then, but it fizzled out.'

'It went to ground,' Latimer said. 'Rossiter set her up in some kind of love nest on the Copper Down estates. Her child, so it's said, is heir to considerable property after Rossiter. And now there's the beautiful Arabella at Copper Down too. Not to mention old Lord Helvyn himself who's an eccentric old recluse these days. It must be quite lively down there. Have you been there recently, Charles?'

Sankey couldn't get over his amazement. 'I've not been there for some time, but I've never heard any mention of Mrs Becket.'

'Well , I dare say he keeps her well tucked away,' Latimer said. 'But it's an interesting situation. Two very lovely ladies and Neville between the two of them – I don't know which I'd put my money on. I think I shall have to make a trip down there before long and see for myself what the score is.'

Sankey just couldn't get over it. He stood speechless for quite a time pulling at his whiskers. He had his own memories of Catherine; once he too had shared in her favours. He's been quite spoony about her, once upon a time. A sweet peach of a woman, he remembered her, with a warm smile of welcome; he had agreeable recollections of the interlude. So agreeable, in fact, that it occurred to him he too might go down to Sussex one day to find out what exactly had become of her.

He said, with a mixture of envy and admiration: 'Well I must say, I must say it – he's a dark horse. All these years he's been rolling it, here in London, and all the time he's had Mrs

Becket quietly stacked away for himself down in Sussex and to top it all he marries Arabella. It's a bit – Wouldn't you say? Don't you think?'

While Charles Sankey shook his whiskers in wonder at Neville's double life, James Conroy reflected on his first meeting with Arabella in Reisbaden and wondered why he hadn't pursued her more positively. There were always so many demands made on him by the beliefs he held so strongly, there was so much to do, so much knowledge to be gained, questions to be answered, theories to be expounded.

And yet – and yet. Now he saw her again, married, he was moved to see her. She was no cardboard beauty, decorating the salons of Society; she had an interesting face. She looked poised, assured, confident, triumphant in her success here this evening, but there was something else about her that puzzled him, a look she had, a way of searching the faces surrounding her, looking beyond them, seeking something, someone. Could she be altogether happy in her marriage? What of this prattle of another woman on the scene?

It seemed to him that there was something solitary about her still, something untouched.

He went over to pay his respects to Arabella. 'Last year in Reisbaden, this year in London,' James Conroy said. 'And now, I hear, you are Mrs Neville Rossiter.'

'You know my husband?' Arabella asked, smiling and happy to see him.

'From time to time we meet and always argue. We are poles apart politically. I will endeavour not to argue with him in future, for your sake, but I usually feel that I cannot agree with him.'

'You would both have strong views about everything, I think,' Arabella said. 'I remember how you inspired me with your views when we met in Reisbaden. I have kept your book and given it much thought.'

'Then I am honoured. I must write another book and endeavour to engage your thoughts still further.'

'If you could endeavour to write it in shorter paragraphs I would be obliged,' Arabella said. 'My brain is not always equal to such a sustained effort as you demand with your paragraphs.'

'None shall be over ten – I promise you,' James Conroy said and they smiled at each other immediately returned to the rapport that had existed between them a year before.

'I was so sorry to hear of the illness of your father that necessitated your immediate departure from Reisbaden,' Conroy said, and he looked so directly into her eyes that he reminded her forcefully of the assignment he had proposed at the Greek chapel in the great forest.

'How Fate does interpose in all our lives,' Arabella said and as he looked at her she felt he was reading her mind, understanding everything about her and knowing that if it had been different she would have been there to meet him beneath the domes of gold.

From the far side of the room, Neville saw the way she smiled at James Conroy and the intensity of the looks they exchanged. Frowning, he in his turn crossed the room to her side.

'There are other people you should meet,' he said.

Many other people she met that evening. By the next day the hall table of the house in Curzon Street was heaped with invitations. Cards and notes had come from Society and from a wide circle of distinguished people.

Lady Despencer called and she shuffled through the invitations with thin fastidious hands, grading them and giving them her seal of approval.

'This is success,' she said to Arabella in her flat voice without a trace of emotion. 'You are a tremendous success.'

Charles Sankey who had called to share in the triumph also, picked up a handful of the cards and threw them in the air letting them fall about Arabella's ears. 'Invitations showered upon you like snowflakes, London at your feet, pretty lady. You will be able to dine and dance and go to three or four parties every evening from now until the end of July. Will you like that? Are you pleased?'

'Am I pleased?' Arabella considered the question seriously. 'I suppose I should be –'

'You suppose. You suppose. Of course you're pleased.' Sankey took Arabella by the hand and swung her round in a brief waltz. 'Look at you – you're dancing with delight. What do you say, my old friend?'

Neville had just appeared in the doorway and he looked coldly at Sankey and at Arabella. The dancing stopped at the sight of him. 'I am, naturally, most gratified,' Neville said.

'I think that means he's pleased,' Sankey said. Neville certainly didn't look it, and Arabella turned away.

Lady Despencer sorted the invitations: these they should accept, these they should consider, these on no account should they have anything to do with. Arabella looked at the choice and wondered if James Conroy would be at any of these dinners, these dances, these parties.

Social engagements ruled their lives for the following weeks and Arabella found there was much she could enjoy on her own account. Visits to the theatre pleased her, from the moment they left the house in the phaeton to drive through the crush of four-wheelers and hansoms converging upon the theatres, where all the world it seemed was in full finery.

At the Opera House in Covent Garden, at the Drury Lane Theatre, the Lyceum, the Globe, the fashionable ladies wore black, and Arabella was well aware that a low-cut black dress showed off her alabaster shoulders and that her beauty shone against the gilt and plush backdrop of a box in the circle or a seat in the stalls.

She was at once susceptible to the magic of the theatre. She loved the anticipation before the curtain rose, the rustling in and out of cloaks as the lights were lowered and the play began. Between the acts she liked the gossiping and greeting of acquaintances, when opinions were voiced and reputations shredded. Arabella would be told confidentially by the dramatist on her left that the play at the Queen's theatre was a failure because the acting was so bad, and then by one of the leading lights of the acting profession on her right that the real reason for its failure was the dramatist's lame story and wooden dialogue.

Once, by special invitation from the actor/manager, she was invited to a party on stage after the performance, and feeling much privileged found that the King of Siam's Summer Palace had miraculously vanished from the stage, tables had been set with silver and fine food, and waiters were on hand. The distinguished company invited included a Minister of the

Cabinet, and a crowd of admirers surrounded Miss Ellen Terry.

Arabella often found that the emotions expressed on stage were emotions which she understood only too well. Watching *Braving The Storm* at the Sadler's Wells Theatre she could sympathize as Widow Green gave full demonstration to the outraged feelings of violent woman whose matrimonial recollections were stormy. Watching *Partners For Life* at the Globe she could respond at once to the smart sentences and witty sayings of the comedy and all her sympathy was with Fanny the married and misunderstood heroine.

She admired the grace and charm of Miss Ellen Terry in *The Merchant of Venice*, but most of all she responded to the romantic talents of Miss Isabel Bateman in *Fanchette* dancing narcissistically with her own shadow in the moonlight. Arabella was reminded of her own ambitions to be an actress, to play a leading role, to be received with rapturous applause. She had no difficulty in imagining herself up there above the footlights, shining forth with brilliance, applauded and idolized. But the theatre stage could not compare with the world stage on which she found herself; she had a role to play in Society and it gave her greater pleasure to play it.

Beyond the theatre of romance and comedy she found there was another theatre of extraordinary power. To hear Henry Irving as Mathias in *The Bells* was an experience like no other. All London marvelled at his amazing voice, sonorous and resonant, it filled the theatre and echoed in the dreams of all who heard it.

Arabella's portrait was to be painted by Tallani and that was a privilege and an accolade, a mark of rare honour, for Tallani's fame had grown so greatly that now he rarely painted any except Royalty and the closest friends of Royalty.

Neville conducted her to Tallani's studio in Chelsea; despite his august patronage Tallani had refused to depart from his Bohemian background, where there were portraits of the great and famous stacked around the walls, and bamboo screens hid bedsteads and washbasins from view.

Tallani was a man of dusky appearance who dressed in sombre style with the exception of his waistcoat which blazed like the setting sun. At social gatherings people were dazzled, first by his waistcoat, then by his genius and reputation. Throughout all the time Arabella sat for him he wore a waistcoat of vivid hue and she grew most concerned for the safety of the garment. In moments of absorbed consideration of his subject he would stroke his Cavalry beard, paintbrush in hand, and she felt certain the waistcoat must become daubed with paint. But amazingly it always emerged unscathed. Tallani was as careful of his waistcoats as he was skilful at presenting his sitter's best features in the portraits he painted.

Arabella found it a pleasant occupation to sit for him. Such concentration solely upon her was always to her liking and she had never known greater absorption in her features, in the proportions of her face, in the tone of her skin and the texture of her hair. It was most pleasing.

He talked continuously. From him Arabella learned much of Society's ways and the latest scandal, who was in favour and who rejected. He identified for her the high-born and the famous she had noted and admired, and often mystified her with initials.

Lady C., he declared, had such poor eyesight she had been known to mistake a footman for her husband; the Honourable Mrs T. went to parties with a parrot on her arm or leading a tiger cub on a chain; one of the Queen's cousins, losing money at baccarat, had gambled away not only his house and his horses but all the household servants; the son of one impoverished duke was to marry an American lady – a novel way to restore the family fortunes. Mr J., he told her, had swum the Thames in evening dress to avoid his creditors and Mr P. had climbed Nelson's column for a wager and a certain Miss W. had attended a fancy dress ball as Lady Godiva, on horseback –

'But she refused to get down from her horse,' Tallani said; he twinkled merrily at her.

'Do you consider that I shall believe anything you tell me?' Arabella said, looking at him out of the corner of her eyes because she could not turn her head.

'You don't like it when I tell you stories to amuse you?' Tallani approached and adjusted, yet again, the exact position of her head and the curve of her decolletage. 'Shall I continue – or no?'

He confirmed for Arabella what she had already surmised, that in this high strata of Society, the rules were broken all the time, but the skill lay in not being discovered. The strict morality she had known in Bishop's Linden's respectable middle class society bore no relation to the upper class world. She had quickly observed that fashionable people were not in the least prudish or puritanical; affairs were common, gossip was rife, known lovers were invited by hostesses to country-house weekend parties and assigned neighbouring bedrooms. She had left the genteel cultivation of virtue behind, in Bishop's Linden. In this world misdemeanours were amusing and indiscretions acceptable, just so long as there was no scandal. Where a man's career could be ruined or a woman find her ruptation in shreds was not because of what they did but because of their failure to keep it out of the public eye.

In all this, Arabella realized, the Prince of Wales was the leader. Tallani talked of the Prince's visits to Biarritz in the spring and Marienbad in the late summer, his fondness for large cigars and pretty women, speculated about who was his favourite of the moment. Tallani had painted all the Prince's favourites and he showed little discretion in his talk of them. This one was a beauty but had not the wit to keep the Prince amused; this one was adroit and nimble with her flattery but too greedy for gain.

Arabella was happy to listen; it was better than reading a novel or a periodical.

When the portrait was finished, she gazed at it in surprise and some confusion. There she was – a girl in a white dress half-drawn from her shoulders, with falling ringlets of curls, a rose in her hands, a dream-like expression on her face, but transformed into a Society beauty.

Neville frowned at the portrait in silence for so long that he caused much disquiet.

'Is it not beautiful?' Tallani demanded.

'Beautiful, yes. But you have made her look – just a beauty. Where is the spirit, the fire, the pride, the character? It is not a true and living portrait.' There was great suppression of

143

feeling in Neville's voice.

'I am a great artist,' Tallani cried, also with great feeling. 'But I am not Almighty God.'

He would accept no fee for the portrait. 'It was painted for love,' he declared passionately and Neville's face hardened so ferociously Arabella thought he would strike the artist. Fortunately Tallani added that all his life he had been a lover of beauty, and when it became clear it was generalized and abstract love, Neville's anger subsided.

The portrait was hung in the drawing room at Curzon Street, but Arabella noted whenever Neville looked at it, he frowned with dislike.

Arabella's taste for quality and style, which had led her to condemn the bric-a-brac of Bishop's Linden, responded to the settings in which she now found herself. She walked through rooms hung with Dutch and Italian paintings, with Gobelin tapestries; there were marble busts set in window alcoves, splendidly painted ceilings, rich Aubusson carpets. Where she had high-handedly rejected the over-furnishing, the pendulous draperies, the assortments of knick-knacks that abounded in her parents' home in Lansdowne Road and so many like it in Bishop's Linden, now she appreciated and admired the elegant eighteenth-century French furniture that she saw in the great London houses, the magnificent collections of Sèvres china, Oriental art, exquisite miniatures, Limoges enamels. It was as though she had been looking for this world, and now felt perfectly at home in it.

It was the same with the fashions she chose to wear. There was much talk among the ladies of couturier gowns by Worth in Paris each costing around £100. 'To be well-dressed by Worth,' said one lady, 'gives one a sense of inner tranquility which religion can never equal.'

But that's not for me,' Arabella decided. She had no intention of allowing any couturier to dress her according to his designs. She had taken note of how many ladies were swathed in costly fabric to below the knee, so tightly that they could scarcely move and certainly not sit down; how many were so tight-laced they could barely breath, and others were overwhelmed with enormous bustle shapes and brilliant contrasting shades of magenta, mauve and peacock blue.

Arabella was most impressed with the style of the Empress Eugenie, and she noted how the most beautifully fashionable ladies were ceasing to wear trains and having the skirts of their gowns the same length all round. She at once engaged the services of the best dressmaker to be found. Mrs Babbacome was a skilled needlewoman with no ideas of her own, or none that she gave voice to. Her value lay in being able to follow exactly when given clear and precise instructions. Arabella was admirably clear, always knew her own mind and exactly how she wished to look.

The gowns she had made for her London season were classical, almost Grecian in silhouette, slimmer fitting, moulded so that her slim shape was not disguised by bunching of skirts, swathing layers and heavy bustles. She had tea gowns made, often of velvet or chiffon that flowed gracefully, and her skirts, without a train, were just short enough all round to show her high heeled boots, and she was one of the first to wear a Dolly Varden hat, tilted saucily forward. Often she was urged by other ladies to confide where she bought her beautiful gowns, but she kept the secret of Mrs Babbacombe to herself.

One of her most favoured outfits was a brown walking costume, a petticoat of brown silk trimmed with three flounces of velvet and over it a tunic and jacket of brown merino of finest texture, the tunic trimmed with flounces of silk in the same shade, the jacket like the petticoat rimmed with velvet. The jacket was simply styled, fitting her superb shoulders to perfection, slashed at the sides and back, trimmed all round with one row of velvet ribbons an inch and a half wide. It had deep pointed cuffs at the wrists, little gold buttons from the bottom of the sleeves to the point of the cuff, a small velvet collar and a white tie round the throat with a large bow in front trimmed with Brussels lace. With this she wore silk gloves, very long at the wrists, of a light buff colour, and a small straw hat, the brim bound with black silk with a large black bow on the left side.

She wore no jewellery of any kind with this outfit. The Empress Eugenie had set the fashion for wearing none.

Dressed in this manner, Arabella acknowledged a feeling of

well-being that, certainly in her experience, religion had never bestowed.

In general she found London much to her taste, an exciting, inspiring place to be. Indeed there were times when she found herself unable to sleep for the social elation that possessed her.

Since they had come to London everything had become far more formal and it was easier in one respect – she and Neville were seldom alone together. The servants at the London house by their very formality imposed a restraint. Ritual morning calls were received and re-paid, she didn't care for those, the conversation was inanely polite), afternoon tea was partaken in fine drawing rooms and was a more genial occasion, then there were luncheon parties, dinners and formal functions every evening and often several functions were attended in the course of one evening. She could be occupied from morning to night and scarcely exchange a word with Neville.

Their relationship itself had frozen into formality. Neville addressed her in clipped, cold tones and he made announcements and gave instructions with little variation in his voice when he spoke to the servants or spoke to her. At breakfast time, on the rare occasions they faced each other alone across the table, he would tell her the arrangements for the day. He had taken to saying 'Oblige me –' an expression his Uncle often used. Sometimes he even addressed her as 'Ma'am'.

He said: he would be calling at Coutts, his bankers; Lady Despencer would be arriving for luncheon with a party which included two leading generals: 'Oblige me by arranging the seating so that they are well separated from each other.' This evening they would be dining at Park Lane House and the carriage was ordered for nine. If she cared to take a drive in the Park earlier, he would escort her himself. 'If that is to your satisfaction, Ma'am.'

Arabella would nod and agree and take note, equally formal, not to be outdone.

A numbness seemed to have overtaken her emotions; she could feel grateful that the intensity of sorrow and the fever of indignation had left her. But instead there was pervading coldness and deep underlying regret for what had been. She was haunted by a dream of a medieval castle in Wales and gently gliding birds on still waters.

She felt herself in a world of splendour that no rooted reality. Every day, every evening she met new people, people of title and quality and power, with noble lineage or fame or great wealth. But in a strange way they seemed to be players on a stage, not flesh and blood people who could engage her affections or emotions.

Sometimes the most real person in her life now seemed to be Becky, her little maid, with her soft Sussex speech and her wide-eyed devotion.

The only other person to emerge strongly from the fashionable crowds was James Conroy ...

During the weeks that the demands of the Season had been occupying Neville and Arabella, it had been very quiet at Copper Down. Altogether too quiet for Catherine Becket's taste, one warm lazy summer day was like another for her in her rural retreat.

She let her thoughts stray to her own triumphant seasons in Society; there had been a time when she had shone there, the wife of a dashing Army officer on the fringe of the Marlborough House set. She had had her crowded hour of glorious life. Then that world had been lost for love – but that was so many years ago now.

A restlessness and discontent began to build up in her. She was not hankering for Society, but she found herself longing for more interesting, stimulating, amusing company. The company she kept was very restricted, parochial, and dull; made up of country bumpkins and tedious individuals whose limits were bounded by the South Downs and the sea and the turnip fields. Even the local clods that represented Sussex society didn't extend invitations to her; they considered she was beyond the pale. When the Prince's party came to stay nearby at Goodwood, she wouldn't be invited.

One sunny day after another Catherine stood at her cottage window looking out at a field full of buttercups and thought how long it was since any man had warmed her with admiration and made her feel appreciated.

She was very pleased indeed to see Latimer when he called

on her. He reminded her of the occasion they had met years ago and how he had recently heard news of her. He reeled off a whole list of people he knew that she would remember – nearly all men, including Neville Rossiter and Charles Sankey – but Latimer included Lady Despencer whom everyone knew to add respectability.

'I don't recall meeting you and I don't remember the occasion,' Catherine Beckett said, smiling with warmth and pleasure. 'But you are most welcome.'

And she made him feel welcome as he sat at his ease in the pretty cottage parlour and drank the home-made wine she poured for him in generous measure. A generous woman altogether, he thought, looking at her in the pale blue dress, a peach-like fullness to her charms, a maturity that was beautiful to see. He could almost imagine himself forgetting why he had come.

'You are most unfair to us all, to hide away here, to bloom unseen like a flower in the desert,' Latimer said. 'Has the world been so unkind to you that you turn your back on it? If it has, I will chastise it for you.'

'How gallant you are. But I assure you I have reason to be content. My life is a little dull sometimes, but I want for nothing. I am well cared for – as you can see.'

'I expect you are often at Copper Down Manor, and at the Grange,' Latimer said with smooth enquiry.

'Often,' Catherine replied smiling airily. 'I dined there only the other day.' In fact it had been last autumn.

'And the little boy – I expect it is a second home to him?' Latimer went on probing gently.

'Exactly. He likes to play there, in the grounds, under the cedar trees, in and out of the gazebo,' Catherine said with a light laugh, though she had last been there with Ralph when she spoke to Arabella in October.

'A very happy arrangement for all concerned,' Latimer nodded.

It was building up to a good story, something he could certainly use, something his editor would be pleased to see. The kind of confirmation she was giving him was just what he needed. Why, it was almost a *ménage à trois* – husband

and wife living at the Grange and the mistress installed in a pretty little cottage just across the park. And Lord Helvyn, a peer of the realm, nearby at the Manor – that gave class. Some salacious little titbit would be nice, for good measure, he thought. But there was no hurry, he could take his time. Catherine was quite forthcoming and he was content to wait.

He talked to her at length, regaling her with the latest gossip and scandal about the people in London Society that she used to know. He was maliciously amusing and very charming and he delighted her. Catherine blossomed in his company, laughing and smiling at him.

'I can see you are a man of the world' she said. 'I haven't been so well entertained for many a long day.'

'You are such a beautiful, receptive audience, that's the reason,' Latimer said in return. 'I have stories enough to amuse you all night.'

'Well, at least dinner,' Catherine said. 'It will be a simple meal, I'm afraid, as Ralph and I live so simply, but you are most welcome, I assure you.'

Latimer accepted with equal pleasure. 'You live here alone then, with the boy?' he asked.

Catherine smiled again. 'There would scarcely be room in this tiny cottage for many more. But room can be found for you.'

There were times, Latimer thought when life could be very pleasant and very satisfying . . .

Arabella and James Conroy met again at an elaborate dinner that went on for hours, a solemn full dress affair, the company gathered round a display of silver and crystal, ruby glass and courtly flowers that seemed to have turned to wax. A large number of candles in cut-glass chandeliers robbed the room of any fresh air and the windows could not be opened or the candles flickered and dropped grease on to the fine clothes of the guests. Footmen brought food on silver trays to serve them continuously.

Arabella looked around her at the distinguished company and listened to the murmur of well-bred conversation. Opposite her, Lady Avon wore green velvet and all the diamonds which unkind gossip had credited to the family financier, and discussed with a visiting Marquis the merits of the play at the Olympic Theatre, Lord Griffiths talked about Africa from which he had just returned red-faced and Charles Sankey talked languidly of his favourite jockey and the prospects for Ascot.

There was mention of the French Prince Imperial now in London, of the garden party to be given by the Prince and Princess of Wales at Chiswick for which 1700 invitations had been issued, how the Emperor and Empress of Brazil were holding a reception during their stay at Claridges, and how there was to be a dinner and ball at Strawberry Hill given by the Rt. Hon. Chichester Fortesque and Frances, Countess Waldegrave.

How fine the talk was, Arabella thought. She could hold her own in the discussions perfectly well now. She had her own views about Mr Vining's performance as Count Fosco in 'The Woman in White', she had attended many of the functions they talked of and would be going to Ascot.

Neville was so far away along the table Arabella couldn't even see him. On her right an elderly gentleman nodded off contentedly between courses; on her left – James Conroy.

'Food. More food. More and more food. Look at it,' James Conroy said to her. 'There's enough here to feed six families for a week. Doesn't it seem to you immoral?'

Arabella stopped with a forkful of salmon mid-way to her lips. 'Yes,' she said in dismay. She put the fork down. 'I can't eat it now.'

'Look around you,' Conroy said. 'Look at the costly gowns the women here are wearing. Do you know how much a seamstress is paid for working from eight in the morning until eight at night? Her weekly wage is five shillings.'

His voice was ardent and urgent at her side where all around her the voices were languid and spoke of leisured luxury. Arabella was confused for a moment. She was not familiar with the earnings of seamstresses but she had experience of the paltry salaries paid to governesses. Thankfully she had left her knowledge of that behind her.

'What would you have me do, Mr Conroy? Why should

these things be? Do you have the answer?' She turned to him, her grey eyes wide and beautiful with concern and James Conroy gazing into her face lost all sight of his theme.

'Forgive me – but I am convinced you have the most beautiful eyes in the world –'

Arabella smiled, her serenity restored. She lowered her eyelids and turned her attention once again to the fish on the plate before her.

Full of fervour, Conroy began to talk to her of an ideal world and a new society. In his enthusiasm he made it sound like the promised land where all shared in the wealth of nations and no one went in need.

'Could this be? Could it really happen?' Arabella asked, interested in the idea and flattered that he should confide his hopes and dreams to her.

'Yes. Yes. It must come.' Conroy talked very quickly in his excited enthusiasm. 'I must give you Engels' book. He charges the middle classes with mass murder and wholesale robbery, condemns the tyranny of mill owners and the cruel oppression of the workers. He says their slavery is more abject than the negroes in America.'

In the urgency of his desire to convince her, Conroy seized her hand and held it close to him, as he had held it long ago in the casino at Reisbaden. Then they both became aware that he was keeping hold of her hand; the intensity of that awareness registered in his eyes and in hers. She took her hand away from him with a sweet deliberation.

'You are very concerned with the condition of people, Mr Conroy.'

'I care deeply about people – not only in the generality, but in the particular.'

They met again in Hyde Park. It was fashionable there and exclusive, at the right hours of the day; in the morning, or between seven and nine in the evening. Arabella liked to ride there or to drive behind a handsome pair of greys or to walk under the trees. Sometimes Neville escorted her, stiffly, silently. Sometimes Charles Sankey, with a lot to say in his affected drawl.

The scene behind the tall handsome railings always fascinated her. The equipages were so various and splendid: man about town in his dog-cart, fashionable toff in a brougham, lady dowager in an open victoria, barouches, curricles with two horses abreast, phaetons, riders on the most magnificent of horses, lady equestrians mysteriously veiled. The carriages had brightly polished lamps and brasswork, jingling harness and smartly trotting horses, some had pedigree dogs trained to run behind them and their coachmen and footmen in livery with top hats and boys in striped jackets perched at the back. The carriage servants were matched to each other in size and conformity as carefully as the horses.

The fashionable young men about town with their white-topped hats and silver-topped malacca canes stood chatting under the chestnuts or leaning over the railing quizzing the elegant ladies riding there. Their heads turned to look at Arabella passing, always. She was the new figure on the scene, the beautiful and stylish Mrs Rossiter.

Once or twice Arabella saw the Prince of Wales and Princess Alexandra driving in the park and she stared at them so wide-eyed that Charles laughed at her and called her a country girl.

'I like the look of them. The Princess has a sweet face. I do so admire the way she wears her hair piled up in curls.' Arabella considered for a moment whether the hairstyle would suit her, and deciding against it, added: 'The Prince looks like an amiable bear.'

'A bear who eats beautiful young ladies, with honey, for his afternoon tea,' Charles Sankey said. 'He is particularly fond of young married ladies, so play your cards with care.'

There were times when she walked in the Park with Neville; her pleasure in the colourful scene made the coldness between them less powerful. She could almost forget their state of separate isolation and sometimes her heart seemed about to come alive again. Then just as the mild or friendly words sprang to her lips, or her hand reached out to his, she remembered the fair figure of Catherine Becket at Copper Down, her small son at her side. The words were never spoken. The gesture was never made.

Neville was with her on the occasion they met James Conroy in the park. They stood together under the chestnut trees, in the form of a triangle, with everyone passing and raising their hats – Arabella in the palest lavender voile, cool and delicate for the warm day, with a lace parasol and a wide brimmed hat, Neville lean and taut and elegant, fashionably attired in a smart, light grey frock coat, and James Conroy dressed darkly as always.

A man of words, Neville thought, regarding him critically, taking his measure. The impression was of great intelligence, the expression of the eyes was intense – there was almost a hint of fanaticism there. He was uncertain what form the fanaticism might take.

'You have abandoned your pen and paper, you have written your masterpiece for today?' He inquired of Conroy, as patronizing and aloof as it was possible to be.

'On the contrary I found it impossible to write or to think or to arrange my ideas. Which is unfortunate because I have a meeting of dock workers to address this evening.'

'Will you find inspiration here?' Neville asked, indicating the fashionable procession with a nonchalant movement of his cane.

'I think I have found all the inspiration I need,' Conroy said, his dark eyes smiled at Arabella.

'How fortunate for the dock workers,' Neville said.

'The time will come when all this,' Conroy in his turn indicated the fashionable scene, 'all this will be impossible. The days of social justice are coming. Capitalism is on the verge of collapse – on the very brink –'

'It seems to be very comfortable there,' Neville said disdainfully. 'You talk radical rubbish. What you are really saying is that you are in favour of a revolution.'

'I'm not in favour of it,' Conroy said, with some warmth. 'But at least I can see that the only way to prevent one is to allow the working man a voice in Parliament. From what I hear, you are thinking of standing for Parliament yourself.'

'It is a possibility,' Neville conceded.

'Then perhaps one day in the future we will face each other across the floor of the House,' James Conroy said and it sounded, in the atmosphere between them, more like a duel at dawn with pistols.

'I think I will join you there,' Arabella said brightly to

lighten the tension. 'I shall form a party to promote the cause of women's rights.'

Her intervention had the effect she desired; they both laughed, in spite of themselves, at the absurdity of such an idea.

But later Neville's feelings became more evident. Arabella with her interest in Conroy renewed, had looked out the treatise he had presented to her long ago in Reisbaden. She had always kept it, and looking at it again now she was still impressed by its intellectual power and baffled by its profundity.

Neville frowned at the sight of it, reading its title and Conroy's name upon the spine with the strongest disapproval in his tone. 'What is the meaning of this?' He demanded, glaring at Arabella.

'Indeed I find its meaning rather obscure –' Arabella began.

'I am referring to this,' Neville said, pointing to the inscription on the fly-leaf. 'Explain this – 'On the occasion of our meeting.'

'I told you that I first made Mr Conroy's acquaintance in Reisbaden. He came to my aid when some of the money I had won at roulette was stolen from me. Later when he was talking to me of his work and his beliefs, he presented to me a copy of his book.'

'And you keep it still. Well, I won't have it in the house.' He threw the book into the grate with such violence that the pages fell apart.

'That was uncalled for,' Arabella cried, but he strode out of the room and she saw him no more that day.

And again they met – Arabella and Conroy – at a ball. It was a very sumptuous and splendid affair in a palatial house in Kensington and its grandeur contrasted in Arabella's mind with the last ball she had attended – in the Assembly Rooms at Bishop's Linden. There she had scandalized local society by dancing five times with Neville Rossiter; now she danced with him as his wife and Society smiled at them.

She danced only briefly with James Conroy. He moved stiffly, awkwardly, and, apologizing for his lack of social graces, suggested that it would be cooler and more pleasant in the conservatory adjoining the ballroom. It was a very hot night and it came as a relief to walk among the green profusion, the smell of the earth and the hot house flowers. Arabella herself looked as cool as a lily in a gown of ivory brocade. She was content to sit in the leafy alcove, sipping iced claret cup, listening to James Conroy talking.

He talked so well, engaging her interest in ideas and theories and abstract things she had never considered before; he stretched her imagination, her reasoning and her understanding to wider horizons than she had ever contemplated. Responding to him, she surprised herself with her own grasp and intelligence. She could feel he brought out the best in her. She hung on every word, so absorbed in what he was saying that she missed the next three dances altogether.

Neville seeking her, found them sitting together in the glassed jungle of palms and pampas grass and tropical flowers. They sat together, their heads very close. Neville could see Conroy's dramatically serious face, his great dark eyes gazing into Arabella's face, earnestly talking to her. He caught a momentary glimpse of Arabella's expression, her hands clasped in a kind of rapture of absorbed interest. It was a long time since he had seen that look of rapture on her face.

Suddenly the sweet scents and the hot air and the sight of the two of them together sickened him unbearably. He could not bring himself to speak to them. He turned away, in the grip of over-powering jealousy.

The guests at the ball were feeling the heat of the night, they stood about in limp groups. They said afterwards that Neville Rossiter as he left the ballroom then, looked like the wrath of God.

Neville walked away mindlessly, striding the hot pavements, ignoring the sauntering women calling out to him and the cabs that drew alongside seeking a fare. The midsummer sky wasn't black at all. London was luminous and glowing, there was a shawl of violet drawn over the house-tops. The leaves of the tall trees along the park hung motionless in the heavy night air.

Neville turned aside into the park, still without thinking where he was going. The paths were gleaming black lines across the grey of the lawns, and the solid shapes of the trees were inky dark. He walked down towards the water and stood there staring at the blank gleam of it, until after a long time the moon came up over London, as full and serene and silver-pearled as over the waters of the lake at Bryder and he thought, with pain, that it was possible that he would lose her.

The prospect apalled him. She was an infuriating, obstinate, damnable woman, but life without her was meaningless. She was his wife. His wife! Impetuous, self-willed, head-strong creature, he thought furiously. The violence of her reaction to her discovery of Catherine Becket's existence and the child's existence had been beyond all reason. The way she had reacted had amazed and infuriated him so much that he had been unable to communicate with her on that subject at any time since.

He had never in his life been called upon to account for his actions, and he had no intention of doing so. He had treated her well, in every respect. He was prepared to admit he had his faults – what man hadn't? – but there were some things a man could not explain to any woman, not even his wife.

Completely unreasonable and wildly headstrong, he thought, with rising anger against her. Like this new concern with James Conroy, allowing him to talk to her endlessly. It was possible she could be rushing into some illicit liaison with Conroy. It might be he could talk her into running off with him. She had looked at Conroy as if she really cared about what he was saying. And she was a passionate woman, none more so. Well he knew that. Was she not his wife?

It was amazing though, that despite everything, all her faults, all his anger against her – he loved her more all the time. It was impossible, but it was so. He felt at times an irresistible urge to take hold of her and shake her, to hit her with his fist. He thought it was quite likely that she would infuriate him to the point of utter madness, and still he would love her.

He walked on beside the water, across the park, as the moon climbed the sky. It was a night for love. The couples walking the hot London streets were drawn towards the cool obscurity of the park like parched desert travellers to an oasis. They walked interlaced ito the dusky shadows and stood in the shelter of the shrubberies or against the trunks of trees, dappled with moonlight, so close that their shadows became one shadow in the soft darkness.

Neville walking on, absorbed in his own emotions, became aware then of the passionate hidden life of the park – a glimpse of a woman's face buried in a man's neck, a glimpse of a hand stroking a head of pale gold hair, whispered sounds, a small cry, a melting laugh, a world of hidden kisses that lingered on and on.

In his fevered imagination each man was intense and dark as James Conroy and each woman dissolving into loving kisses was Arabella. He thought of the times she had melted in his arms, the lotus-dream of the days and nights in Bryder, the inward beauty and the unimaginable joy, the deliciousness of the sensuous revelation, the love – the love.

'If that was not real, nothing is real,' Neville said aloud and with all his force he beat his fist against the trunk of a tree, so hard that blood trickled down his fingers, but no feeling penetrated the greater pain in him.

At the sound of his voice, a woman materialized out of the low slung branches of a grove of trees. 'Come with me. Won't you come with me?' She was a woman of the streets, but quietly dressed, dark-haired, soft-spoken. Something in the way she moved her head, tilting her long neck, for a moment was like Arabella.

Arabella. No one else. No other woman was any use to him now. He brushed the importuning woman from him like a moth of the night. Images of Arabella swam in his brain – Arabella with her head held high; Arabella standing with her back turned saucily to him while he hooked up her bodice for her; Arabella standing irresolute in her chemise, trying to decide which dress to wear; Arabella waking in the morning her body soft and warm, surrendering. That another man should know that sweet surrender . . .

Without a word he changed direction, strode full of formidable purpose, with no thought but her, back to the house in Curzon Street.

Arabella had returned from the ball, without escort, made

uneasy by Neville's sudden unexplained departure. She had waited up for a time, not knowing what to do, not knowing why he had gone or where. Then she had gone up to her room, telling Becky to go to bed.

Neville found her bedroom door locked, as it was always locked. All the nights he had ignored it, let it stand unchallenged between them. Now that time had come to an end.

The first Arabella knew of his return was his voice outside her door.

'Open this door, do you hear?'

Arabella pressed her hands to her mouth. For so long she had gone on with her rebellion and not been called to account, it had become established, routine, something she had come to accept, that he had seemed to accept. She was alarmed now by the deep menace in his voice, by the prospect of a battle for which she felt unprepared.

Uncertainly she crossed the room to the door. Her brocade ball gown lay like a fallen flower-head across the arm of the chair where she had thrown it aside carelessly. She was half undressed and wore only her corsets and her petticoats, her hair dark and loose about her shoulders, the silver-backed hair brush still in her hand. She stood beside the door and made no move, said no word.

'I have put up with this state of affairs quite long enough,' Neville said and she could hear the resolution in his voice. 'You are to open this door this instant.'

Still she made no move. But in the moment of silence that followed she could feel her heart pounding painfully and her legs seemed to weaken under her.

Neville threw all his weight against the door, and the lock held. She stood staring at the door, helpless, hypnotized, listening to the sound of his attack. The frame of the door was solid enough, but there were four panels of thinner wood and Neville kicked the panels violently until the wood splintered with a terrifying sound.

When he had kicked the door down, they stood staring at each other. At the sight of her, lovely and vulnerable and afraid, he was shaken in his resolve, but the thought of James Conroy and their heads so close together was a driving force that pushed him as relentlessly as the existence of Catherine Becket had been driving Arabella.

She fought him with all the strength she had. The heavy silver hair brush was a powerful defensive weapon but the blows that she struck at his shoulders and his back were utterly futile and he seized her wrist and pressed her arms behind her until they ceased.

She fought silently without a sound or a cry, but with a passion as fierce and powerful as his own. Only his superior strength forced her back, yard by yard across the room until he could press her back on to the bed and her rustling white petticoats fanned across the crimson silk of the quilt, where the maid had turned down the sheet so neatly, her flowing hair spread wild on the pillow.

She went on fighting and struggling to the last, her head turning this way and that, her hands scratching and clawing and pushing at him, her knees, her feet, her elbows making every move as difficult for him as it was possible to be. Silk and cambric was rent and torn aside. Once when his arm came across her mouth, she bit into the flesh and made him curse. But she made no sound, never cried out, made no appeal.

Right to the last, there was no sweet surrender, no moment at which she gave up hope and gave in to him. This was brute force, animal supremacy, an exercise of superior strength and power. Now he was the jungle tiger possessing his mate and he was the Victorian husband asserting his rights and claiming his property.

When it was over, he left behind him a shattered door and a ravaged bed and a woman who wept, on and on until the morning hours, as if her heart had broken.

CHAPTER NINE

'May I give you some tea?' It needed all Arabella's concentration not to spill the tea as she passed it to Lady Despencer.

That esteemed lady had been paying her calls to the house in Curzon Street earlier and earlier in the day since she had been organizing Arabella's Society debut, and this morning she was particularly early. She sat erect in her black bombazine, a mauve triangle filling the neckline of her dress and a black velvet ribbon round the base of her thin throat, and she breathed the dry and dessicated air of well-bred refinement.

Arabella dispensed tea and listened, while Lady Despencer talked, for sounds in the house. She didn't know where Neville was and she felt uneasy to think of him anywhere near, terrified at the prospect of meeting him. At any moment he might come into the room and she would have to face him.

Above them on the first floor, two carpenters were removing the shattered bedroom door at the hinges and fixing a replacement. At the faint sound of hammering a shudder Arabella couldn't repress made the fine porcelain tea-cup rattle on the saucer in her hand.

Lady Despencer said: 'I am most concerned that you should be at Nelson House this evening, at nine. You must not be late, that is important. I cannot tell you more just yet, but there is someone for you to meet.'

Arabella nodded and murmured agreement, but the words floated past her.

'You are looking rather pale,' Lady Despencer said, critically, without sympathy. 'You must not overtire yourself; you must look your best this evening. Wear white, it becomes you well. We are all feeling a certain weariness by this time in the season, and it has been so hot this summer, but it is nearly at an end. On the last Friday in July there is the end of season ball at Marlborough House and then three days later everyone goes to Goodwood.'

Against my will, Arabella kept thinking, to be forced, against my will. To be treated like a possession. That he could treat her in such a way.

Neville Rossiter came into the room then and at the sight of him, she was seized by a kind of panic of dismay that left her speechless. She gripped the arms of her chair so tightly that she hurt her hands. She couldn't bear to look at him.

Yet when she did look, she found that he was engaged in formal conversation with Lady Despenser, they were discussing the evening function, just as if everything was normal. There was nothing else to do. She could never speak out or cry out her anguish and despair. She could only agree, as coldly formal as Neville himself.

She listened to Lady Despencer talking with Neville of the prospects for Goodwood, of the Prince of Wales and the house Ferdie Rothschild would be renting near the race-course for the Royal party, and how conveniently near that was to Copper Down, and how with the end of the season Arabella and Neville would be returning there.

She couldn't consider that future they were discussing for her. She thought, it is impossible for me to go on with this life because I cannot bear it. There must be some way of escaping from it, escaping so that she would never see her husband again.

The feeling she had for him had become a kind of fever of hatred. Though her manner to him was more coldly distant than ever, it concealed a consuming flame of hatred now.

All that she could hope for this evening was that she would see James Conroy at the reception. He was someone who would understand, perhaps the only person in the world who could.

All the world, said Lady Despencer, went down to Goodwood at the end of July. Charles Sankey, for reasons of his own, headed in that direction a little earlier.

For many weeks ever since Latimer had produced news of Catherine Becket he had been contemplating a plan of seeking her out. Memories of the time he had spent in her company were very pleasant memories and he had been intrigued by the news of how she was living now. He considered mentioning Latimer's information about her to Rossiter himself, but he had then thought better of it. Rossiter's taciturn demeanour never invited comment or question and recently it had become positively forbidding, even to Sankey. The idea of talking to Catherine was more appealing to him than the idea of talking to Rossiter.

'Anyway, she's much prettier,' Sankey said to himself as he made the decision to travel to Copper Down. Competition for Catherine Becket's favour had always been keen, but he himself had won the day on quite a few occasions in the past. 'Quite a few, quite a few,' Charles said with remembered satisfaction.

Recalling the delights of that interlude reminded him that he had been quite a fellow himself in those days – 'Quite a flyer, quite an out-and-outer'. That, of course, was before he had made the mistake of getting married and saddled himself with a fretful wife. 'Marriage is the trouble,' he said to himself with deep regret. 'Ruined me, it has. I don't hold with it at all. Don't do any man any good.'

Sombre and gloomy thoughts of the punishments of matrimony occupied him throughout the train journey from Victoria to Chichester. There the much advertised Mr Wm. Powell, private and Livery stable keeper, fly and job master, was able to hire him a fly and a flyman to drive him to Copper Down, though at a very leisurely country pace. When at last he reached Copper Down and the flyman found for him the cottage at Bassetts, Sankey saw Catherine Becket in the garden gathering roses and he leapt out as lively as any young blood.

'Pretty cottage, pretty lady, pretty flowers – all pretty as a picture,' he called out exuberant and enthusiastic.

'It must be Charles Sankey behind all those terrible whiskers,' Catherine said and she came smiling to the gate.

'On my way to Goodwood, don't you know. Thought I'd pay you a call. Are you at home at all?'

'To you always.' Catherine was as sweet and kind and generously welcoming as ever he'd remembered her. He threw his hat in the air with a gesture of abandoned gaiety and missed catching it. 'You'd better come in and hang up your hat.' Catherine said laughing.

'Let me just send the gee-gee away,' Sankey said, indicating the fly. He went over to the flyman and said pulling at his whiskers: 'Go on, down to the village. Put up at the inn and don't come back until – um, until you're sent for.'

'Now you must come and tell me all about yourself,' Catherine said, leading the way into the cottage. 'Such a lot of news there must be in all the long time since I last saw you.'

'Such a long time,' Sankey mused, his gaze resting on her with great pleasure. 'And you look more beautiful than ever.'

A pleasant hour passed in the small parlour, drinking the home-made wine that Catherine poured so generously, and talking over their salad days and the people they had both known. Sankey kept off the subject of Rossiter, thinking it might be better not to know too much. As it became dusk, Catherine offered him a meal and he accepted with even greater pleasure, but the first soup-spoon had scarcely touched his lips when there was a violent interruption.

Lord Helvyn walked in on them, throwing the door back with a heavy crash. He looked enormous in the lamp light, bowing under the low beams of the cottage. Charles Sankey leapt to his feet, scalding himself with hot spilt soup, but Lord Helvyn wasn't concerned with him. He was holding a folded newspaper and pushing it threateningly at Catherine, shouting at her incoherently.

'Scandalmongering gutter press. Who have you been talking to? How did he get hold of this? Who the hell is he?'

Catherine was on her feet too, trying to make sense of what the old man was shouting. She didn't seem overwhelmed with alarm at Lord Helvyn's arrival. She went to him and tried to calm him and talked reasonably.

'Some nonsense they write in the newspapers – what does that matter? I haven't seen it and I don't want to. You don't care about what they say.'

She coaxed him like a fractious child and Lord Helvyn's tone quietened a little. But he went on muttering angrily: 'They spread their lies and their scandals for everybody to read – they print just what they like.'

Lord Helvyn seemed to sway on his feet and several times he hit the side of his head with the flat of his hand. Then he saw Charles Sankey. Sankey had been standing still and keeping quiet, but the sight of him incensed the old man all over again.

'Who the hell are you? What do you think you're doing here? Well I won't have it. You can get out. I order you out of this house. Go on – get out, or I shall throw you out.'

For Sankey it was deuced awkward. To stay meant to put

that threat to the test and he didn't relish it, but it wasn't the thing to leave a lady in this sort of situation. Catherine solved the dilemma for him.

'It's better if you go,' she urged him. 'Do as he says. I can calm him. It's easier for me if you go.'

Charles Sankey acted promptly and thankfully on her advice. Clearly it was no place for him. But he didn't like it and he didn't like having to walk all the way to the village to find his flyman, and the more he thought about it all the less he liked it. Lord Helvyn had always had a reputation for eccentric behaviour, but now he seemed to have gone beyond the bounds.

One conclusion Charles Sankey did come to, he must tell Neville Rossiter what was going on down there, it was the least he could do. That pretty little woman, he kept saying to himself, trying to manage that old brute. He didn't like to think of it. Neville was the one to do something about it, though. It was family business. It was his Uncle ...

Arabella prepared mechanically for the function she must attend that evening. As she stepped into her petticoats, as Becky laced her corsets and arranged her hair, she moved like a doll. She sat staring at her reflection in the glass with a blank stare as though the woman reflected there was nothing to do with her. For the first time in her life she found no pleasure in the sight of her own reflection.

'You are not well, Ma'am?' Becky asked her, familiar with all Arabella's demands and caprices, but not with this strange, detached remoteness.

'I am not well,' Arabella said, as though she had no spirit to do anything but agree. There was no way in which she could describe her feelings; they had been assaulted and trampled into numb desolation.

'But I won't wear the white dress. Take it away. Give it away. Get it out of my sight,' Arabella said with sudden force.

She rejected every one of the costly gowns that had been purchased for her Society season. She wore instead the crimson dress that she had first worn long ago in the gaming rooms at Reisbaden.

Then in the mirror Arabella saw Neville himself come into

her room. He stood at the door, which now showed no scar from his onslaught upon it, stood there looking at his wife as she sat at her dressing table and she looked at his reflection in the glass before her. No sign, no signal, no acknowledgement passed between them. He came across the room towards her and Becky, without waiting for her dismissal, slipped away.

As he came near her, Arabella felt oppressed by his presence and an unbearable tension. It showed in her shadowed eyes and her quickened breathing, but she didn't move and she couldn't speak to him. Last night, only a matter of hours ago, they had been fighting like animals here in this room. The silver-backed hair brush she had used as a weapon to defend herself, lay mute witness to the deed, beside her on the dressing table.

In the taut silence, Neville's voice had a hollow sound, but it still had the familiar note of command.

'Do you know what time it is? We are expected. We must leave at once.'

'And if I choose not to?' Arabella said, still regarding his reflection.

Stiffening even more, Neville said: 'You are free to choose –'

'Surely not. My freedom of choice seems to be entirely subject to yours,' Arabella said coldly, but she rose to her feet and stood facing him with her head held high and her face showed no emotion at all.

Then he led her down to the waiting carriage and the reception at Nelson House. I am a prisoner, Arabella thought, and the cage is made of glass.

Their host was Sir Francis Brook and the reception at Nelson House with its gathering of fashionable women and distinguished men, was the scene that had thrilled her on her introduction to London society. The luxury and the splendour had now become familiar.

The elaborate self-indulgence of Society, its rules and its frivolity, its brilliant wit, its fashions and favourites, had interested and amused her, but not dazzled her. She had liked the satisfaction of making her mark, but she had not been seduced by Society.

The atmosphere at Nelson House that evening seemed

tense, as if host and guests were waiting for something to happen. Sir Francis conferred closely with Lady Despencer, and Arabella's arrival with Neville was greeted as though it was of special significance. So much attention was paid to her that it was some time before she could discover James Conroy's presence, and with some difficulty that they managed to have a conversation apart. They withdrew into a window alcove, to stand half hidden by hanging draperies and potted palms.

'I needed so much to see you,' Arabella said, breaking out of her reserve and speaking with anxious eagerness. 'I don't know how to begin to tell you –' Her voice faded with the feeling that she could never tell anyone, not even him.

James Conroy took both her hands in his with reciprocal eagerness. 'And I needed to see you. It was most important for me to speak with you. I must tell you at once – I have had dramatic news from Paris. There has been a workers' uprising. This is the beginning and I must go there –'

'But when is this?' Arabella asked, dismay sweeping over her, a personal sense of loss because she needed his presence.

'At once. As soon as it's humanly possible,' he spoke more ardently than ever. She had not the least idea of what he meant when he spoke of a workers' uprising, but she caught the spirit of his zeal and responded in some admiration of his free spirit. He talked of justice and of truth, of a society in which all men – and all women – would be free. And as she listened to him, Arabella began to see a solution to her own plight.

'Could I be a part of that?' she asked.

'In theory it's possible. Certainly possible.' He smiled at her with grave indulgence.

'Then let me come to Paris with you,' Arabella said, her hopes rising buoyantly and her enthusiasm rushing ahead impetuously.

Conroy looked at her in complete silence. Then he said: 'I don't think you have any idea what you are saying.'

'You have no idea of what I have endured.' Arabella cried, 'Listen, I must explain to you. My marriage – it has become intolerable.'

Conroy thought of what he had been told of Neville Rossiter's mistress said to be installed on the very threshold at Copper Down, of Rossiter's arrogant possessiveness, and as he looked at Arabella he guessed something of what she had to endure.

'But it is unthinkable,' he said. 'You may have every reason to wish to escape from what seems to be an intolerable situation. But there is no solution in France. How can there be? Already thousands have died in the streets of Paris in their efforts to form a Commune; and against that your unhappiness does not compare. I must hasten to give all the support I can, but it is no place for you, believe me.'

'But that is theory – words!' Arabella cried in exasperation. 'Is an abstract idea the most important thing in life to you? What about people? What about me?'

Conroy looked more serious still. Then he said: 'The most important thing in life, I consider to be the brotherhood of man. You must understand – that is why I must rally to the support of the cause in Paris.'

'Don't you have any feelings for me?' Arabella asked.

'Great admiration and great respect,' Conroy replied sombrely. 'But – you are another man's wife.'

Arabella felt utterly amazed. Conroy had preached to her the downfall of the capitalist system and all bourgeois rules and values, he believed in a new religion yet he spoke with the same established assurance Neville himself would have used. It seemed she had no existence except as Neville's wife, and Conroy's free spirit was political and intellectual, it didn't extend to emotional freedom.

Conroy went on talking, of events in Paris and the war that must be waged against reactionary government, but he found no receptive audience in her now. Arabella was puzzling over her own mis-reading of his character and the rapport between them. He had gazed at her as if she was his heart's dearest desire, he had sought her out, he had come to her aid when the thief purloined her winnings on the roulette table, he had presented his book to her, he had proposed an assignation –

Was it all then a fleeting impulse, a passing thought, an idea that had appealed to him in the moment and been as quickly forgotten. 'A man of words', Neville had described him contemptuously. Effectual in terms of theory, ideas and ideals, but lacking in positive action and force. If he had really cared deeply about her, he would have pursued her, he would grasp at this chance.

If it were Neville in his place now, she could but think, he would have pursued his desires through to a conclusion, he would have persisted, demanded, insisted. Sadly Arabella saw the ramparts of her romantic dream crumble away and with it the bond between them.

'I wish you well with your efforts in Paris,' she said, and it was farewell.

'Where is she? Where is she? Where is she?' On all sides anxious voices sought Arabella. Lady Despencer found her and seized her arm. 'I have found her. Here she is,' she called urgently to Sir Francis and he came up and took her other arm.

'What is it?' Arabella asked, looking from one to the other.

They led her between them to the doors of the main salon. 'You must not be hidden away out of sight,' Lady Despencer said in a hushed but urgent tone.

A hush had fallen over the assembled company, a ripple of expectancy ran through it, a whispered excitement. Then a warm and guttural voice sounded outside the doors and Arabella saw the reason for the excitement. Tubby, bearded, amiable, glittering with decorations and the Order of the Garter, the Prince of Wales had arrived from some diplomatic function.

'I'm afraid I'm a little late,' he said as Sir Francis hurried forward in a bowing position and Lady Despencer melted quickly away. Arabella found herself left in solitary state in the middle of the floor. Sir Francis Brook beside her was saying smoothly: 'Your Royal Highness, may I introduce Mrs Neville Rossiter.'

The Prince's pale and protuberant eyes rested on her and registered immediate Royal approval.

'Yes. And what do you talk about?' The Prince asked her with that formidable roguishness that had devastated legions of dull, polite young men and agitated bevies of shy, conventional young girls.

Arabella replied to him with a recklessness born of her despair: 'Myself, mostly. I begin to find other people's emotions impossible to understand and I find my own quite fascinating.'

'Then shall you and I discuss the subject of you? I feel sure that I shall find it quite fascinating also.'

And despite everything, Arabella was impressed. To meet a member of the Royal family and to be singled out for his attention was a new and gratifying experience. She smiled, and she was most charming.

'Tell me, how are you enjoying London this season, Mrs Rossiter? It is new to you, I think.'

'I find it diverting, Your Highness. And that pleases me.' Arabella spoke with honesty for the events and activities of the season had distracted her from her personal unhappiness.

'From what should a pretty woman wish to be diverted, I wonder? I must ponder on that. And where have you been hiding up to now? Where were you born and bred?'

'Bishop's Linden,' Arabella said, dismissing Lady Despencer's ruling that the town was too middle class to be mentioned.

'Bishop's Linden? I have some knowledge of it,' The Prince said. 'A dull place, as I recall it. What happens there?'

'Remarkably little happens there, Your Highness.'

'Not the place for you then. Nothing to do but read poetry and dream of meeting a handsome prince, I shouldn't wonder.'

'But dreams are such pale and ineffectual occupations, not to be compared with reality,' Arabella said. Her mood was all careless boldness. So much had happened to shatter and disturb her that caution seemed irrelevant. She spoke simply and instinctively, for it had never been in her nature to consider her words and she was not given to feelings of awe.

The Prince was clearly much taken with her, focusing all his attention on her alone. They were the leading players on the stage, the rest of the company had withdrawn to the background, watching.

At a reception of this kind there was constant arrival and departure of guests, for the event would be one of several functions they would be attending during the evening. The stairs would be crowded with people coming and going and the hostess would be wearied by standing for three hours shaking hands, welcoming to the arrivals and bidding farewell to the departures.

Arabella had lost all sight of Neville for some time. As she looked round for him, Sir Frances Brook approached her with a discreet air.

'Mrs Rossiter, there has been a message left for you. Your husband has been called away unexpectedly.' He added no further-explanation.

'Don't trouble yourself about that. The lady is in my care,' the Prince said. 'I'll tell you what, Brooke, we'll play a few cards. A few cards, Mrs Rossiter? What d'you say?'

As she took her place at the card table in an adjoining room, with a grace that would have done credit to any member of royalty, Arabella experienced the joy of sheer triumph. The Prince smiled at her, watching her over his hand of cards, addressed her in tones of obvious approval, almost as if she were alone with him. Arabella knew herself to be on the highest crest of social success, proud and poised there; she spared a thought for all the people she had left behind, and how impressed they would be. All her life she had dreamed of shining, leading, being the foremost and the chosen. At that hour on that evening she reached a high point of social triumph and took it at the full.

By next morning an air of triumph reigned at the house in Curzon Street also. Every servant in the household worked with a fever of industry and excitement. Everything in sight and out of sight was being polished. Lady Despencer, who had arrived extremely early, breathed triumph down her well-bred nostrils.

The cause of all the excitement was a small, gold, embossed card. It had been sent round by hand from Marlborough House and it advised Arabella that the Prince of Wales would be pleased to call on her that same afternoon.

'There, I thought it would be so,' Lady Depsencer said. 'Everything has gone perfectly.'

'I feel most honoured, of course,' Arabella said. She couldn't help thinking how overjoyed her mother would be at the very idea. 'I liked him,' she added.

'He liked you, that is the point,' Lady Despencer corrected her. 'I thought that was how it would be, I thought you would appeal to him. Now you have the chance to become his favourite. It is the pinnacle of success.'

'A chance to become his favourite?' Arabella said, frowning a little.

'Yes, indeed. Yes, of course, child. This is what we have all been working towards. How right we were. How right.'

'We?' Arabella said.

'Yes, child. All your friends.'

'And my husband?'

'Neville? Ah, yes, he must make himself scarce this afternoon,' Lady Despencer said, and she rang peremptorily for the servant to discover Neville Rossiter's whereabouts.

'Why do you say that?' Arabella asked, her tone sharpening.

'My dear child, you know what this means. You do understand, surely? It is court etiquette when anyone is engaged with the Prince of Wales, all outsiders, even husbands must depart. Neville must arrange his absence so that you and the Prince can spend a congenial afternoon together.'

The servant who had been summoned returned to report to them that Mr Rossiter had already left the house. He had been called away on some urgent business.

'That,' said Lady Despencer with satisfaction, 'is just his way of saying he will not be intruding on this afternoon's appointment. He has foreseen and already withdrawn from the scene. So it is all arranged for you.'

Arabella thought that though Neville was the man she hated most in all the world, yet at the news that he had left, she felt very alone. She found it hard to believe that Lady Despencer was right, that Neville had intended her to catch the Prince's eye, that it had been in his mind too that she should attract Royal favour. And yet he had escorted her to the reception and he had disappeared during the course of the evening and left her to meet the Prince alone. And now he had gone.

A wave of shocked dismay swept over her.

'No,' she said suddenly, interrupting Lady Despencer who was discussing what she should wear. 'No, I will not do it.

It is immoral and impossible.'

'Immoral?' Lady Despencer said with straight-backed in-dignation. 'This is the Prince of Wales we are talking of.'

'Then it is a royal whore we are talking of,' Arabella said.

'Lower-class morality,' Lady Despencer said, clicking her tongue and very much on her dignity. 'You seem to have your ideas rather muddled.'

'I am not in the least muddled,' Arabella replied, very much on her own dignity. She could consider ending her marriage because it had become intolerable to her and love had died; she could consider running away to Paris with James Conroy, if they loved each other enough, but she could not consider this kind of arrangement in which love had no part at all. 'I know exactly what I am doing. I am refusing to have anything to do with your plan. You had no right to assume my acquiescence.'

Arabella swept to the writing table with a proud swish of her skirts. She sat on the edge of a chair and quickly wrote a note of polite regret to His Royal Highness saying that she would not be at home this afternoon as she was leaving London.

Lady Despencer came and stood over her. 'This is foolishness beyond all reason. The Prince will not take no for an answer at all agreeably. I warn you, you are overplaying your hand. You cannot play at being unavailable. No woman can do that and expect to be invited to Marlborough House.'

'I am not playing any game,' Arabella said coldly.

When Lady Despencer realized she was determined upon her course, she had her final word. 'Lack of true breeding always shows itself in the end,' she said.

Arabella gave instructions for her note to be sent round to Marlborough House by hand, then she gave orders for the carriage to be made ready for her departure.

On a high note of proud rejection, Arabella made her departure – but unfortunately she had formulated no plan as to where she was going. The phaeton remained stationary outside the tall house in Curzon Street, her instructions were awaited. Where could she go? At last in exasperation and from lack of an alternative, she decided she could but go to Bishop's

Linden. Becky must be summoned to accompany her and there was more delay.

'Now drive me to Charing Cross,' she said with an imperious gesture, flicking her wrist. 'And find me a train.'

Even as they proceeded to the station though her spirits began to sink at the prospect of the reunion before her. To be going home to her mother, admitting failure and defeat was an unbearable prospect. In a flash of vivid foresight she could see them, all gathered together in the over-crowded sitting room – her mother, fond, foolish and frumpy, her hair hanging down either side of her face spaniel-like and her bustle on crooked, so pleased to see her and so utterly incapable of comprehending anything of Arabella's plight. Her mother had been so gratified by Arabella's impressive marriage; she was so content with her guaranteed six hundred pounds a year from Neville Rossiter. How could she advise, sympathize, console? The impossibility of explaining and making her understand filled Arabella's heart with deep despair. She thought of her sisters all giggling together, remembered that at this time of year Uncle Edward would have arrived to pay them the summer visit he never admitted was a holiday.

The girls would be overcome at the very mention of the Prince and the idea that Arabella had exchanged a word with him. Uncle Edward would have only one word of advice – humility. And her mother, if she grasped the issue at all, would in her genteel way seize on the dreadful impoliteness of Arabella's not being at home when the Prince came to call. Then could she go to Ashley House, to her old friends the Faver-shams? Unhappily she could imagine also what their reaction would be. They would be pleased to see her, certainly; a little put out perhaps that she had not forewarned them of her coming, but pleased if she entertained them with lively chat about her season in Society. If she talked to them of her troubles though, they would not want to know, they would brush aside her anxieties, saying she must surely be mistaken.

'No, not there, not there,' Arabella cried to herself as the phaeton reached Charing Cross. 'I am not going to Bishop's Linden after all.' She gave instructions to proceed instead to Victoria Station. She would take a train to Chichester and return to Copper Down Grange.

Travelling southward into Sussex she had plenty of time to think and wherever her thoughts turned there was sadness, disillusion, disappointment, regret. She had married almost exactly a year ago and it was no anniversary to celebrate.

Becky looked very bright eyed and cheerful at the prospect of Sussex for she had been homesick in London, but Arabella watched the strong, smooth line of the South Downs come into sight without any enthusiasm. The patriarchal trees of Sussex, elms and spreading oaks, stood out majestically green against the backcloth of golden corn. Across that richly undulating landscape she had travelled last year after her wedding, and how gold the corn had been then. Now it stood ripe and glowing in the fields again. The harvesting would begin early this year, on the sloping fields below the chalk line of the Downs, it had been so fine a summer. Arabella sat idle and abstracted, feeling solitary, and limp with a terrible mental and emotional fatigue.

Copper Down where Lord Helvyn lived his lonely and eccentric life, the Grange where she must live in estrangement from her husband, and Bassetts where Catherine Becket lived in a picturesque cottage with her small son – Copper Down was waiting for her, it was at the heart of her problems and her unhappiness. She had no will to go there, and no idea where else to go.

The hired fly from the station at Chichester conveyed her to Copper Down and as soon as Arabella stepped out on to the gravel drive of the Grance she saw at once a black horse tethered at the steps and knew that Lord Helvyn was there. It was such an enormous black animal he always rode, with a shotgun always strapped to the saddle, there was no mistaking it.

She entered the Grange with her spirits very low.

She found Lord Helvyn in the hall, towering over the frail figure of the old housekeeper, Miss Baker, storming and shouting at her. Miss Baker was shaking her head and twisting her hands over and over in her agitation. Lord Helvyn was gesturing wildly with a newspaper, and it might have been a dagger the way he used it.

'Uncle? What's going on here?' Arabella rushed forward. For a moment it seemed to her, the Uncle was going to attack Miss Baker with the newspaper as a weapon, but at the sight of Arabella he forgot all about the old housekeeper.

'Hah! You've come back then. Well, where's Neville? What? What?'

'Neville is still in London. I've come alone –' Arabella started to say, but he wasn't listening.

'He's never here when he should be. I never know where he is. Do you know?' He glared down into Arabella's face and his eyes between the heavy eyebrows and massive beard had a look of fury and despair in them.

But he always is fiery and angry, Arabella thought. He's rude and arrogant and shouts at everyone. She was in no mood to be shouted at.

'I know he's in London. Why do you want to see him?' She sounded crisp, cool and in control and Lord Helvyn seemed to accept that. He backed away and his whole powerful frame seemed to slacken. Instead of threatening her, he began to walk to and fro aimlessly, muttering to himself.

'I don't know. It's a bad business. Terrible. Spreading lies and scandal like this. The family name. All the world reading this. And no way out that I can see.'

'What are you talking about?' Arabella said impatiently. 'I don't understand.'

Lord Helvyn looked at her, stared at her as if he didn't know who she was. Then he thrust the newspaper at her, pushed it at her as he had pushed it at Catherine Becket in the cottage the day before: 'Look at this then. You're in this too.' He wandered aimlessly away still talking to himself, going from room to room. 'No end to it – terrible business – family name dragged into the gutter – what can I do? What? What?'

Arabella looked blankly at the crumpled newspaper he had thrust at her. Baffled, it meant nothing to her, then she looked again and her own name sprang from the page, her eyes raced across the newsprint.

'Earl's heir in *ménage à trois* ... The new Mrs Neville Rossiter has been widely seen and admired in fashionable London circles this season ... when she returns to rural

Sussex, to Copper Down where the Earl of Helvyn has his family seat, she is part of an unusual domestic arrangement ... while Mr and Mrs Neville Rossiter reside at the Grange, across the park lives Mrs Catherine Becket whom many will remember for her grace and beauty ... Mrs Becket it was once rumoured was seeking divorce from her husband in order to marry Mr Rossiter herself ... now she dines with the family, walks and talks with Mrs Rossiter in the grounds of the Grange while her young son who, rumour has it, will one day inherit a considerable part of the estates, plays happily in the gardens of his inheritance ... a charming scene ... Golden haired Mrs Catherine Becket told me that there was complete harmony between the parties concerned. 'I am well looked after, as you can see,' she said. And were there no objections from the elegant, dark-haired Mrs Neville Rossiter, who as Arabella Curtis was unknown in Society until she married Lord Helvyn's heir in Bishop's Linden last year ...

Arabella drew in her breath with a great gasp – to see it all written, printed, published aboard. The effrontery of it, the innuendo, the descriptions – every word of it was salt on the wounds she had suffered. Arabella threw the newspaper down with a movement of complete rejection.

'I will have nothing more to do with this place – these people – any of it. I am going –'

Urgently, Arabella called for the housekeeper and rang the nearest bell and shouted for Becky. The maid had been hiding behind a door watching what was going on from a safe distance. Poor Miss Baker appeared looking more agitated still. 'Ma'am, I'm so anxious. His Lordship – he's acting so –'

Arabella no longer cared how his lordship was acting.

'Call the coachman here,' she said. 'I'm leaving. Now! Why don't you get him?'

In the back kitchens the elderly coachman had just got his boots off and his hands round a mug of tea. He was slow to react to sudden orders for the dog-cart to be brought round, far too slow for Arabella's demanding impatience, but within a very short time she was on her way again, back to the station, heading back to London, accompanied by a doleful Becky.

But now she had a determined plan in her mind. She would

return to London and then she would set forth again and begin the long journey to Castell y Bryder. For Arabella, it was the only place left to go.

CHAPTER TEN

Neville Rossiter had his attention drawn to the offending newspaper story on the evening of the Nelson House reception. His reaction was immediate and forceful. He went at once to the newspaper offices, discovered that Latimer was the man behind the by-line of Onlooker and sought him through a progression of London clubs and drawing rooms late into the night.

He tracked him down at a club in Jermyn Street. There he had seized the smooth and languid Latimer by the scruff of the neck and thrown him to the ground, then picked him up in order to repeat the process with violent satisfaction. The members of the Club stood round him in astonishment and most of them were inclined to applaud his action. But finally they had been moved to restrain Rossiter before he did irreparable damage. No good could come of actually killing the man, they said, and Rossiter appeared quite capable of it.

Charles Sankey had considerable difficulty in locating Rossiter. He finally ran him to ground conferring with his lawyers on legal action against the newspaper.

'Your Uncle was going berserk about a newspaper,' Sankey said. 'I couldn't make it out, but I decided I'd better warn you. Something has unhinged him and he's gone quite gaga.'

'Good God – I never thought he'd get to see it,' Neville said.

Immediately he put everything else aside and gave instructions that he was leaving at once for Copper Down. Then he discovered that the phaeton had taken Arabella to Victoria Station earlier in the day. If Arabella went to Copper Down and Lord Helvyn was there.

'I don't like it,' Charles Sankey said. 'The way he was ranting and raving.'

Neville in his turn made all haste to the station and caught the next available train. Somewhere on the way he passed Arabella making her impetuous journey back to London. At Chichester he was too impatient to wait for the return of the hired fly that could take him to Copper Down. Instead he hired a horse from the redoubtable Wm. Powell and covered the remaining miles at his own furious pace.

He was met at Copper Down Grange by a distraught housekeeper almost beside herself with agitation.

'Is Mrs Rossiter here, Baker?' Neville demanded.

'No, sir, she's gone. And his Lordship's gone too. He seemed to go quite mad, sir, and he took his shotgun.'

Miss Baker could not possibly describe how terrified she had been at the sight of Lord Helvyn swaying on his feet, hitting his head violently with the flat of his hand, shouting and bellowing: 'It's no good, it's no good.' He had stormed out to his horse, taken the shotgun from the saddle and galloped off.

'Which way did he go?' Neville shouted to her. He was already back in the saddle.

'Across the park, sir, towards Bassetts –'

Across the twilight of the park, Neville raced in pursuit, with only one thought now, to reach his Uncle. Catherine Becket's cottage was just in sight as he reached the hazel copse and he heard a shot ring out, then another.

Cursing, he whipped the horse into the last hundred yards and as he reached the lane, the door of the cottage opened. His Uncle stood there, stooping under the low lintel, and his shotgun still in his hands. At the sight of him, Neville had pulled on the reins and for a shocked moment of time they stared across at each other – the old man in the doorway, defeated by a terrible madness, and the nephew who understood the violence and had been too late to prevent it.

In the seconds it took for Neville to reach his Uncle, the old man turned the shotgun to his own forehead and fired. He fell across the path at Neville's feet, crashed to the ground, like a felled tree, a mighty Sussex oak laid low.

Then, a man in a nightmare, Neville went into the cottage. They were both dead, mother and child. Horror-stricken he looked from the body of Catherine Becket to the pathetic body of the boy and found no life, no hope. He held on to the wall as he staggered outside, shocked at the terrible finality.

The sound of the shots had brought men running from the racing stables, but as they approached he couldn't speak to them, he could only convey with outstretched hand his own helplessness and shake his head because it was hopeless and it was all over ...

The hills of Wales were shrouded in mist, when at last Arabella reached them. Clouds of hill fog had descended over the green land; the sheep wandered in and out of trailing wreaths of mist and the trees appeared like skeletons taking a step forward out of the shrouds.

The difficulties of the long journey into remotest Wales had in itself been a challenge to her and she had been thankful to apply herself to that, to the exclusion of all else. Becky had trailed along with her, amazed at the prolonged train journey through the night, the many dreary changes that imprisoned them in comfortless waiting rooms or left them abandoned on bleak forgotten platforms listening to the sound of night trains fading away into the distance. Then she was even more amazed at the journey they must make by coach.

Arabella had found that it was impossible to hire a conveyance to take them all the way to Castell y Bryder, they were forced to put up at an inn twelve miles away and wait while word was sent ahead to bring the Helvyn carriage forth to collect them.

Becky could not understand her determination to go even further into the wildness of Wales when it seemed such a lost and misty place, with rough and mountainous roads and barbarous inhabitants speaking a strange tongue.

White clouds had blotted out the outlines of Mynydd Maw and Mynydd Bach; sky and lake at Bryder had joined into one white nothingness in which no swans moved; the waterfall sounded muffled below the castle walls and the stone of the castle itself seemed as if it would dissolve away into the substance of clouds.

Mrs Williams, whose voice had lifted in a sing-song lilt of happy greeting a year ago, was full of gloom and dire prophecy.

'You coming here alone, are you? What is this then? No good will come of this, will it?'

Arabella slept off her exhaustion in the brass bedstead, and then for hours on end she stood staring out at the lake. She had travelled so far that the worlds of London Society and Bishop's Linden and Copper Down might have ceased to exist. Here there was nothing but the featureless mist filling the lake valley and nothing but her thoughts of the time she had spent there with Neville.

She walked on the terrace, her shawl wrapped about her, the strands of her dark hair curling in the damp air and sprinkled with moisture. A year ago she had stood beside Neville on that terrace, watching the last light fade from the lake and one bright star appear. She could hear again the tenderness in his voice then, and somewhere deep, deep inside her an ache began, an ache of longing and regret.

She thought of the glory of their nights, in the brass bedstead here at Bryder and under the ornate canopies of the marital bed at Copper Down. Such riches they had, such joy, such immeasurable joy –

As day became night she didn't lift her eyes, she was lost in the sadness of her thoughts and unaware of the changes surrounding her until suddenly the radiance of moonlight washing over the waters of the lake astonished her.

She looked up then and saw that the mist had cleared and a full and glorious moon was riding the sky, serene above Mynydd Maw and Mynydd Bach, and something in her lifted in response.

Just so had the moon shone down on them in their joy last year, some things were constant and unchanging. The moon waxed and waned but always returned to shine again silver-pearled above the mountains, just as the spring at the heart of the hills where the cascading river had its source, bubbled for ever clear and pure. She remembered then that the ultimate moment had been there where the stream began, at the heart of everything. She thought, there is still one place further I must go.

She rode there next day, alone and purposeful, riding up from the shores of the lake through the oak woods where the deer glanced away at her approach, up and up the valley where the hills folded one after another, up the rocky steepness till the last of the sheep was left behind sounding plaintively to its echo and there was only the river itself for company, a bright and tumbling stream in a chasm beside her with deep rock pools. When she reached the amphitheatre in the centre of the sunlit hills there was complete quiet, complete peace.

The spring bubbled from its green turf bed and once again she knelt to cup the water in her hands to throw it into her face. It was all as before – but it was not the same. She was alone. The answer struck home with the cold shock of the spring water. She had been so happy here with Neville last year, happy because she was with him, because of their love. She had been truly alive then when they were at Bryder and during the early days at Copper Down – gloriously alive when they were together, and never alive in the same way since.

Love was at the heart of everything, as they had said then. Love such as she had known with Neville must endure in the face of everything and override everything, the greatest pain was in denying it. If they held fast to their love no outsider could destroy it and if their love was supreme in their lives then pride itself must be subjected.

She was so sure of the answer that all perplexities and indignations fell away. A confusion of inheritances and rivalries and mistakes – mistress and child, Prince and radical, were as nothing.

She rode back with calm decision in her heart.

She would write at once to Neville making it clear to him that her love for him was true and enduring and more important to her than anything else in her life. She would ask him with all her heart to come to her at Bryder.

She was so convinced now, so certain in her love, that she walked out on to the castle lawns confident that now, now there would be sight of the black swans on the lake coming steadily towards her over the water, confirming her love and convincing her of the rightness of her course of action. She strained her eyes across the brilliance of the sunlit water but the lake was a shining expanse as empty as the sky. All she found, lying at her feet at the lakeside, was a solitary black feather.

She was standing, stroking the feather against her cheek,

when they came to tell her that a messenger had arrived with a letter for her. A letter from her husband.

Arabella's hands were shaking as she took the letter. Suddenly she was clumsy. Almost she was afraid to break the seals. She had been apart from him for so many days, alone with her thoughts for so long, completely unaware of what he was thinking and doing and feeling. He was so far away, yet with this letter he was close to her.

Trembling she unfolded the letter and stared at the words on the page. Stared, and couldn't believe what she saw. Read the words but couldn't comprehend them. Catherine Becket – dead. The boy – dead. Lord Helvyn in his final madness taking his own life. Such terrible news set forth on the page. The shock of it overwhelmed her. Alone with the horror and the grief of it, she wept because there were no words, only tears. Death and its sorrow could not be comforted.

It was a long time before she could take up the letter again and read Neville's words to her:

'. . . This letter which must bring you this terrible news also contains explanations that are long overdue. They are your right and I should have acknowledged that a long time ago.

'Catherine Becket – she was my mistress. But it was many, many years ago. The affair burned brightly for a time, she left her husband and there was a plan of taking steps towards divorce. In the tortuous business of arranging this, emotions faded; she turned to others, many others, and so did I. I did not see her again for two years, though I heard of her.

'Then she came to me saying she was penniless and had nowhere to go. She was my responsibility. Without me, she might have still been happily married to her Army husband. I found the cottage for her at Bassetts and there she met my Uncle.

'The child, Ralph, was his, Arabella, not mine, and that was why he stood to inherit some property.

'I can understand now your feelings of outrage. I understood when I felt the full force of my own outrage concerning Conroy.

'My actions then sprang from my love, Arabella. I am making this statement of my love for you because you must

182

have doubted its existence. Do not doubt it. I beg you to believe in it. It is more important to me than life itself.

'But you were right to leave and I do not ask you to return. This final madness and violence has proved to me that the black blood in this family is still strong and terrible. I recognize that same violence in myself and you must never be subjected to the chance of its infliction.

'I give you your freedom. Whatever divorce arrangements you want I will put in hand. There will be no coercion from me of any kind. I will make arrangements for your financial independence at once. Be assured that you will never want for anything. You are free to remain at Bryder if you so wish, or to return to the London house. But do not come here to Copper Down.

'There is just one request I would make of you. That you will allow me to see you, finally, that there may be words of farewell between us, and our marriage does not end with cruel recrimination or hostile silence. I suggest that we meet in London, on neutral ground, with others present if you so wish. I would not ask that you come here to Copper Down where this is so much sadness. It is not possible for me to come to Bryder ever again.'

Arabella's immediate reaction was to seize pen and paper to declare her love and understanding. But with the pen in her hand and the paper before her, the tumult of her feelings could not be given expression – so much, too much – it was impossible. She pressed both hands to her face in a kind of despair – and then saw on the table before her, the black feather she had found at the lake side.

She took the feather and sealed it into the envelope with a paper that said: 'Please come.' Then she addressed it to Neville and urged the messenger to hurry on his journey, for the message was most urgent.

She almost set off herself to travel to Copper Down, to reach him sooner, so great was her need to see him. But her feeling was even stronger that here in Wales in this enchanted valley was their greatest hope of happiness. If he would come to her here. Somehow she must wait, somehow she must have faith and patience. Never had it been so difficult to restrain herself from action and await the action of another.

As she paced the rooms of the castle and the terraces by the lake there was an unnatural stillness everywhere. The wide surface of the lake was mirror still, becalmed and tranquil, the woods and mountains around it as if they were painted, and the reflection of the castle walls and the summer sky scarcely stirring in the water. In the cool rooms of the castle the tapestries hung motionless in the quiet air and the dark medieval furniture seemed to be waiting, expectant. Scarcely a footstep sounded on flagged floors and stone stairways. Not a sound from the servants, they were all keeping out of sight, shutting themselves away in the back kitchens as though it was safer there.

Mrs Williams was so distressed and fearful at the news of Lord Helvyn's madness and the three terrible deaths that she gave Arabella renewed alarm. The mournful dying fall of her sing-song speech, her gloomy recollections of the past and her foreboding of the future, the tears in her eyes and the wringing of her hands were uneasy accompaniment to the time of waiting.

'I've always known it would happen, haven't I told you? A curse on the family, generation after generation. When Fate has a hand in it there's nothing anyone can do. You can't change your luck. Lord Helvyn had the madness in him, God rest him. And now I'm so fearful that his lordship will go the same way.'

'His lordship?' Arabella said, startled. She hadn't realized until that moment that Neville Rossiter was now Earl of Helvyn.

'He's got the same look as his Uncle. He doesn't speak to anyone, no one knows his real feelings until suddenly they explode and there's violence. I've known him since he was a child. I've seen this coming. You mark my words, he'll go the same way.'

'That's nonsense,' Arabella said crisply, reassuring herself at the same time. 'When he comes you'll see —'

'He won't come here now. Not now. He'll be like his Uncle and his father, bury himself away at Copper Down, never come back here after what's happened now.'

184

There was something witch-like about Mrs Williams' moaning cadences. Arabella wondered how she could ever have liked the rising and falling of Welsh speech and thought it was like the wind in the trees.

'Why should you say that?' she said impatiently. 'It was in Sussex that the dreadful things happened. Not here.'

'It's part of the curse, isn't it? All part of the legend. The bad luck of the family because they should never have left Castell y Bryder. When something happens like this they forfeit the right to come here. An unlucky family, they can't escape it. And have you seen the black swans?'

'No,' Arabella said startled again. 'No. I haven't. Not since I've been here this time. Why?'

'No. And you won't, will you? Not after this. No one will see them. They won't return now.'

However much she might dismiss Mrs Williams' omens and prophecies, Arabella's uneasiness was increased by her words. She spent the rest of the day walking restlessly on the lawns and terraces by the lake. White roses hung on the stone of the ancient walls, full blown white roses and there was heartbreak in their fragrance that filled her thoughts with half-remembered poetry – the lines that Neville had repeated for her walking there, calling it Lotus land. 'There is sweet music here that softer falls. Than petals from blown roses on the grass Or night-dews on still waters between walls of shadowy granite, in a gleaming pass. Music that gentlier on the spirit lies Than tir'd eyelids upon tir'd eyes Music that brings sweet sleep down from the blissful skies.'

She found no comfort in the lines now. Lotus-land he had called it; a place where one would wish to stay for ever, but could not.

She stared out at the still waters of the lake with tenderness and longing, gazing at sedge and island and overhanging trees, willing the black swans to appear before dusk fell. But only coots, moorhens and tiny water-birds busied themselves at the edge of the lake.

Disturbed at their failure to appear, Arabella picked up a handful of small pebbles and threw them into the lake to release her feelings. She would give no further consideration to omens and legends and fate controlling destinies. Good luck, bad luck, it was all nonsense. She watched the spreading rings of ripples on the lake widening and joining, then she turned briskly indoors.

'I would like a light supper served on a tray,' she said to Mrs Williams. 'Then I shall retire to bed.'

Becky was summoned and Arabella was installed in the brass bedstead. Her dress replaced with the cool ease of a pale pink nightdress, cobweb fine, a lace shawl draped lightly round her shoulders, her hair released from its pinnings and brushed to a fine gleam. She was propped up regally with a mountain of pillows. Then Becky too was dismissed and she was alone with her thoughts and fears. She had given her instructions and the servants had responded, grateful it seemed for the normality. She could speak with decision and act the part of Arabella, Countess of Helvyn, but the strangeness was still about her.

Her thoughts went back to other nights in that brass bedstead, nights of such tender and passionate revelation, and to other times when she had awaited Neville's coming – in her home at Bishop's Linden when he first sought her hand, then again when he returned from abroad to claim her. Vividly she recalled the night he had come from London and she had rejected him with violence for she had spoken with Catherine Becket, so terribly the night he had forced his way into her room, kicking down the locked door –

She hid her face in the pillows, remembering too much, too painfully. Then she took out his letter again. '... My actions sprang from my love, Arabella ... Do not doubt it. I beg you to believe in it. It is more important to me than life itself.'

She lay awake for a long time, trying to guess how long she must wait, how long it would take for her message to reach him, how long the journey took from Copper Down to Bryder. She fell asleep at last with the letter clutched in her hand.

The room was full of moonlight when she woke. She knew at once that he was there. It was not possible – but he was there. He stood at the door, very still, dark and formal still in his riding cape. Arabella sat upright against her high-banked pillows, pulling her lace shawl round her.

If she had thoughts that he was a part of her dreaming or an apparition of the night, she knew when she heard his voice that it was not so. His speech was as clipped and cold and distant as ever.

'I have come, as arranged, to take my leave of you. It was not my wish that the meeting should take place here.'

'It was my wish. I must thank you for acceding to it. And I must also thank you for your explanations to me in your letter.'

'They were due to you as of right. And now I give you your freedom from this marriage.'

'I wish to remain here.'

'That I accept. You may stay here as long as you wish. It is impossible for me to do so.'

'Why? Why? Why?' Arabella cried. 'You surely don't believe this story about a curse on the family. You are the proudest, most obstinate, arrogant and impossible man alive, as I know to my cost, but you are not usually stupid as well.'

'Stupid!' The fury of the word broke the icy formality into angry outrage. 'How dare you. You're the one – you. If anyone is headstrong, obstinate and impossible it is you.'

'Yes. But I know that I love you, so help me.'

The stiff, fierce, proud figures moved at last. He came to her and on the snowy whiteness of the quilt he laid the black swans' feather she had sent to bring him. He took her hands and knelt to bury his face down on to them and she bent her head and rested her cheek against his hair, as if for all time.

When he raised his head to look at her, the words came slowly. He said: 'You can have no idea how greatly I needed to see you. I sent the messenger ahead with the letter. I have been waiting at the inn at Hereford. But it was because I cared so much, because I loved you so dearly, that I wanted you to be free – of me and of all this.'

'It is over now and in the past. The future is ours, we can shape it for ourselves.'

'So much bad blood in the family. It would be better if the family line came to an end.'

'No. It is a great family line, we must restore it. We must

have so many children that the family tree blossoms as never before and bears enough fruit for a whole orchard. Our children will be half you and half me and all the better for it.'

'You are right,' Neville said. He looked into her eyes with a subdued kind of joyousness. 'You are absolutely right. You are amazingly, incredibly, extraordinarily, beautifully right.'

She smiled for the first time and saw his answering smile. Then still looking troubled, he said: 'Sometimes I can see my Uncle in myself. You must have seen. There are resemblances. You have known the violence of which I too am capable, that I am driven to destroy even when I love.'

'You had cause,' Arabella said. 'There will be no such cause in future. No more misunderstandings, pride, false pride. We will both believe in our love now.'

Neville reached out to stroke her cheek with gentle fingers. 'I have always believed in it.'

The frozen emotions, the icy formality, the cold clipped tones had melted and he talked to her then as she had not known him talk since the first months of their marriage.

He could talk to her of his Uncle: 'I can remember him when he was truly an impressive man, with great energy and strength.'

He could even talk to her of Catherine: 'She was unhappy, and I think everything I did made it worse. What should I have done?'

Arabella could only shake her head, for sometimes there is no good a particular man can do for a particular woman, only harm.

'And the Prince of Wales?' Arabella said as an afterthought; and it was not often the Prince of Wales was anybody's afterthought. 'Was it your intention that I should capture the Prince's attention? Did you tactfully withdraw so that I could be *tête à tête* with the Prince when he came to call?'

The look on Neville's face told her nothing had been further from his intentions. 'What the devil gave you that idea?'

'Lady Despencer mostly,' Arabella said with a certain timidity. 'And the circumstances did seem to suggest –'

'Circumstances! Circumstances! I shall shake that damned old griffin until her teeth drop out. I shall kick that Teutonic

Casanova into the reign after next.' His eyes were flashing with anger, immediate and forceful as ever. 'What did he say to you?'

Arabella produced a fair mimicry of the fiercely guttural Royal accent: 'I dare say you've been dreaming of meeting a handsome Prince.'

Neville's anger disappeared as quickly as it had come, dissolving into laughter, and tenderness. He took her hand to his lips. 'I love you, Arabella,' he said, and she felt weak at the sweet sound of it.

A languorous feeling was stealing over her with the warmth of the summer night and a deep sense of pleasure. She slipped the shawl from her shoulders and moved her limbs luxuriously between the cool sheets. It was a feeling of such goodness, such richness, such delight.

Neville continued to regard her gravely, unsmiling now but as if he would never take his eyes away from her. Arabella found the intensity of his gaze so great that her eyelids flickered and the long dark lashes rested for a moment on pale cheeks.

'You are exhausted by so much drama and distress,' Neville said. He spoke with a great effort; such restraint seemed greater than flesh and blood could stand, but the memory of the terrible night he had attacked and forced her against her will held him in a grip of iron self discipline. 'You want to sleep now, you need to rest,' he said.

Arabella hastily opened her eyes, for he was as good as his word. He was already on his feet, preparing to leave her. Holding his gaze Arabella sank deeper into her pillows, stretching out her arms to him. In the incandescence of the moonlight there was all the warm radiance of her beauty.

'I need you,' she said, and found his arms about her. All her seducing sweetness was gathered up into a powerful embrace. Her only desire was to be lost in his arms for ever.

It was a kiss of such unbounded joy, a greater joy than happiness springing from a deep well of tenderness, warm as a homecoming and mixed with the delight of sensual revelation. It acknowledged life's greatest gift, to love and to be loved, and spoke for each of them: 'you and only you.'

All that had occurred to separate them heightened the sweetness of that moment. Once again with his arms about her, Arabella had no thought but her own warm-hearted surrender to the passions enfolding her, to be close, so very close, that no one could ever divide them, to be a part of this most glorious flowering.

For them both there was a feeling of renewal and overwhelming thankfulness that they should know such exceptional good fortune, to have and to hold, from that day forward.

The moonlight faded while they slept in close embrace. Morning broke over the Welsh hills and the sunlight reflected from the waters of the lake on to the ceiling of the room where they lay. Arabella waking reassured herself that it was not a dream.

It was a return to a kingdom from which they had been exiled. Bryder was waiting for them, sunlit and serene. There was a special quality to the light in that idyllic place, it was mystical, translucent, a suffusion of enchantment spreading over the ivied castle walls rising from the lake like the battlements of a fairy tale, the water frothing down the deep ravine, the hills folding gently one after one. The oak glades on one side of the lake were green and gold haunts of deer, the dark mountain crags on the further side were tasselled with the silver of cascading streams.

Arabella and Neville looked with happiness out at the wide lake shining in the sun. Then they looked at each other and smiled. There were two black swans coming towards them over the water.

Victoria Holt

The supreme writer of the 'gothic' romance, a
compulsive storyteller whose gripping novels of the
darker face of love have thrilled millions all over
the world.

FONTANA PAPERBACKS

Fontana Paperbacks

Fontana is a leading paperback publisher of fiction and non-fiction, with authors ranging from Alistair MacLean, Agatha Christie and Desmond Bagley to Solzhenitsyn and Pasternak, from Gerald Durrell and Joy Adamson to the famous Modern Masters series.

In addition to a wide-ranging collection of internationally popular writers of fiction, Fontana also has an outstanding reputation for history, natural history, military history, psychology, psychiatry, politics, economics, religion and the social sciences.

All Fontana books are available at your bookshop or newsagent; or can be ordered direct. Just fill in the form and list the titles you want.

FONTANA BOOKS, Cash Sales Department, G.P.O. Box 29, Douglas, Isle of Man, British Isles. Please send purchase price, plus 8p per book. Customers outside the U.K. send purchase price, plus 10p per book. Cheque, postal or money order. No currency.

NAME (Block letters)

ADDRESS
